I0576395

JUSTIFY MY DESIRES ROGER & LEONIE PART III

STEELE INTERNATIONAL, INC. A BILLIONAIRES ROMANCE SERIES BOOK 5

CHARMAINE LOUISE SHELTON

ISBN: 978-1-7363429-0-9 (Paperback)
ISBN: 978-1-7352917-9-6 (eBook)
Published by CharmaineLouise New York, Inc.
Sexy Fantasies Fulfill Your Desires Publications

CONTENTS

FREE BOOK

Get the start of the STEELE International, Inc. A Billionaires Romance Series with *Discover My Desires Sebastian & Lola Prequel* **FREE!**

Click Cover Below or visit **bit.ly/CLBooksNewsletter** to subscribe to my newsletter for latest news and launches, books from my author friends, and sizzling reads in book promotions. Plus, start reading the steamy billionaire romance *Series Prequel* of Sebastian Steele and Lola Lewis.

Their stories. Their discovery of unknown desires...

FREE BOOK!

PREQUEL
NEVER
RELEASED!

EXCLUSIVE FOR SUBSCRIBERS!

STEELE INTERNATIONAL, INC.
A BILLIONAIRES ROMANCE SERIES

ABOUT STEELE INTERNATIONAL, INC. A BILLIONAIRES ROMANCE SERIES

Welcome to the titillating world of the multibillion-dollar global company and the love affairs of the family that controls it.

STEELE International, Inc. is a series of interconnecting Billionaire romance. Follow the Steele family as they fly around the world chasing the women they love and their happily ever afters. Get ready for glitz, glamour, and steamy romance books. What's better than that? The Jet-set Lifestyle has never been hotter...

The Desires Series is not for the tea set; it's for the top-shelf vodka straight up in a pretty crystal glass coterie!

Don't miss any of the sizzling romance books in the STEELE International, Inc. A Billionaires Romance Series:

Discover My Desires Sebastian & Lola Prequel
(Available Exclusively to Subscribers)

Fulfill My Desires Sebastian & Lola Part I

Heighten My Desires Sebastian & Lola Part II

Ignite My Desires Roger & Leonie Part I

Stoke My Desires Roger & Leonie Part II

Justify My Desires Roger & Leonie Part III

Deepen My Desires Sebastian & Lola Part III

Capture My Desires Malcolm & Starr Part I

Embrace My Desires Malcolm & Starr Part II

Cherish My Desires Malcolm & Starr Part III

A Trilogy of Desires Sebastian & Lola Parts I-III

A Trilogy of Desires Roger & Leonie Parts I-III

A Trilogy of Desires Malcolm & Starr Parts I-III

Series Extras

Series Playlist

ABOUT JUSTIFY MY DESIRES
ROGER & LEONIE PART III

The smoldering love affair of Roger The Responsible and Leonie The Lion concludes with their struggle to make lightning strike a third time for their happily ever after in their second chance billionaire romance story.

The loving duo may be heading down the aisle in a winter wonderland wedding with their adorable twins, but will the shadow of Roger's legal woes follow them?

Come along for their steamy holiday romance as they travel to Verbier for a sizzling Merry Christmas & New Year, personal fireworks in Southampton for Labor Day, Capri for yachting, Paris for home sweet home, and wherever their rendezvous take them!

Their love story is a standalone second chance romance trilogy in the series. Get a glimpse of their dynamism in other books.

Anthem: "Justify My Love" Madonna
https://www.youtube.com/watch?v=Np_Y740aReI

Playlist:
https://www.youtube.com/playlist?list=
PLXwYvn0e218CZOKMieHtBQ3QRL3xlxMA8

Visit CharmaineLouiseBooks.com

ROGER

"*B*ecause *of the testimony provided by both the plaintiff and the defendant, the evidence brought forth, and of my careful deliberation, I determine* Roger Steele *and* STEELE *International, Inc. should—*"

"AAAH... MON DIEU!!"

"*Qu'est-ce que—*"

"*Oh, Mon Trésor!!*"

"*Leonie!! What's wrong?!*"

"ROGEEERRR!!!"

My fiancée Leonie Beaulieu's ferocious roar of my name snaps me back to the Parisian hospital's bustling operating room and out of the hell of the pretrial courtroom.

What an emotionally charged day...

From making love to Leonie so intense it felt as though our souls blended to the rollercoaster ride of the courtroom right before the pretrial judge's determination on the prosecution of the case and now she's in labor.

Damn.

WHOMEVER SAID money is the root to all evil wins the gold medal.

Delia Fucking Shaw wanted more than my billions. She had her sights set on the ultimate prize... Roger Steele of the media-dubbed STEELE Quaternity.

They consider my three brothers—Sebastian, Malcolm, Harris—and I the most sought-after of the world's eligible billionaires. Although not a part of the group, Haley, our youngest sibling and the fraternal twin to Harris, has a multibillionaire status that attracts men to her like bees to honey. Not that we allow just anyone access to our baby sis —no fucking way!

I should have known Delia was up to more than simple flirting with the professor when I guest lectured one of my then girlfriend Leonie's classes at the Paris American Academy.

As my family's multigenerational multibillion-dollar company STEELE International, Inc.'s President of Residential Properties Division, Leonie thought I would impart some of my knowledge on her classmates. She was in her last year for her interior design bachelor's degree.

Wanting to help her make a good impression on her professor, I agreed.

Leonie has always had an eye for design. The combination of being the world-renowned megamodel *The Lion* for almost nineteen years and as the daughter of an old, wealthy Parisian merchant family that travels seeking antiques, antiquities, and fabrics instilled in her a love for the aesthetics. Transitioning into interior design has been her dream for years. And in any way I could help her, I promised I would.

Unfortunately, it came at a price.

During the class, Delia flirted with me, and Antonio Velasquez flirted with Leonie. I gave him the look of death, and he backed off. Or so I thought...

The dick didn't learn his lesson then. So I had to teach him at their end-of-the-semester reception when I caught him kissing my girlfriend—MINE!

My training with a former heavyweight boxing champion primed me to knock Velasquez on his ass and then some.

Which led to restitution as a vast sum of money for him and a STEELE internship program with the Paris American Academy for two of their students in perpetuity. Unluckily, the first two recipients turned out to be none other than Delia and Velasquez. Pain in my ass number one and pain in my ass number two—initially in either order.

Now, Delia takes the top spot.

Although I'm sure she would have preferred the bottom position with her writhing beneath me... Billions and a ten-inch cock.

Despite my best efforts to elude her unwanted attention, she managed to get at me twice.

The first with an unannounced and unapproved visit to my offices on the executive floor of STEELE Paris. My take-no-shit personal assistant, Françoise Faucher, thwarted Delia's double entendre comments and advancement. Françoise made it her personal mission to escort the intern from my offices to security for the reprogramming of her ID card access and to human resources for a refresher in protocol with the president.

The proverbial nail in the coffin came in the form of Delia insisting I speak with her on my way to the Interior Design Team's weekly meeting, at which she was a participant.

Against my better judgement, I allowed her to ride up to the conference room on my private elevator with me. Said elevator oddly malfunctioned, and we were stuck together in the dark for twenty minutes—no cameras, no help, nothing but the two of us. No one knows how the hell my elevator went on the fritz.

Delia's interpretation of the events on the elevator differs so greatly from mine. She filed a legal petition. A petition against me for sexual assault and harassment and against STEELE International, Inc. as co-defendant with a civil claim for none other than… a vast sum of money.

Meanwhile, for the last eleven weeks, the love of my life has had to cope with the stress of this bullshit while pregnant with our twin boys. Already struggling with the fear of her mother's experiences with multiple miscarriages before giving birth to Leonie and her parents' subsequent inability to ever have children again compounded by Delia Fucking Shaw.

So instead of having her water break under normal circumstances at her family's ancestral estate *Le Beaulieu*

Manoir—where we're staying to avoid the rabid media and stalkers—it happened in the fucking pretrial courtroom. Surrounded by protestors, onlookers, Velasquez, and Delia, Leonie screamed in anguish from the contractions and the ensuing gush of amniotic fluid protecting The Twins.

Pandemonium broke out.

I gave zero fucks about Judge Favre's pronouncement. My baby was in pain, and I would be damned if I didn't go to her.

Without approval from the judge or STEELE General Counsel Albert Perry, who's representing me and the company, I rushed to Leonie's side.

The expression of fear and hurt on her beautiful face struck me in the gut like a sledgehammer. Her pitiful cries galvanized me.

My eldest brother Sebastian and I carried her between us while my other brothers, our male friends, and security detail cleared a path for us. With Lola Steele—Leonie's best friend and Sebastian's wife—leading the way, we exited out the back of the courthouse. Then we hurried into one of the Mercedes-Benz Sprinters I leased to transport everyone during the pretrial.

Starr Knight—Leonie's friend, yoga teacher, and doula—called her OB-GYN Dr. Pierre Berger. Starr confirmed he was on his way to the hospital as the five of us sped off. My trusted driver Eric Vogler maneuvered the crazy Parisian traffic to get us to the hospital in record time. Thankfully, Starr kept Leonie relatively calm during the ride.

Luc Montaigne—Leonie's mentor and friend and the

multibillionaire CEO and Chairman of the Board of his family's multigenerational, global banking empire Banque Montaigne—once again used his considerable influence as the major benefactor of the hospital to garner approval for a custom suite. This after he procured Dr. Berger as her doctor.

When we found out Leonie was pregnant, Luc demanded the top OB-GYN attend to her. Not just of the hospital, but of all France. Since this is the most esteemed hospital in Paris, Dr. Berger has his affiliation with it and serves as their OB-GYN department director and a practicing physician.

No sooner had the nurses settled Leonie in her suite did Dr. Berger arrive with his team. An anesthesiologist, two pediatricians—one for each Twin—two labor and delivery nurses, an OB tech, and a nursery nurse followed him into Leonie's suite.

They went to work in prepping her for the first stage of pregnancy, pre-labor. Dr. Berger explained in twin pregnancies, it can take up to thirteen hours for her body to be ready for the actual delivery. He expected the first Twin within two hours after and the second Twin less than twenty minutes later.

Leonie was a lot less fearful now that she was in the hospital's safety and under the doctor's care. She may have been better prepared, but still in the throes of labor as she experienced acute contractions.

Her golden caramel complexion flushed rosy from the sensations overtaking her body. Her feline amber eyes glowered at my wolfish gray ones, while French curses spilled from her lush lips. Her ass-long mahogany waves once pulled in a sleek ponytail, now in one thick braid thanks to Starr.

She and Lola fussed over Leonie as Sebastian and I hovered around her bed. Soon the rest of our family and friends arrived from the courthouse. Leonie's mother Josy and my mother Shelley hurried to her side, hustling Sebastian and me right out of their way. Haley joined them at the foot of Leonie's bed as she massaged her feet and calves to comfort her.

Surrounded by the most important women in her life, Leonie braved the pre-labor stage for just over twelve hours. Now, the ferocious Lion is loose…

"ROGEEERRR!!!"

"Oh, mon Dieu!!! Aidez moi!!!"

She squeezes the fuck out of my hand.

I wince from the bite of pain, but persevere. If she has to go through contractions and all, I won't wuss out and will remain by her side.

At this stage, besides the medical team, Starr is the only person with us in the operating room. Dr. Berger moved Leonie from her suite to here since twins can have complications during delivery. He wants to ensure all equipment and support are available with no delay.

Thank fuck since I would lose my shit if something happens to Leonie or to our babies. My thoughts drift back to the conversation we had early in her pregnancy before we knew we were expecting twins.

"Leonie, understand me clearly. If for any reason I have to choose between you and this baby or any other, I choose you always. You mean everything to me. We can try for another baby, or we can adopt a baby in need of a wonderful home. But you... You are irreplaceable, my love. Call me selfish. But I will not live without you, Leonie."

She speaks. But I cut her off with a firm shake of my head. I don't give a damn how harsh it may sound. But it's the damn truth.

"No! This is nonnegotiable. And we will not speak of such things ever again. Do you understand?"

Leonie nods, still sad.

"Words, Leonie. I will have your words," I demand.

She takes some time to consider.

I feel her body stiffen, and she sits up tall. The surrounding energy vibrates anew. Then Leonie stares me straight in the eye with a fiercely determined expression.

"Oui, Roger. You are right, Mon Cœur. We will move forward from this moment on with only positive thoughts and words of love. You are the most responsible person I know"—she smiles brightly as she strokes my cheek—"But we will share the responsibility of our blessing together. I don't want you to think you have to be strong for both of us. I will not neglect your needs either."

So, God forbid, anything goes wrong, I set my mind. But I push the negative thoughts out and return Leonie's bone-crushing squeeze of my hand with a much gentler version to hers as I stroke her reddened cheek.

"Yes, my love? You're so brave and strong. We are so lucky to have you—"

"BULLSHIIITTT!!!"

Leonie snarls and swats my thumb from her face. The golden flecks in her eyes flash dangerously as she glares at me.

An unceasing slew of French curse words follow a particularly painful contraction.

Starr turns her head. But not before I glimpse the smile on her face. Her dimples deepen as her sorrel-brown eyes dance with mirth.

Even Dr. Berger coughs to hide his laugh.

I glance around the room, and others avoid my gaze. Suddenly everyone has an important task...

"Oooh... How much more?" Leonie huffs huskily. *"Mon DIEU!!!"*

Dr. Berger peers between Leonie's legs—the caveman in me wants to carve his eyeballs out with a flint knife—to check.

"One more push, Leonie. You can do it. He's almost here," the doctor states, back to business. "Now!"

With what must be a Herculean effort, Leonie delivers our first Twin. Their piercing cries mingle in the tense air of the operating room.

Rodolphe Beaulieu Steele enters our world.

My eldest son. Named for me. Leonie nicknamed me *Mon Loup*, my wolf. His name translates to famous wolf.

Tears fill my eyes at the sight of mother and son.

My protective instincts kick in. I follow his pediatrician —Dr. Constance Taylor recommended by Dr. Berger—as she carries my son off to the side in order to care for him. I split my gaze between her actions and Leonie, who's being comforted by Starr. I confirm she's fine, then turn my full attention to Rodolphe.

"How is he?" I ask as I watch possessively over the doctor's shoulder while she tends to him.

She smiles at me and responds, "He's in excellent health! All ten fingers and toes! He weighs 5.2 pounds. An acceptable size for a twin. Congratulations, Mr. Steele!"

Relief washes over me. Then anxiety sweeps in when she places a freshly cleaned Rodolphe in my arms. When I look at her in a panic, Dr. Taylor smiles encouragingly.

I glance down at his red face. He may be tiny, but the weight of responsibility hits me in that moment. This is one of my sons, the fruit of my loins. I am his father. His safekeeping ranks as my utmost priority along with his soon-to-be-born brother and their mother.

"Roger? What's taking so long? Is he okay?"

Leonie's soft voice filled with concern calls me back to the operating room.

"He's perfect, my love. See for yourself," I respond as I stride over to her and place Rodolphe on her chest.

Leonie's face lights up with such love and joy when she stares at our son. Tears stream down her cheeks. Her fingers tentatively touch his soft jet-black hair, and his eyes open slowly.

Gray eyes and black hair. The Steele family traits continue.

Leonie peers up at me and smiles.

"*Mon Loup,*" she whispers.

I bury my face in her damp hair and cry.

· · ·

"FUUUCK... YOU!!!"

Stage three begins...

Rodolphe sleeps in a warm hospital crib while his younger brother is being born. And his father is being cursed out by his mother.

I learned my lesson the last time. Instead of speaking sappy words, I go for the Alpha male route.

"Leonie. You will push when Dr. Berger says and not a moment before. Do you understand—"

I didn't even see it coming.

Leonie slaps the shit out of me.

"Don't you dare pull that dominant bullshit on me right now, ROGER STEELE!!!"

She bellows, eyes shooting golden fire.

Struck speechless, I can only stare at the wild Lion before me. The tame and loving new mother of ten minutes ago disappears in a puff of smoke.

Yeah, fuck me...

THIRTY MINUTES LATER, a fatigued, not ferocious, Leonie rests in her suite's bed with our sons in skin-to-skin contact against their mother's body as she breastfeeds them.

The sight is so poignant; I have to capture it with a few photos by my mobile. The clicking attracts her attention, and she lifts her weary gaze to mine.

"Hi, baby. I love you so much," I breathe. "Do you need anything?"

Leonie shakes her head and pats the bed beside her.

I sit and brush my fingertips across her cheek.

She closes her eyes and nuzzles against my palm; a soft purr slips past her lips.

"*Non, merci, Mon Cœur, je t'aime aussi,*" she whispers, followed by a yawn. "Only you and our sons."

Gaspard Beaulieu Steele, my second son. Named for Leonie. Her parents nicknamed her *Mon Trésor*, and we name our son treasure bearer. His gray eyes and jet-black hair mark him as a Steele. A perfect baby who weighs a healthy five pounds with all ten fingers and toes.

A beautiful fiancée and identical twin sons. My heart swells. My family.

MINE!

LEONIE

"*T*he next generation of Steeles is born! May they carry on our clan name and STEELE and Beaulieu forever!"

Declares Morgan Steele as he holds his day-old grandsons proudly.

"*Oui, Mon Trésor* extends her family's line with males, one for Beaulieu and one for STEELE!" My father Guy adds proudly as he plucks Gaspard from Morgan's arm.

The two titans refer to the alliance forged between STEELE International, Inc. and Beaulieu Enterprises, SAS by Sebastian as CEO of STEELE and my father as Président of Beaulieu. Morgan approved it since the deal was Sebastian's first major one after taking over from his father.

My family's company is privately owned, and I am the heir apparent. After my engagement, my father expressed his wish for Roger to take on the helm with me when he retires. I made it clear I was not interested in running the day-to-day responsibilities as I prefer to focus on my interior design career.

We agreed we would incorporate Beaulieu within the STEELE organization. But I will maintain majority control, with our children taking on the company at the appropriate time. The Beaulieu company will continue to pass on to the next generation as it has for centuries.

The future addition pleases everyone. It's the perfect solution for both companies and families.

Now my sons are but a day old and their *grand-pères* reaffirm the partnership and The Twins' future roles.

I shake my head and smile.

Roger slips his hand in mine and dips his head to kiss my lips.

"Let them have their fun, my love. You've made them so thrilled," he murmurs.

"And you? Have I made you happy, *Mon Cœur*?" I ask softly as I lean into him, seeking his warmth and strength.

Roger straightens and cups my chin. His signature intense gray-eyed stare pins me in place.

"Absolutely. With no doubt. Once you bear my name, as our sons already do, you will make my life complete, Leonie," he responds in a voice thick with emotion.

I whimper and bury my face in his neck as I sob.

So much has happened so quickly, I feel overwhelmed. From the highs of graduating from the Paris American Academy, learning I'm pregnant, and becoming engaged after a tumultuous on-again-off-again relationship. Then the lows of being apart from Roger, the scandalous false allegations of she who shall not be named, and the as yet announced determination.

Throw in the hormones raging through my body, and I can't control my emotions.

Merde…

"Oh, sweetheart…"

Roger's comforting murmurs of love and support boost my spirit. He's my rock.

"Let's give them some privacy—"

My best friend's suggestion reminds me I'm surrounded by my loved ones. My babies are healthy. My true love is by my side. I have a lot to be thankful for.

With fresh resolve, I face my family and friends.

"*Non, non,* stay. Don't mind my blubbering," I say as I dab my face with Roger's handkerchief. "You do not understand just how much I love and appreciate you. It's been a trying time. But new life brings great joy."

My mother comes over to the bed and clasps our hands before she kisses them. I see my amber eyes reflected in hers, set in the same oval-shaped face. Her fawn-colored complexion deeper than my caramel skin tone due to the combination of her Tunisian ancestry and my father's Parisian pedigree.

The power of genetics to pass traits from parent to child amazes me. Just as illustrated in The Twins and the Steeles. I smile at her.

"*Mon Trésor,* never make excuses for your emotions! Your body is going through a lot"—she turns to Shelley and gestures for her to join us—"I may have had only one baby, but I know how you're feeling. Shelley, who's had five, will agree."

Roger's mother, or my *Maman Aussi* as I call Shelley, smirks and strokes my cheek.

"Yes! And you thought you had some choice words for Roger. Well, let me tell you, I laid Morgan out each and every time!"

The room fills with our laughter, Morgan's chuckles loudest of us all.

It's even more funny since Roger swears our fathers are Alpha Doms and our mothers are subs. The visual of the men being in a submissive circumstance cracks me up.

"I agree! Norman may have been the champ in the ring. But I won by a TKO when he dared to utter one word while I was in labor," Anita says from the sofa.

Norman feigns the impact of a crushing blow and collapses against the armrest. The same king of the boxing ring who plays dress up and has a tea party with his toddler daughter.

Again, the tough guys are always the softies at heart.

"—YOUR *Maman* is resting now, Rodolphe. You and your brother wore her out coming into this world, you know... Yes, I know. You're tired too... Tell me all about it, *mon fils.*"

The low drone of Roger's words enters my dreams.

It's later in the evening and our family and friends have gone home. The quiet of the room makes it easier for his voice to carry.

I awake to find him pacing the floor with a small

bundle bouncing in his arms. For a few minutes, I watch transfixed by the sight of my six-foot, three-inch, powerfully built Alpha male negotiating with our eldest newborn son.

Rodolphe responds with low-pitched whining, just as engaged in the conversation as his *Papa*.

My gaze leaves them to find Gaspard still tucked in his crib, covered in a soft, white cashmere blanket and matching beanie. They're a gift from his *Oncle* Luc. Gaspard sleeps peacefully. So I return my attention to my man and other son.

"—Do you know how much I love you and your brother? A whole lot, Rodolphe. The two of you are an unexpected joy. The thought of having children anytime soon never occurred to me. But your *Maman* stole my heart the moment I heard her melodic laughter outside of my offices. She says it's *un coupe de foudre*. I have to agree it was love at first sight. It took us a while. But here we are and here you and Gaspard are, too. I will do all in my power to protect and care for your *Maman*, Gaspard, and you…"

Roger's voice cracks, and I realize he's holding back tears.

I'm not the only one on an emotionally charged ride. He needs me, too.

"*Mon Cœur*," I call to him softly.

Roger stops walking and lifts his gaze from our son's face to mine. In the low light, his eyes sparkle with unshed tears.

My heart clenches.

"Come," I say, opening my arms to welcome both of them.

Roger sits beside me, and I lean forward to kiss his lips. Then place my forehead against his.

Rustling from the crib draws our attention to Gaspard. Our other bundle must sense he's missing family time as his movements escalate to cries.

I take Rodolphe, and Roger rises to bring our Treasure Bearer to me. Time for The Twins to drink from the golden chalice.

Roger watches us with such love in his weary gray eyes. He told me he still can't believe we're parents and have healthy identical twin boys. The day he found out about my pregnancy—when I was rushed to the hospital—was like a bolt of lightning to his heart, again.

He understood then the importance of providing a safe and happy home for us—his own little family, one he created from his heart and loins. Without saying it, he alluded to the pretrial needing to complete posthaste in his and STEELE's favor so we could move forward with our new life together.

Nothing and no one would come between us. We would be an impenetrable unit powerful enough to withstand any assault—she who shall not be named included.

I wholeheartedly agree with the love of my life. We will get through this nasty pretrial and have the life set for us even before we knew one another.

Our *coup de foudre* proves it, I smile to myself as I watch Roger stare at our sons and me.

Once they're fed, changed, and tucked in their cribs, Roger takes off his robe and returns to the bed.

With the custom suite, we could bring in a larger sized hospital-style bed that could accommodate both of us. Why should Roger cramp his large frame in a convertible chair? Many thanks to Luc!

"Your words were so sweet, *Chéri*," I tell Roger as I snuggle against his shoulder.

He wraps his arm around me and pulls me closer as he kisses the top of my head.

"I didn't mean to wake you," he responds quietly.

I lean back and cup his face in my hand. His clean-shaven face now with more than a five o'clock shadow is weary, too.

"Hey, we made them together. We care for them together," I tell Roger. "You've been just as stressed, if not more... So you need a break, too."

I rest my head again and continue.

"*Maman Aussi* told me the secret is to get sleep when they sleep. Sooo, *bonne nuit mon amour et fais de beaux rêves*," I say as my eyelids close.

Roger chuckles and murmurs his love for me, too.

The rhythmic beat of his heart lulls me into a peaceful sleep where I dream of our return to *Le Beaulieu Manoir* tomorrow.

ROGER

"*Fortunately, Judge Favre made an exception for Leonie going into labor and allowed a medical recess. However, he called for the court to return to session tomorrow morning. He requires your presence.*"

Albert's words play on repeat in my mind since his call yesterday afternoon.

The delight of my sons' births hours before dims from the shadow of these bullshit allegations. I didn't mention the call to Leonie, just to my father and Sebastian.

I will not allow the news to lessen Leonie's joy of her new motherhood no more than I allowed the pretrial to overshadow our wedding day. I can't postpone my return to the courtroom like I did our ceremony. But I chose not to discuss it then.

Now, I have to tell Leonie where I'm going.

Although I'm sure she's been thinking about it. I've caught her peeking at me with a wistful expression before she can cover it up with an overly bright smile or avert her gaze.

It's not as though we can completely ignore the situation. Fuck the elephant in the room. It's a ginormous blue whale.

I take a last glance at my reflection in the bathroom mirror. I shaved after two days and my collar-length hair is well-kempt. But the angles of my face emphasize the shadows beneath my dull eyes.

It's not that I've given up. Rather, I'm tired of the shit and want to enjoy my new family without wondering if I'll get to see them beyond a partition in some French jail.

Albert and the legal team remain confident. They were certain it wouldn't go to pretrial too...

But as Leonie says, stay positive and no negative thoughts!

With a deep breath, I resettle myself and repeat my mantra.

Inhale, I am.

Exhale, innocent.

Pause.

Inhale, I am.

Exhale, innocent.

Pause.

As I open the bathroom door, I hear Leonie's giggles as she coos at one of our sons.

But her smile fades when she glances up to see me in one of my bespoke three-piece suits, custom dress shirt, silk tie, and Oxfords. Gone from the room is her laughter, just like my long-sleeved t-shirt, joggers, and soccer slides.

We stare at each other in silence for a moment before we speak at once.

"Where are you going—"

"Judge Favre called court—"

Leonie nods as her shoulders slump. Tears fill her eyes, and she glances away, biting her lower lip.

"Baby, remember only positive thoughts," I say as I turn her face back to mine. "The judge will make the determination. No matter what he says, know that I am innocent of any wrongdoing."

She whimpers and closes her eyes.

I brush the tears from her cheeks and kiss her lips gently.

Leonie sobs. But wraps her arms around my neck to pull me closer as she deepens our kiss. Her passion ignites a fire within each of us. The heat that always simmers between us roars to life, engulfing us.

I tilt her head to take control.

A knock on the door brings us back.

"I love you and our sons, Kitten," I tell her gruffly before I kiss Rodolphe and Gaspard on their foreheads.

Their baby smell fills my nostrils, and I close my eyes to inhale it deeply.

Inhale, I am.

Exhale, innocent.

Pause.

Inhale, I am.

Exhale, innocent.

Pause.

.   .   .

Fucking déjà vu.

Hecklers and protestors scream false accusations and obscenities as I make my way to the courthouse doors. Once inside of the courtroom, I notice Delia who sits prim and proper, dressed like a mousy elementary-school librarian. Velasquez sits behind her in the gallery, smirking at me.

Everyone except for Josy and Starr return with me in a show of support. Lola wanted to stay at the hospital. But Leonie insisted her best friend go with me since Dr. Berger hasn't discharged her from the hospital yet. My parents, Guy, siblings, Jackson cousins, Luc, Blair, Billie, Joel and Hettie, Norman and Anita, Françoise and other STEELE employees sit in the gallery on my side.

"All rise... This court is now in session. The Honorable Judge Favre presiding."

Good. Let's get this over with already.

I say a silent prayer as I rise and watch Judge Favre enter the room.

He sits stoically on his bench. Then his eyes scan the courtroom before they flick to me with his analytical stare.

"I understand Mademoiselle Beaulieu is in good health?" The judge asks without preamble.

"Yes, Your Honor, thank you," I respond, surprised by his unexpected question.

"*Très bien*," he nods formally. "We shall begin."

Judge Favre leafs through the papers in front of him and scans the documents. Then he summarizes the claim and the parties involved, similar to his opening statement. When he pauses, a hush descends on the crowded room.

In my periphery, I notice Delia stare at me long enough that her attorney nudges her and whispers in her ear. With a shrug of her shoulder, she faces forward again.

Judge Favre raises his eyebrow and turns a blistering stare on Delia as he speaks.

"Because of the testimony provided by both the plaintiff and the defendant, the evidence brought forth, and of my careful deliberation, I determine Roger Steele and STEELE International, Inc. should not face prosecution and the claim dismissed with prejudice. I shall make these proceedings into a written record immediately afterwards. Court is adjourned."

Pandemonium breaks out again in the form of Delia Shaw.

"What?! No!! Roger Steele tried to—"

Bam bam bam!

"Silence!!"

Judge Favre's command stuns Delia. She gapes at him as he pins her with a glacial gaze.

"You will control your client and her outbursts or face a fine, Counselor," he says in a chilling tone.

Delia's lead attorney sputters as his eyes bounce from the judge to her. Then he nods and offers his apologies. One of his associates bustles Delia out of the courtroom, followed by Velasquez, who scowls at me as he passes by.

Good fucking riddance to bad fucking rubbish! I'm free of this bullshit!

The din of the courtroom increases once the group exits out the side door.

"Excellent outcome!" Albert says as he shakes my hand. "I will finish with the paperwork now."

I shake his hand and clap his back as I nod, "Thank you, Albert! Well done!"

Albert smiles, and I thank the legal team before I turn to my family and friends.

"Congratulations, Roger!"

"Hell yeah! It's over!"

"You're innocent, big brother! The world will know, I promise!" Haley declares as she hugs me tightly.

Everyone whoops and claps as they share their glee.

I smile and answer on autopilot. While my mind swirls with emotions of relief, thanks, and elation. It's all behind us now. We can move forward unencumbered by the malicious accusations and the vicious commentary.

My thoughts move to Leonie, Rodolphe, and Gaspard. It's time I get back to my little family.

"—HEARD anything, yet? I'm worried sick—"

Leonie stops speaking when she sees me standing in the suite's doorway. Her eyes widen and her mouth forms a perfect O before she claps her hands over it.

"Hello, my love," I say gruffly as I step into the room. "It's over."

Leonie gasps and closes her eyes as she falls back against the pillows. Her body shudders as her sobs increase in her hands.

I rush to her side and pull her into my arms, kissing her face as I murmur words of love.

The click of the door's lock draws my attention back to the room. Josy and Starr left. When I walked in, I glanced at them barely. My sole focus was Leonie.

Now, as I hold her in my embrace, I look around to see Rodolphe and Gaspard asleep in their hospital cribs. Swaddled, they lie quietly. My sons.

No longer do I have to worry about not being with them and their mother. We're free to make our family official. I won't wait long to claim Leonie as my wife.

ROGER

"This chalet hasn't sold yet. It's the largest with five stories, twelve bedrooms, sixteen bathrooms, four fireplaces, an oversized ski room, and the usual entertainment rooms including a sixteen-person cinema room, game room, gym, and wine-tasting cellar. The indoor-outdoor heated pool pavilion with spa is an added bonus. Staff quarters are above the six-vehicle garage."

I barely hear the project manager rattling off the details of the luxury chalet. The spectacular view of Verbier and the Swiss Alps through the floor-to-ceiling windows capture my attention.

After a month of being with Leonie, Rodolphe, and Gaspard—we only left the *Manoir* to attend Joel and Hettie's wedding—I couldn't put off the final walk-through of STEELE's latest Swiss project.

The STEELE Verbier Hotel & Resort had its grand opening during last year's ski season. We planned the Residential Properties Division's completion of the by-application-only compound of ten state-of-the-art chalets and private clubhouse to take occupancy for this year's season.

Verbs, as the in-the-know jet-set call it, is a town in the Swiss Alps. A part of the Valais canton in the southwest of Switzerland, France borders Verbier to the west with Italy to the south. It's the most exclusive ski destination in the world.

It's the winter version of Monaco, with the difference being people who go to Monaco want to watch or be watched. Whereas Verbier has an understated style where wealth is glamorous, stylish and tasteful. People are here for the reasons one goes to a ski resort—the superb skiing. Not to mention the phenomenal bars and restaurants; the après-ski is perfect for party lovers. Verbier is a glamorous winter playground.

The luxury chalets occupy the area south of the Médran lift. They're slightly away from town along Rue de Médran, where the extra space means they are rarely overlooked and have a private, exclusive vibe. The residential compound is opposite to the STEELE Verbier that's closer to the heart of the village square. The concept is for the STEELE Verbier Chalets to access the resort for its five-star amenities. The most important include the luxury thermal bath spa and the three Jackson Corporation restaurants headed by our cousin Lucien *The Sexy Chef* as he's known by his millions of followers.

I'm surprised this chalet is still on the market. The decor is modern Alpine chic with traditional materials of timber and stone complemented by the high-quality fixtures and fittings and custom furniture. Combined with the view, it's an incredible property.

"Well, damn. Maybe I'll buy it."

I glance over at Malcolm and raise my eyebrow questioningly.

"Why not? We all ski and could use a place here to hang out," he adds with a shrug.

At only two years apart, he's Sebastian's doppelgänger: same six feet, four inches in height; gray eyes; black hair; clean shaven or 5 o'clock shadow covers a firm jaw. As kids, Malcolm strove for his own identity, hating being in Baz's shadow. Fortunately, they grew past their teenage angst to develop a close relationship.

We're all close. And close enough to hang out together regularly. We even spend lots of time with our parents going on vacations, the holidays, birthdays. What can I say? The Steeles enjoy each other's company.

An idea hits me. I'll buy the chalet and gift it to Leonie for Christmas. She loves to ski, and winter is her favorite season.

We can have our wedding at *Le Beaulieu Manoir* as planned two days before Christmas Eve. The next day we come to Verbier to celebrate the holiday and New Year's Eve with our families, then our honeymoon alone. We didn't want to travel too much with The Twins since they will be with us. Perfect!

"I'll buy it. It'll be my Christmas gift to Leonie. Plus, we can all come here after the wedding for the holiday. Afterwards, Leonie and I wills stay with The Twins for our honeymoon," I say with finality.

Malcolm cocks his head to consider my pronouncement. Then he nods.

"Sounds good to me, bro," he responds. "Leonie will love it. Man, what a way to celebrate, new babies, new wife, new beginning. I'm happy for you, brother."

I smile at my second oldest sibling. We're only a year apart, so he's never lorded over me with an age difference. Harris and Haley get ribbed the most for being the youngest, especially Haley for being the only girl. Her declaration that we're not her father never gets old.

"Thanks. Sebastian, me... Now it's your turn..." I say waggling my eyebrows.

I'm on a roll with my love matches—Luc and Blair, now Malcolm and Starr. He thinks no one's aware of his feelings for the beauty. But he made it clear at Baz and Lola's wedding Starr was on his radar. Neither has said much recently. But oh well. That ends now.

"How's Starr by the way?" I ask.

Malcolm dodges the answer with a conference call he claims he has to take. Then hightails it out of the chalet with a promise to meet me for dinner later.

The project manager hides his laugh with a cough.

I turn to him and nod.

"Let's get this deal closed now. I'll need a copy of the promotional video emailed to me pronto," I tell him.

Yeah, Leonie is going to love it. She jokes about hanging out with the glitterati—as though she's not a part of that clique—when she's at her penthouse in Monte Carlo. Here she'll rub elbows with British and Danish royalty and others of the jet-set who prefer Verbier to Gstaad and Zermatt as their ski destination.

What's also great about it is the family friendly atmosphere. Not only the royals holiday with their children. But other high-net wealth clans hit the slopes with their toddlers and teens.

Rodolphe and Gaspard will join them. I can't wait to watch my sons zip down the trails and toboggan in the winter, then hike and swim in the summer. This will be another great vacation spot for us to make memories.

The ringing of my mobile breaks into my reverie. A smile big enough to split my face breaks out. I excuse myself from the project manager and move closer to the wall of windows.

"Hey babe. What's happening?" I answer. "I was just thinking about you and The Twins."

Leonie's laughter warms my heart as I stare at the snowy vista.

"You better be Monsieur Steele! Who else should occupy your mind?" She responds.

I chuckle and shake my head. Feisty as ever.

My father was right when after the pretrial he told me:

"You go to Leonie and your sons. Important bonding occurs in the early days with newborns. Plus, your fiancée needs you."

The past four weeks will forever remain etched in my memory. Each milestone from The Twins lifting their heads on their own to watching me more intently than I watch anyone to cooing and smiling.

And Leonie... Well, her tits blew up several cup sizes, and I have the privilege as the breast masseuse to care for them. She started on a postnatal routine designed by Starr and Anita. Leonie is determined to get her pre-Twins figure back before our wedding. She declared:

"Well, now that they're born, I want to look fabulous in my gowns and wherever you're taking us on our honeymoon!"

"No one but you, Chocolate Bonbon. Who might compare to you, my love?" I murmur.

Leonie laughs again. The seductive, husky sound makes my cock throb.

We haven't fucked since the morning she went into labor. My fist has been pretty busy in the shower each morning, beating my morning wood. I don't bother Leonie about it. Hell, she has enough to handle. Besides, she came up with the crazy idea to wait until our wedding night to make love again.

And like a wuss, I agreed. Fuck!

"Absolutely no one," she purrs. "I miss you, *Amoureux.*"

Yup, another twitch.

"What are you going to do about it?" I taunt.

Leonie purrs, "Are you alone?"

I pivot to face the project manager, who's busying himself on the other side of the great room.

"I'll meet you back at your office at the hotel to complete that paperwork," I tell him hurriedly.

Shit, if Leonie wants me by myself, it must be for an NSFW reason. My dick lengthens down my thigh in anticipation. Yeah, buddy!

With a nod, he leaves, and I jog up the stairs to one bedroom.

"Are you there, *Amoureux?*" Leonie asks.

I damn near throw myself onto the bed, kicking the paper booties off I changed into when we entered the mudroom.

"Yes!" I respond as I lean back against the pillows and adjust my thick girth.

"Mmm mmm *bon*... Call me back on FaceTime. I want to see you naked, *Amoureux*..."

Leonie's lusty growl ignites my passion as I race to strip at her command.

Without hesitation, I pull the black cashmere turtleneck over my head and toss it to the floor. The pile grows until I'm free of my trousers, silk boxer briefs, and even my damned socks. Not one thing will hinder the satisfaction Leonie is about to bestow upon me.

When she answers the FaceTime video call, she's a delight to my eyes. I can just make out her plump brown nipples and now DD-cup breasts beneath a semi-sheer gold dressing gown. Her ass-length mahogany mane cascades around her shoulders and down her back in shiny waves. The gold flecks in her amber eyes dance in the candlelight.

My baby set the scene with our bedroom darkened except for candles placed around our bed where she sits on her heels in the middle. The sultry sound of *"Je T'aime,... Moi Non Plus"* by Jane Birkin and Serge Gainsbourg plays in the background.

Fuck me! I wish I were between Leonie's hips coming right now!

I growl in frustration and throw my head back against the pillows of the big empty bed.

"Oh, *Chéri*, don't despair. I've got you," she coos. "Open your eyes and look at me. I want to make up for all the time we've missed. If only for a moment…"

The temptress seduces me. Caught in her thrall, I obey.

"Take you dick in your hand. Pretend as though it's mine. See let me show you, *Amoureux*" she says.

My mouth drops open when she takes one of our sex toys, a custom replica of my ten-inch dick in her hand. It's crafted from a mold and mimics every vein and ridge along its length. Leonie's long fingers cannot circle its girth as she strokes it from the base to the tip.

I glance from the pseudo-cock down to the real deal. It lays heavy along my six-pack abs to above my navel. The bulbous tip glistens with a bead of pre-cum. I use the natural lubricant to coat the head and slide my fist to the base.

My hooded eyes watch Leonie as she continues to stroke the toy. Typically, we use it for double penetration of one of her holes while I pound another—toy to ass, cock to pussy; cock to throat, toy to pussy; or any combination. Now she uses it for our long-distance tryst.

"That's it, *Amoureux*," she purrs. "Pinch your tip for me just… like… this…"

I follow suit and grunt as my balls draw up. Damn, I want my dick buried deep within her wet pussy, feeling her inner walls milk every drop from it. Fuck!

Leonie guides me for a few more minutes as my groans fill the air.

Then my eyes pop out of my head.

She opens her dressing gown only enough to show the

curve of her ample tits. While she watches me from beneath her long eyelashes, she slides the toy between her mounds. Then with the sides of her arms she pushes her breasts around it as she leans forward biting her full bottom lip. When her little pink tongue darts out to poke the slit at the tip of the toy, I lose it.

FUCK. ME.

On a roar, I vigorously pump my cock and thrust my hips up with my muscular thighs spread wide, heavy balls hanging between them. I don't stop until ropes of my creamy cum shoot all over my bare chest, pecs, and abs tight with tension. I throw my head back as I squeeze my eyes shut and yell Leonie's name. The vision of my girth stretching her throat appears in my mind.

The intensity of my release ricochets through my body. My heated skin tingles. Spots appear behind my closed eyelids. The weight of my head too much as the light-headed sensation takes over. My curled toes relax as I allow myself to recover.

"Feel better, *Mon Cœur?*"

Leonie's voice is low and throaty. The same as after she's swallowed me whole.

An entranced, lopsided grin spreads across my face as I nod like a bobblehead. My temptress has me under her spell.

LEONIE

"*H*ow excited are you to get married and to become my sister officially? I mean, we've been best friends and the closest we've ever had to flesh and blood siblings for over eight years. But now on paper! Woo—"

"You mean my sister, too, Lola!"

I smile at Lola and Haley, my future sisters-in-law.

Lola and I share a special bond forged from the first day I met her. I remember Luc insisted I meet a new lingerie designer, and I thought, *mon Dieu*, really?

At twenty-five, I was at the height of my modeling career with well-established designers pleading with my agents to book me to open and close for their shows. Global cosmetics companies clamoring for me to represent them with exclusive, multimillion-dollar, multiyear contracts. The face of *The Lion* graced hundreds of billboards and magazine covers.

So, an up-and-coming designer like Lola was far from

my radar. Luckily for her, Luc knew me through mutual acquaintances and insisted that I meet with Lola. I chuckle to myself as I remember how persistent Luc was for me to give her a chance to discuss me being the spokesmodel for Lola's Coterie. The very handsome and sexy nobleman— or *Le Renard Argenté,* the Silver Fox Lola and I nicknamed Luc—can be very persuasive. How could I say, no? But really, I knew that if he said she was worth it, she must be special.

Now who would guess we'd go from a relationship just as strong as sisters to marrying brothers making us true sisters-in-law!

Haley. Well, the first time Roger and I dated Haley, and I didn't spend any time together. The brief love affair of two months was fast-paced and all-consuming. It didn't allow for time with others except for a business trip Roger accompanied me to Las Vegas for the opening of a Lola's Coterie boutique.

My relationship with Haley developed over planning Lola's wedding since Haley was a bridesmaid and I was the maid of honor. Even though Roger and I weren't together at that point, Haley and I bonded, especially during another business trip cum Girls' Get Away to Los Angeles.

Over the past fifteen months since Roger and I reunited, Haley and I have grown closer. She's become as much a part of our girls' crew as Billie, Blair, and Starr. From our trip to Buenguerra Island off the coast of Mozambique to her support during the pretrial when she came and stayed at the Manoir to being at my side with the pregnancy.

Between Lola and Haley, I won't ever lack a sibling I can rely on and love.

"*Mes chères sœurs...* My dear sisters, there's more than enough of me to share!" I tease, laughing. "No need to squabble, little ones!"

Sure, I'm only a year older than Lola and two more than Haley, but I rib them anyway regarding them being younger.

"Little ones, my butt!" Haley retorts with a roll of her gray eyes behind her glasses. "Don't even try it. I don't need another big brother slash sister..."

We crack up as the door to the private room in my fashion designer friend Elie Saab's Parisian atelier opens.

"So much joy, my love!"

My gaze shifts to the voice, and I smile at my friend.

"Elie! How good to see you, *mon ami!*" I exclaim as I rise to greet him.

Throughout my modeling career, I opened and closed his runway shows and was the feature model in many of his campaigns. Over time, our business relationship developed into one of close friends. Often I spend time with him, his wife Claudine, and their three sons at their home in Lebanon.

For Lola's wedding, the bridesmaids and I wore Elie Saab custom creations. Since he has a studio in Paris and is my good friend, he made my gown specifically for me matching Lola and Baz's color palette. It's a dreamy strapless column of silk organza layers in various shades of the orange and fuchsia hues.

Haley's design is a halter-top column dress and

follows the same layers as mine. Billie and Blair's were similar in fashion and feel, accentuating their curvy assets.

Now, it's my turn for my wedding gowns!

"Congratulations on your sons! Claudine sends her love and a gift from all of us," Elie responds as we embrace.

One of his assistants steps forward and hands a large gift-wrapped box to me. The giant navy blue velvet bow drapes over the matte platinum paper.

I smile and thank her, then open the gift and gasp.

It's an extraordinary jewel-encrusted copper box. The handcrafted piece has a hinged lid that opens to a ruby-red velvet-lined interior. A removable tray lifts out to reveal another compartment. A parchment with The Twins' names and date of birth written in a beautiful calligraphy script rests on the bottom. It's the most exquisite gift we've received.

"It's a keepsake box for you to put your most treasured memories of your sons. It's over a hundred years old and a rare piece made by Lebanese artisans," Elie says.

Tears fill my eyes as I thank him for such a thoughtful gift. He knows my family's history as merchants and my innate love for the aesthetics. What a perfect way to commemorate The Twins' milestones, especially Gaspard, whose name means treasure bearer!

"Oh, Elie! How lovely!" My mother adds as she hugs him.

She's joined me on some of my trips to visit him and his family. They've become close, too.

I introduce him to Shelley, and he greets Lola and

Haley, remarking on how good it is to see them again. Then we get down to the business of my gowns.

This is my second fitting and the first with the actual dresses. So I clap my hands and do my happy shimmy dance with Lola when another assistant rolls two garment racks into the room with the haute couture pieces hanging from them.

We incorporated my Christmas wedding palette of cranberry, burnished gold, champagne, and ivory into the colors of my gowns. Touches of platinum will add shimmer and match Roger's gorgeous eyes. The fiery and cool colors symbolize all the blazing levels of our white-hot romance.

Roger, our fathers, and the groomsmen will wear white-tie attire to go along with our ultra-formal evening wedding. So debonair!

The first garment rack has my reception and party dresses on it. For the reception, it's a one-shouldered, backless mermaid gown made of tiny platinum elongated beads stitched onto silk. A double fan shape forms the neckline at my shoulder and rises to one side of my jaw line. The body-hugging silhouette clings to my waist and hips, then drapes around my knees to the floor in front. The back of the gown has three bands of the beaded mate-rial crossing from one shoulder down to the other side, exposing my back to end in a vee just above my ass. The mermaid tail flows from the vee to trail on the floor in a sweep length.

Here's to the endless hours of working out with Starr and Anita! Even Norman gave me conditioning lessons.

The party dress is not so much a dress, but a bodysuit with an open-front skirt attached to a two-inch gold metal band. Sheer champagne tulle netting covered with intricate gold filigree makes up the bodysuit that features a deep-vee halter top with an open back framed by two strips of the material. The gold metal belt holds the skirt up with a large appliqué at the side of my waist. The skirt made of more sheer tulle with veins of gold sequins embroidered on it flows from my waist to pool in a train behind me. My legs left bare save for the gold double ankle strap sandals on my feet.

Talk about *Goldfinger*! The outfit inspired by the sexy femmes fatales in James Bond movies—my favorite delectable secret agent.

The second garment rack holds my wedding gown and veil.

To pay homage to my family's height of success as members of Louis XV's courtiers and when he awarded some acreage for *Le Beaulieu Manoir* to add to its existing land, Elie designed a ball gown of the era. With its wide silhouette and gold and platinum detailing, the ball gown embraces the Rococo style, which is highly ornamental and popularized in France, then spread to Central Europe.

The intricate bodice features an illusion neckline of sheer tulle that finishes in long sleeves with shimmery platinum embroidery covering the netting. Then it has a sweetheart dip at my bosom. Gold lace covers the gown from the dip to below my waist before the lace mingles with more of the shimmery platinum embroidery over sheer champagne tulle. Underneath the sheer tulle is a champagne silk chiffon skirt with layers upon layers of crinoline beneath to emphasize the wide silhouette.

From behind, the illusion material continues until it meets the gold lace midway down my back. The silk chiffon skirt flows to the floor in a circular train behind me to a chapel length with the sheer tulle a few inches beyond.

The pièce de résistance is my exceptional veil. It comprises two parts. An elbow-length blusher that will remain over my face until Roger lifts it during the ceremony. Then, for the most regal entrance and exit fit for *The Lion*, I had to have a cathedral-length veil.

The blusher ends in a raw edge of the sheer champagne tulle that has the shimmery platinum embroidery covering the netting to frame my face. The cathedral portion also has the embroidery throughout its length. It falls elegantly from a cap of elaborate platinum appliqués that starts at the crown of my head. The artisans stitched diamonds from my family's heirlooms collection throughout the cap to add to its luster.

The entire ensemble is absolutely breathtaking.

I try on each gown, and the seamstresses make adjustments. They used my pre-The-Twins form with room for my much more ample bust line to make the muslin test garment to check for the fit. Again thankful for my hard work and dedication to getting the babies weight off in time, the seamstresses have minor changes to make.

"You go, Girl! Peep you rocking your *The Lion* hot bod just as fierce as ever!" Lola whoops as she high fives with me as I stand in the party dress. "Your legs look phenomenal!"

Playfully I give a Moulin Rouge-worthy kick, and everyone laughs.

"Roger is going to lose it when he sees you!" Haley adds, giggling. "We may not get to see you on the dance floor!"

Elie claps his hands, and all eyes turn to him.

"Ladies, now is the time for Leonie to don her ball gown!" He exclaims.

Cheers and claps fill the air as I step off the fitting platform and sashay to the dressing room.

When I emerge, everyone sits in silence. I glance from one face to the next. Each makes my emotions run high.

My mother is the first to sniffle, then sob. Elie hands a handkerchief to her and pats her shoulder. Soon we're all bawling like Rodolphe and Gaspard before I feed them. The assistants rush about handing out tissues to dry our eyes. The seamstresses fuss over my gown and drape it with a silk smock to keep my tears from splattering on its beautiful surface.

"Oh, *Mon Trésor... Comme tu es belle dans ta robe de mariée!*" My mother says through her tears.

I brush a tear from my cheek and reply, "*Merci, Maman.* I feel beautiful."

"Roger will be so pleased, Leonie," Shelley whispers as she dabs her eyes. "You look amazing, sweetheart."

I nod my thanks, too overcome with emotions to respond verbally. The thought of Roger chastising me with his Alpha-male demand for my words makes me smile. My heart leaps knowing we'll marry next month!

While I changed into my regular clothes, Lola and Haley went to their dressing rooms to put on their matron of honor and bridesmaid dresses. They come out and we clap in delight.

Both of their dresses have a rich cranberry base with different details. Lola's dress has an off the shoulder sweetheart neckline with a bodice encrusted with gold and champagne shimmery beading. The embroidered skirt flares from her narrow waist, cinched with a gold belt to widen at her hips down to the floor. The silhouette similar to my ball gown harkens to the Rococo period.

Haley's strapless dress has layers of silk chiffon with a neckline of a confectioner's sugar swirl of the silk. An intricate appliqué of gold, champagne, and touches of cranberry attaches at her waist and crosses her body from one hip up to cover the opposite breast. The skirt mimics mine, too.

"The two of you are divine!" I squeal, clapping my hands and beaming. "I cannot believe what a fantastic job Elie did just from our conversations! *Merci! Merci!*"

"Thank you, my friend! We had video conferences with Billie and Blair for their fittings. The seamstresses enjoyed their trips to Las Vegas and New York City, taking private jets and staying at STEELE hotels!" Elie responds. "We'll do the final fittings here two days before the wedding. All will be spectacular, I promise!"

My mother and Shelley chat with Elie while Lola and Haley change.

Meanwhile, my mind whirls with happy thoughts.

I'm so excited everything is going to plan from the

decorations to the food and drink—thanks to my mother and Lucien—to the musicians and the DJ. Roger spared no expense to bring my fairy-tale wedding to fruition. That's my man... *Roger The Responsible*. And I cannot wait to make him mine all MINE!

ROGER

"Cut it out, Harris! Pass the cranberry sauce to me already!"

Haley growls, frustrated with her twin's antics as he teases her relentlessly. Her gray eyes flash like a stroke of lightning as she glares at him.

"Harris Steele! That is enough, young man. Stop taunting your sister and give her the platter at once," our father commands in full-on Alpha Dom mode.

Immediately Harris complies—albeit grudgingly, with a smirk on his face—and hands Haley's favorite Thanksgiving side dish to her.

"Jerk," she mutters under her breath as she snatches it from him.

He in turn mimics her response wordlessly lest our father hear his new gibe. I hide my laugh with a cough and shake my head at Harris. He smirks until our father pins him with a steely stare.

Then I can't help myself, and I laugh out loud.

Leonie peers at me questioningly, and I shrug as I continue to chuckle.

Those two will never stop. It's their usual behavior at any of our family gatherings. When we were younger, Haley would sometimes leave the dining room in tears. Our parents would chastise Harris and send him to his room.

I was always the one to go after her and offer comfort. Yeah, the responsible one.

Now it's our first Thanksgiving as a family with Leonie, Rodolphe, Gaspard, Guy, and Josy. Even Luc joins us. My gaze travels around the dining room table of my parents' new penthouse on the twenty-eighth floor at The STEELE Tower Paris designed by Leonie. Everyone smiles and appears peaceful. The atmosphere is one of gratefulness and happiness.

The pretrial judge declared me innocent; The Twins at two months are our new bundles of joy; I'll marry the love of my life in a few weeks. All is right in the Steele-Beaulieu World.

"Leonie, you did such an incredible job with the redesign of our penthouse!" My mother declares as she raises her glass of Chateau Lafite Rothschild. "*Merci ma fille aussi!*"

"Well done, Leonie!"

"It's marvelous!"

"Cheers!"

Leonie preens.

I lean over and kiss her temple. Then inhale her classic sultry perfume, Dior's Pure Poison. She tells me it makes her feel powerful, like a woman who commands attention. The blend of florals with amber and musk is the perfect balance of femininity and masculinity. My cock twitches.

"It was an honor. Thank you for entrusting me with your home," she responds humbly.

Luc shifts in his seat to face her and asks, "When do you expect to return to your new career, *chérie*? We know how important interior design is to you."

Leonie glances at me, then turns to Luc.

"Roger and I haven't spoken about it yet. But I was thinking once Rodolphe and Gaspard reach six months, I could return to STEELE's Interior Design Team part-time as a project designer."

She glances at me from beneath her eyelashes and smiles.

I return her smile and kiss her hand.

"Whatever you want, my love. We have Nanny Grace to help us. Plus, you can even design a nursery for The Twins next to your office if you want to keep them close," I say.

The adoring smile that brightens Leonie's face makes my heart swell with love.

"Oh, *merci, Mon Cœur!*" She squeals as she pulls my mouth to hers and plants a toe-curling kiss on my lips.

We get ribbed for the PDA. But we're in France, so *c'est la vie*!

"Well, that means you have to make time for your Lola's Coterie campaigns, too! And we need to work on more designs for the pre- and post-natal collections. They've been a colossal hit!"

Leonie and I separate so she can answer her best friend.

"*Oui, oui! Absolument!* I cannot wait. I have some new sketches for you, *Chérie*," Leonie says giggling as I continue to plant kisses on her cheek.

Fuck, I love this woman! I cannot wait until our wedding night so I can ravage her until she can't move a single muscle—well, aside from her pussy walls...

"*Très bon*! That's splendid news," Luc says. "Excellent idea, Roger. Leonie, you should consider a specialization in interior design for children. What I've seen of three of the... What is it? Nine? Nurseries for The Twins, they're incredibly well done. You could design nurseries, play-rooms, bedrooms—"

"Ooh, and playhouses that match the families' mansions!" Haley adds. "I've read they're extremely popular with chichi parents."

I have to give it to Luc; his thoughts are never far from revenue-generating ideas. Haley, the nerd, more than likely read about the mini mansions during one of her many Internet searches.

"That's an area STEELE International doesn't cover. The focus has always been on the main properties and amenities. Perhaps you'd like to lead your own division?"

My intense stare meets Sebastian's.

With a nod to me he adds, "If Roger is game, we can set it in motion as a subset of his division."

"That would add another offering to our clients, and we would include it in future projects. Another revenue stream," Morgan adds, ever the CEO even while retired.

Leonie looks at me, her amber eyes glow with excitement.

I pretend to consider the idea with a scowl on my face. But I can't hold it and start to chuckle.

"How can I deny my love anything? Not to mention the CEO and Steele Patriarch... Thanks, Luc, for an excellent idea!" I proclaim as I raise my glass of Chateau Lafite Rothschild. "Here's to Leonie's new division!"

"Hear, hear!"

"*Félicitations!*"

"Cheers!"

Leonie claps her hands and does that shimmy with her hips that makes my cock come to life. She turns to me with a grin and kisses me silly again.

This will never get old.

"How DID you like Thanksgiving dinner, Josy?" Shelley asks as we sip Rémy Martin digestifs in the library.

Josy gestures to my mother with her Baccarat snifter, "It was delicious, *merci!* Guy and I spent Thanksgiving with Lola at her Parisian penthouse on many occasions. She would cook a delectable multi-course meal. Luc would bring scrumptious pastries, and I would bring my double-chocolate soufflés for dessert."

She turns to Leonie and quirks her elegantly arched eyebrow at her daughter.

"Leonie, however, brought the wine since she doesn't cook despite my best efforts to teach her our Tunisian family's recipes."

Lola scoffs, "That's a wasted effort, *Maman* Josy! I've told you so for years!"

Leonie's golden caramel cheeks flush red, and she shakes her head.

"Don't tease her, *Mon Amour*. She takes after her Beaulieu side with her love for beautiful things," Guy responds as he winks at Leonie.

Daddy's Little Girl blows him a kiss in thanks.

"Well speaking of food, Nanny Grace just sent a text to me. The Twins are ringing their dinner bell! So pardon me," Leonie says.

I rise with her, but she pushes me back to my seat gently.

"Stay, *Chéri*, Nanny will help me," Leonie says as she smiles lovingly at me while she runs her fingers through my hair, massaging my scalp.

Malcolm claps his hands, and we glance at him in surprise.

"Do bring my nephews back. I haven't spent enough time with them," he says. "I don't want them to forget their favorite uncle!"

Sebastian sputters on his sip of cognac.

"Hell no! I'm their favorite uncle. So bring them to me!" He exclaims.

Harris and Luc join in, all proclaiming their place in The Twins' lives.

Leonie laughs, and her eyes twinkle.

"Simmer down, boys! You're all their favorite!"

I chuckle as she leaves the library.

"Well, don't get me started on their favorite aunt!" Lola adds.

"Yeah… Me!" Haley cuts in, lifting her snifter in salute.

Everyone laughs good-naturedly.

"Since Leonie is out of earshot, I'll tell you some stories about her as a child," Josy says gleefully.

We listen and laugh some more until Leonie returns with The Twins.

I go to Nanny Grace and take Gaspard from her arms with a word of thanks. Then I kiss his rosy cheeks as he coos happily.

"That's it. Hand him over, bro," Malcolm hustles over and plucks Gaspard from my arms just as Sebastian scoops Rodolphe from Leonie.

I roll my eyes at my siblings and shake my head.

"Hey, you could have your own, you know..." I rib them.

Baz smirks and inclines his head towards Lola.

"Yeah, no need to tell me. Have that conversation with your sister-in-law," he retorts.

Lola gives me the stink eye, and I opt to not comment. Instead, I cock my head at Malcolm.

"So what's your excuse, lover boy? How're things with—"

"You mean the sexy AF yoga teacher? Because if you're not interested, I'll step in without hesitation!" Harris says.

A growl comes from Alpha Dom Malcolm as he glares at our youngest brother.

Harris snickers and pulls out his mobile, typing on the screen.

"Oh, hi Starr... Yes, Happy Thanksgiving to you, too... I wanted to wish you a wonderful holiday and ask how the new surveillance system is going... Mmm... Right... Okay, great! I'm looking forward to the retreat, too. Thanks for inviting me... See you soon."

Silence descends on the library, making the sound of Malcolm's ragged breathing loud.

10... 9... 8...

"You. Little. SHIT!" Malcolm explodes.

I reach for Gaspard. But Malcolm pulls away and turns his glare on me.

"I know what I'm doing with a baby! Lest you forget, I used to wipe the snot from your nose," he snaps before he pins Harris with another heated stare.

"You'll pay for that when you least expect it, little brother. And lest you forget, I'm. Not. Haley," he snarls.

Harris' smirk falters since he knows Malcolm is *The Enforcer* amongst us. Damn. I feel right sorry for the jokester.

"Ha! Good! Get 'em for me too, Malcolm!" Haley shouts, punching the air in victory.

Malcolm winks at her and responds with a dark chuckle, "Will do, Baby Girl, will do."

"One day you'll learn, little bro," Sebastian laughs. Then leans over to Gaspard and adds, "Just ignore your *Oncle* Malcolm's foul mouth..."

Now Malcolm looks chagrined and glances at Leonie.

"Sorry, sis. It won't happen again," he promises.

Leonie's laughter morphs into snorts as tears fill her eyes. She shakes her head and waves her hands in front of her flushed face.

"No worries, *mon frère*! They don't understand words

yet, just emotions," she tells Malcolm as she pats his shoulder. "But, Harris, boy oh boy, I feel bad for you!"

LATER WE GO UP to our redesigned triplex penthouse to give everyone a tour.

Leonie did another excellent job with combining my parents' former penthouse below my duplex to create one large home for our growing family. It's on the top three floors, thirty through thirty-two.

Located in the Front de Seine district of Beaugrenelle in the *quinzième*, the property, like The STEELE Tower New York, is mixed-use with commercial and residential space plus the largest mall in Paris. The views of the Seine and of the Eiffel Tower are incredible, especially now at night when the spectacular light display flits across the monumental iron structure.

We decided to move into our new home when we return from our honeymoon. While we're gone, Josy agreed to oversee the move. Until then, Leonie, The Twins, and I will remain in Leonie's East Wing at *Le Beaulieu Manoir*.

The spacious wing is more like a house within a house. We took over her former bedroom suite and the nursery Leonie designed for The Twins. The rest of the wing comprises several bedrooms and bathrooms, kitchenette with eating area, library, art studio, media room, and living room.

It was all hers before she bought her duplex. It's where she stayed when she visited her parents. The maids maintain it. So it only required the arrangement of our personal items and clothing.

"Nicely done, Leonie," Luc says when we return to the main living room on the first floor. "*La Tour Eiffel* resembles a sparkling Christmas tree!"

"My favorite room is your Pilates and yoga studio," Lola gushes. "I need one! Then I can get a good workout at home."

Sebastian snorts and whispers in her ear.

Lola blushes scarlet red, but her hazel eyes spark with desire. Playfully, she swipes at Baz. He chuckles, wrapping his arms around her waist and pulling her back to his front. He places his hands possessively on her lower belly as he nuzzles her neck.

Leonie slips her hand into mine and smiles up at me knowingly.

Yeah, it won't be long before Baz and Lola have their own bundle of joy.

LEONIE

"Guess what today is, *mes beaux fils?* ... What did you say? ... *Absolument*! Your *Maman* and *Papa* become husband and wife forever and ever... And the two of you have starring roles!"

At three months old, The Twins are more active and react to sounds. The singsong of my voice attracts their attention as they lie on their tummies in front of me on the bed.

Gaspard lifts his head and laughs out loud. Drool spills from his Cupid's bow lips. Rodolphe rolls over onto his back and turns in the sound's direction. Wide gray eyes fringed with thick ebony lashes so like his father's sparkle as he studies me intently. Their serious personalities so similar.

I reach to pick him up, and he lifts his arms. It's amazing how quickly they develop.

"I know! I can't wait either!" I tell him as I nuzzle his tummy through his onesie.

His ah-goo vocalizations make me laugh with him.

I nestle Rodolphe in the crook of my knee as I sit cross-legged and lift Gaspard in the air to nuzzle him, too.

He squirms and laughs some more. It's delightful music to my ears. His carefree personality, so like mine.

"You agree, *Mon Petit Amour?*" I ask, giggling.

My mobile buzzes with "Big Poppa," Roger's ringtone. When we found out we were having twins, I dubbed Roger Big Poppa after my favorite rapper, The Notorious B.I.G.

"Speak of him, and he shall appear," I say sagely as I scoop my mobile from the pillow beside me.

No sooner than I press to accept the call, Roger's deep baritone filters through the speaker.

"Good morning, my love. Are you ready to become Mrs. Roger Steele?" He asks.

I close my eyes and take a deep inhale.

My mind wanders back over the last sixteen months we've been back together and then the twelve months prior. For over two years, it's been a roller coaster ride of highs and lows.

The best parts being our *coupe de foudre* when we met during the Lola's Coterie meeting with STEELE International, Inc. in New York City; reconciling after Lola and Sebastian's wedding in Dubai; our trip to the South of France where I became pregnant in Cannes; the birth of our Twins and our subsequent engagement here in Paris.

The struggles of our opposite personalities, with Roger being so intense and inflexible and me being more apt to go with the flow—sometimes too much so. The time we were apart was like a dull blade in my heart, constantly twisting and causing me sheer agony. To learn Roger felt the same made the ache less severe. We realized we need each other and will adjust to make our relationship work. The turmoil only made our love for one another stronger.

In the end, our initial love-at-first-sight passion proved justified.

So, am I ready to become Mrs. Roger Steele?

HELL. YEAH!

I exhale, then open my eyes and tell the love of my life just those words.

Roger guffaws. I hear Joel cracking up and Harris whooping in the background.

Oops… Did I roar it?

My cheeks heat, but I don't give a damn. I'll shout it from the top of *La Tour Eiffel* with a bullhorn proudly! By the end of this fairy-tale day, I'll be MRS. ROGER STEELE!

"It was a good idea to keep the boys busy at STEELE Place Vendôme overnight and until the ceremony this evening. Tradition is important, *Mon Trésor.*"

I nod and smile at my mother as we sit in the living room of the East Wing at *Le Beaulieu Manoir.*

Roger had it transformed into a mini spa so my girls and I could get pampered before the wedding. He arranged for my favorite day spa in Paris to set up multiple stations and rooms for our treatments.

My mother and I have facials done in an area separated by an antique, hand-painted Chinese partition. While Lola,

Shelley, Haley, Starr, Blair, Billie, Anita, and Hettie have five-star massages, scrubs, and waxings. We'll all end up together in the manicure and pedicure chairs.

We started the day with a vigorous yoga flow led by Anita, followed by meditation with Starr. So this is a much-needed respite. So relaxing and rejuvenating!

"*Oui, Maman*, I agree. We don't want any bad vibes on our wedding day!" I giggle. "We only want good times for sure!"

The aesthetician tsks when my giggles turn to snorts, causing her application of cream to miss its mark. Which in turn makes me laugh even harder. I can't help the giddy feelings swirling through me. I'm just so ecstatic!

"What's so funny, love bunny?"

Billie's silly question evokes more snorts to the point I have to sit up from the table and fan my heated face. The cucumbers roll off my eyes and plop onto my lap.

"Ha! She's hysterical! Leonie is losing it, folks!" Lola says, bouncing on her feet and clapping her hands.

Everyone laughs, even the aestheticians, albeit discreetly.

Again, I don't care. Call me mad because I'm crazy in love with Roger Steele!

Shelley walks over and plucks the cucumbers from my lap and says, "Oh, let her be. It wasn't so long ago you were in the same position, Mrs. Sebastian Steele."

Then with a wink, she adds, "Although I can understand why... My sons are fine catches!"

She glances at Starr, and her smile broadens.

Starr, however, bites her lower lip and suddenly finds interest in the nail polish selection.

Shelley snickers and helps me from the table.

"I remember how nervous I was before I walked down the aisle to Joel," Hettie starts. "It terrified me he'd get cold feet and duck out of the church!"

We laugh, and I think about how I encouraged Hettie to move out of the flat she shared with Joel and back into hers. The separation gave Joel a reason to pursue her. It worked, and after a Guys' Night Out, he bought her an incredible diamond engagement ring from Harry Winston at Roger's urging.

I too benefitted from the spontaneous shopping.

Roger bought me an extraordinary *toi et moi* ring. Two large pear-shaped diamonds with a platinum band set in pavé diamonds. The identical, flawless stones act as a reminder of our identical twins every time I see it on my right ring finger.

I gaze down at it now. My heart warms with love for my man and my babies.

"Up and at 'em! We've got a schedule to maintain," my mother says as she slips off her table and joins the others at the mani/pedi chairs.

Lola and I glance at each other and bust out laughing. We thought Shelley was a sergeant with Lola's wedding. Well... my mother is just as bad!

As our nails finish drying, one servant enters the living room-cum-spa with a beautifully wrapped box in her hands.

Throughout the day Roger sent gifts to me. A painting

of a golden lioness with two cubs trailing behind her as they amble through the grasses of the African savanna. A red suede bound book filled with love letters he'd written to me, but never sent while we were apart. A themed playlist of love songs he curated. Each precious and heartfelt.

I thank the servant. Then I lift the top—of course Roger The Responsible thought to make the gift easy to open after I had my nails done. Inside is a flat blue velvet box. I press the sapphire cabochon closure, and the lid lifts to reveal an exquisite suite of diamonds set in clusters of pear-shaped stones in various sizes: a pair of earrings; a bib necklace; a bracelet. They glitter as the light bounces off their flawless surfaces. Simply dazzling.

"Whoa! Someone pass my shades to me, stat!" Exclaims Blair as she shields her eyes from the brilliance of the diamonds.

Haley claps and adds, "My brother knows how to treat a lady!"

Indeed, he does. I smile to myself as tears of absolute joy fill my eyes. Sure, the jewelry is phenomenal. But it's the entire package—a man who loves me and our sons and with whom I'll spend the rest of my life.

It doesn't get any better than that.

"Shelley, *chérie*, you are right. Your sons are fine catch-es!" My mother says.

We head to the solarium in the East Wing that faces the Bois de Boulogne for the bridesmaids' luncheon. To go along with the spa theme, the menu comprises green salads, grilled herb-crusted salmon, roast chicken, and citrus-infused water. We prefer to eat light before putting on our gowns. Besides, I've waddled enough during my pregnancy. No need to waddle down the aisle...

I giggle at the thought.

"There she goes, again," Lola says gleefully as she twirls her finger in a circle by her temple. "Looney Tunes alert!"

"HOW CUTE ARE THEY?!"

"OMG! Hey, Little Fellas!"

Rodolphe and Gaspard look like two Christmas angels in their cranberry velvet onesies with gold bib fronts dotted with Swarovski crystal buttons. Their cleft chins bob as their eyes light up dancing from the face of one adoring woman to another gathered around them.

I smooth their silky ebony hair with the hairbrush, and it gleams. My boys are gorgeous like their father.

Even though Nanny Grace is on hand, between The Twins' *grand-mères* they were bathed and dressed in moments. Now they're ready for their official debut.

Roger and I chose to keep them out of the media. The Steeles, like many old wealthy families, prefer to stay out of the limelight except for business purposes. Being that I'm a world-renowned supermodel, I can't help but be front and center. However, our children are private to us and will remain out of the media as much as possible.

The wedding is a family affair, even if we have three hundred guests in attendance. It's not public per se. Photographers and videographers have followed Roger and me separately all day and captured images of The Twins. But again, the images are for our private albums.

I smiled when I glimpsed some photos of Rodolphe and Gaspard. They could easily model just as their father did with me for the last Lola's Coterie collections we shot in Beverly Hills, Las Vegas, New York City, Abu Dhabi, and Dubai.

Lola insists they join me in the upcoming campaigns with their faces not appearing on camera. More authentic to the post-natal vibe, she claims. I told her Roger and I would let her know. She convinced Roger with the others; we'll see if she's successful with his sons.

"Leonie, it's time for you to get dressed, my friend."

I turn to the doorway of bedroom we converted into a dressing room for me.

Elie strides inside with his two assistants and several dressers ready to help the girls and me get into our gowns.

My heart skips a beat as I realize it's almost time to say I do to the man I love.

As I stare out the window past the pristine snow-covered grounds to the forest beyond, I reflect on my childhood here in my ancestral home. With the next generation of Steeles and Beaulieus sleeping peacefully beside me in their bassinets, I imagine them running and playing on the lawns or riding their horses on the trails. The Twins will grow up and explore just as their ancestors and I did before them.

However, they'll have the added benefit of growing up

in New York City and spending time at other Steele family properties around the world. Roger and I decided we'll globe-trot while The Twins are young, at least until they're of school age.

We want them to experience different cultures and lifestyles. See the off-beat places and the conventional destinations. It's the traveler in my DNA.

A soft knock on the door brings my attention back to the room. I peer over my shoulder to find my father smiling at me with tears in his eyes.

"How beautiful you are, *Mon Trésor*"—his voice hitches and he clears it before he continues—"So regal and stunning… My baby girl."

Tears threaten to spill from my eyes. But he raises his hand and shakes his head.

"No crying. Only laughter and joy!" He proclaims.

I nod and suck in a shaky breath as I bow my head to gather myself.

A moment later, my mother and Shelley enter the room to pick up The Twins. They'll enter the Beaulieu Chapel in the arms of their *grand-mères*. Bundled in their snowsuits, they'll stay nice and warm on the drive over.

I give them hugs and wave as my mother and Shelley go through the door.

"Your turn, *Mon Trésor*," my father says as he drapes the custom cape over my shoulders carefully.

The dresser plans to add my veils once I arrive at the Chapel. We didn't want the delicate piece to sustain any damage before I walk down the aisle.

I place my hand on my father's arm, and we make our

way through the house to the ornate horse-drawn coach out front. The gold leaf and cranberry lacquer glimmer in the glow from the fairy lights strung on the palatial French Rococo mansion and throughout the estate's twenty acres.

A footman helps me up the step, and I settle on the soft leather seat.

My father joins me and beams.

"My little princess on her way to her prince," he says, his voice gruff with emotion.

I nod, too overwhelmed to speak aloud. I take the time of the short ride along the path to our family's Chapel to practice my deep breathing, hoping to calm my racing heart.

The surrounding land and the facade of the Chapel also have strings of fairy lights. The sound of a harpist with the angelic voices of a choir singing Christmas carols fills the air. The atmosphere is heavenly.

Once I alight from the coach, I pause to take it all in. My pulse races again as my face threatens to split from the smile that breaks out. I glance up at my father and he's grinning, too.

Then the wedding planner spies us, and she ushers us into a side room. The dressers remove the cape and rearrange my gown. They place the diamond-encrusted cap of the cathedral-length veil on my head before they add the blusher.

Lola walks in and adjusts my train and the veil over my gown.

I peer into the full-length mirror. Then smile at the sparkles that bounce off my opulent gown, my head from the cap and my ears, décolletage, and wrist from the suite Roger gifted me. I feel like a princess bride and I'm more than ready to marry my prince.

Lola dabs her eyes and air kisses near my cheeks before she leaves the room to line up behind the rest of the bridal party. The pairs formed by Luc and Blair, Malcolm and Starr, Haley and Lucien, and Harris and Billie.

My father holds out his arm, and we follow Lola to the wrought-iron gates at the entry to the Chapel's primary room. My breath catches at the sight of my fairy-tale wedding come true.

Thousands of fairy lights twine with the dark greens leaves and red berries of holly around the gates, the columns, and up the walls to the ceiling bathing the Chapel in a soft, golden glow. An abundance of wreaths and flowers ranging in hue from deep cranberry and burgundy to champagne and ivory fills the Chapel. The sweet, hot spiciness of cinnamon mixed with the floral scents waft through the air. The space is at once elegant and festive.

The bridal party turns to me and everyone smiles as they murmur praises. Then the music changes for the start of the procession. The Trans-Siberian Orchestra perform their "Christmas Canon." The strains of the violins swirl around me and the sweet voices of the boys bring tears to my eyes as the Chapel fills with the sounds.

When the last verse ends and the instruments continue to play, my father walks me down the aisle—the most important runway of my life—to my prince, my love, my Roger.

ROGER

"Well my friend, this time tomorrow you'll be a happily married man and join the likes of Sebastian, Norman, and me in the bliss of wedlock. Here's to you and your beautiful bride-to-be!"

Joel raises his Baccarat crystal snifter in a toast.

The glint of the amber liquid reminds me of Leonie's twinkling eyes after I've wrung multiple orgasms from her sweet, juicy pussy, and we—

"Damn, man! Get a grip on yourself with that goofy ass smile on your face!"

Along with Joel and Norman, my brothers, Luc, Lachlan, Lucien, and Laurent guffaw.

The tantalizing image of a sated Leonie spread before me dissipates as Norman's bellow and their resulting laughter resound around the room.

I heave a disappointed sigh at the loss and refocus on my bachelor party or Bro Bonding, as Laurent calls it. The youngest Jackson is their company's director of cigars and a rebellious playboy who loves to party. He's game for any opportunity to drink and have fun.

We're at Jackson Smoke&Scotch Lounge Paris—what's quickly become my favorite spot to unwind with my boys as we partake of their top-shelf Scotch offerings. I rarely smoke their fine Cuban cigars, but tonight is a special occasion.

I take a long draw on it and settle back in my leather club chair. The tasting notes of the spicy, earthy, and woody flavors linger on my palate. They blend well with the smoky, dark berries flavor of the Jackson Reserve Scotch. Its trademark bite drags along the back of my tasting.

Much like my delectable and tantalizing Leonie. As Pam Grier says in *Foxy Brown,* "the darker the berry, the sweeter the fruit, honey." And Leonie is all that, and then some...

The thought makes my mind drift, again.

The lounge is near where we're staying at STEELE Place Vendôme while Leonie and her girls stay at the *Manoir.*

Leonie and her traditions. First no more sex until our wedding night. Then I couldn't see her before the ceremony, which meant no wrapping my larger frame around her lush curves in an attempt at relief for my aching balls last night...

Fuuuck.

"Who would have thought from one meeting over two years ago would bring us to two Steele men capturing the hearts of my mentees and friends?"—Luc shakes his head and his navy blue eyes sparkle with mischief—"Roger, *oui*. But Sebastian… mmm mmm. A surprise!"

Malcolm, Harris, Lachlan, and I chuckle remembering how jealous Baz was of the Silver Fox's relationship with Lola.

Luc may be in his early fifties. But as Leonie and Lola pegged his nickname, he can go toe-to-toe with any of us for a woman's affection. Hell, he may even win! An Alpha Dom at six feet, four inches with salt and pepper hair, a clean-shaven face that highlights the cleft in his chin. He could pass for a movie star. Not to mention being a billionaire duke, the last of his noble line.

We laugh some more when Baz bristles.

Only after he put his ring on Lola did he loosen up a smidgen on Luc. Obviously, it's still a touchy topic…

"Ha! Just fucking with you, Steele," he chuckles. "I trust you and your brother will do well by Lola and Leonie. That is, if you know what is best for you."

He pauses to pin both of us with a don't-fuck-with-them stare, then raises his glass for a toast.

"*À la tienne, mes amis!*" He proclaims with a smirk.

I laugh and raise my snifter high, knowing I will forever cherish Leonie, the one and only love of my life.

ENCHANTING.

That's the only word to describe the sight of my precious love walking down the aisle towards me as the Trans-Siberian Orchestra performs her favorite Christmas song. With the Chapel alight with tiny lights and covered in flowers as the background, she looks like a dream. An unforgettable fantasy.

It takes all of my well-known self-discipline to anchor my feet to the Chapel's stone floor to prevent myself from rushing to Leonie and sweeping her into my arms. I want to carry her and our cubs away to my den.

"Slow down, bro. She's yours forever."

Sebastian, as the eldest who's always felt responsible for his younger siblings, must sense my caveman need to claim my mate. Right. Now. Plus, his being an Alpha Dom makes him very familiar with my need to mark what is mine. He chuckles and pats me on the shoulder.

I relax a bit and watch enthralled by my princess bride floating towards me on an ethereal carpet of fragrant white rose, camellia, and gardenia petals.

Through Leonie's veil, I can see her brilliant smile rivals the diamonds in her ears and on chest. Our eyes lock, and the grin that spreads from one ear to the other threatens to split my face; my cheeks hurt.

Slowly, I pull my gaze from Leonie to travel down her body, taking in the opulence of her regal gown.

The demure neckline can't hide the voluptuousness of her full breasts. The rounded tops peek above the sweetheart shape, held back by sheer material. More sheer material with shimmery silver lace covers her toned arms to her wrists where her diamond bracelet glitters. Her narrow waist appears smaller than before she gave birth to The Twins. The slimness enhanced by the flare of the skirt from her hips to the floor.

Leonie's presence captivates not only me, but our guests. Locked in an awed silence, their eyes follow her down the aisle.

Guy pins me with an intense stare before he answers firmly, he and Josy give this woman to be married to this man. Then he turns to his *Trésor* and embraces her.

I remember his words when I first met him.

He leans forward. His obsidian eyes bore into mine.

"Do not fuck my daughter over or you will pay the price."

He rivets me in place for a full minute.

Now, he extends his hand to me, and we shake as he nods his acceptance of me as Leonie's husband.

First Luc, then her father. The men in her life are protective of her, but not as much as me. I will keep her and our children safe from harm, and they will want for nothing. They are mine.

At last I have Leonie's hands in mine as we listen to the officiant, then recite our vows of everlasting love. Leonie tears up, as do I when we each say I do.

But a squeal soon replaces the tears when Sebastian presses the clasp on the blue velvet jewelry case.

Leonie sparkled before, but the enormous diamonds of the custom hand harness and her eternity band make our guests find their voices as they exclaim over the jewelry. I took a page out of Sebastian's book with a twist. I designed it to take her *toi et moi* ring symbolism to another level, including myself with our sons.

The chain of diamonds connects to her eternity band on her middle finger by three pear-shaped diamonds in a row that rest atop her hand attached to a diamond triple bracelet. Her engagement ring sits on her ring finger. The harness is removable. So she can wear her band and ring together.

I slip the entire piece on her and Leonie gasps along with her bridesmaids. Her feline eyes fly to mine, and I cock my head as I raise my eyebrow. Marked as mine for all to see.

She lifts her hand to admire the harness. Sparks fly from the flawless diamonds, even more blinding than her suite.

A ripple goes through the Chapel as the guests whisper about the magnificent piece.

Leonie winks and says, "My turn to claim you, Monsieur Steele!"

The gathering laughs and I join in.

Smiling, she places my classic platinum band on my finger. She holds my gaze and adds, *"Pour toujours, Mon Amour."*

The officiant pronounces us husband and wife.

My heart bursts with joy. Ecstatic to complete our bond after twenty-nine long months. This can only be the bliss Joel talked about. I rejoice at joining Sebastian and him.

With a smirk, I lift Leonie's veil then lift her in my arms to kiss Mrs. Roger Steele until she's breathless.

The guests stand, clap, and whoop.

I growl and end the kiss with little nips to her swollen lips; she purrs. Damn. We may not make it to the reception as strung tight as I am right now from the caress of Leonie's luscious body against mine.

With a Herculean effort, I step back.

Leonie whimpers, and my cock twitches.

Fuck. Me.

I take a deep breath to clear my head and send a silent prayer that no one notices the enormous bulge in my tuxedo pants.

Lola places Leonie's bouquet in her hand and straightens her long veil and the hem of her gown as we turn to our guests.

My gaze zooms in on our sons, who are just as much a part of our nuptials as Leonie and me. I grin when I see my mother holding Rodolphe and Josy—my new mother-in-law, so cool to say it at last—cradling Gaspard.

My sons are adorable as fuck in their bespoke formal onesies designed to match the wedding colors. Might as well get them used to dressing in the finest garments men of means can purchase.

So attentive at three months, they move their heads to take in the world around them, attracted to the sounds and lights. I swear Rodolphe's eyes widen in recognition of me when I pluck him from my mother's arms. I laugh and snuggle him close to my chest.

A small hand rubbing my lower back, then circling around my waist draws my attention to Leonie who holds Gaspard in the crook of her arm. She beams up at me with a radiant smile, and I kiss her full lips.

I grasp her hand in mine, and as a family, we stroll down the aisle to the cheers of our guests.

"You're all mine, now, Madame Roger Steele," I tell her as soon as we pass the wrought-iron gates at the entrance to the Chapel's primary space.

Leonie giggles and tugs my hand as she leads me to a separate room.

Once inside, she wraps her arm around my neck and pulls my mouth to hers. This time, she kisses me silly, and I groan into her mouth. Our tongues tangle as she deepens our fiery connection.

"And you are all mine, Monsieur Roger Steele. Never forget it!" She commands as she presses her forehead to mine.

We stand in our own little family bubble until a knock at the door interrupts us.

I call out to come in, and Sebastian followed by Lola and the rest of the bridal party barge in.

"Yeah, yeah, yeah... Time for pictures in this Winter Wonderland Chapel, Love Birds!" Lola calls out. "The guests head back to the *Manoir's Grand Hall*. The wedding planner said to hang out in here until they're all gone."

Starr laughs, "Lola, you are no good!"

I notice Malcolm stands close to Starr with his front inches from her back. His focus remains on her the entire time we're in the room.

He might as well admit something's up with the two of them. They can't keep mum forever...

I glance at Luc to see him and Blair in a tête-à-tête near a corner. She giggles and covers her mouth with her hand after he whispers something in her ear. Her face flushes a rosy pink while he smirks down at her.

What's it about weddings?

Hell, I know I couldn't take another moment without Leonie at Sebastian and Lola's nuptials. It's hard to evade love when it swirls around you. The very atmosphere charged with the electricity of two people deeply in love.

I chuckle at myself, waxing poetic.

"What's so funny, *Mon Cœur*?" Leonie asks, staring up at me while she bounces Gaspard on her hip.

I bend over and kiss the tip of her nose, then whisper, "Love is in the air..."

She follows my line of sight and takes in first Luc and Blair, then Malcolm and Starr—now facing one another, lost in their own world.

Leonie turns back to me and whispers, "Who do you think is next?"

I consider, then waggle my eyebrows.

"Double ceremony?"

Leonie cracks up, drawing everyone's attention to us.

Fortunately, the wedding planner enters and ushers us into the primary space. Hairstylists and makeup artists touch up the girls' before we pose for the cameras.

The Twins steal the show. The photographers and videographers came prepared with colorful fuzzy balls suspended from sticks to keep Rodolphe and Gaspard looking toward the cameras. They reach for them and track the balls as an assistant moves them through the air. Pros just like their *Maman*!

Since Leonie avoided me like the plague all day, a photographer and a videographer captured the guys and me in candid and posed shots. The girls did the same. So we spend little time on the group photos.

When we exit the Chapel, I laugh at the golden coach led by four horses with a driver and two footmen waiting to take us back to the mansion. Their liveries just as formal as my white-tie attire, harkens to days of the centuries past.

The beauty of the snow-covered lawns and twinkling trees remind me of being inside of a snow globe for a wintry fairy-tale. The stars glitter in the ink-black sky and the air is crisp. Sound muffled by the falling snow. It's fantastical.

Once settled in the coach, I lean over to Leonie and ask, "How's your fairy-tale wedding so far, my love?"

Her smile shines brighter than the stars and millions of tiny lights. I warm in its luminosity.

"Unbelievable! Better than I ever imagined! *Merci, Mon Cœur*," she responds breathlessly. "But nothing will compare to the consummation of our marriage..."

Forget twitching. My cock lengthens down my leg in anticipation of a warmth even better than Leonie's smile.

I smirk and respond, "What are you waiting for?"

Leonie's laughter rings out. Then she replies, "Soon *Amoureux*, soon."

ROGER

"*L*adies and gentlemen, presenting Mr. and Mrs. Roger Steele and their sons Master Rodolphe Beaulieu Steele and Master Gaspard Beaulieu Steele!"

Leonie glances up at me. Another of Cupid's arrows hits its mark and dings me in the heart. She lifts her stunning face up for a kiss. Without hesitancy, I indulge my wife—I can refuse her nothing. Our guests rise to cheer as we enter the *Grand Hall* through the screens passage.

The room is resplendent in our wedding colors of cranberry, gold, champagne, and ivory. Each table feature towers of flowers as centerpieces with cranberry and champagne colored crystal glasses, ivory plates, and gold napkins and tablecloths. Even the silver utensils have gold accents.

They covered the walls in silk drapery the color of champagne with swathes of cranberry. Christmas wreaths hang vertically in groups of four. They didn't miss the magnificent chandeliers and three-story-high ceiling either. Garlands of flowers, golden glass balls, bows, and tiny lights twine overhead.

As we pass the ornate stone hearth, I glance up at the elaborate overmantel with stone carvings on top of which the Beaulieu coat of arms and heraldic mottoes adorn the space. Even there, miniature topiaries mimic the table centerpieces and tiny lights make them glow. The fireplace is large enough to walk in and stand inside. But tonight, a roaring fire fills the grate.

Leonie smiles and nods at our guests as we make our way to the other end of the *Grand Hall* to the dais where the high table waits for us. Flanking it just below sit two tables for our bridal party on one side and for our parents with their closest friends on the other. My Uncle Connor and Aunt Lucie Jackson—parents of Lachlan, Lydie, Lucien, and Laurent—join them as the women have been best friends since before either married their billionaires.

Just beyond the dais, Nanny Grace and another nanny wait in one of the private rooms. She's a temporary helper for Nanny Grace while Leonie and I enjoy our reception. We trust the temp since she's from the same agency as Nanny Grace that the überwealthy and celebrities use to hire staff for their children, including nannies, nurses, and governesses.

However, Harris set up one of his high-tech video monitoring systems so we can check in on The Twins right from our table. Our parents have one at their table, too.

Mine to protect and all.

Before Leonie and I sit, we place The Twins with their

grandmothers so we can have our first dance, and they can watch.

Leonie wanted to surprise me with the song, so I don't know what to expect as I pull her into my embrace on the dance floor. But as the opening strains of "La Vie en Rose" by Édith Piaf play, I glance up at the minstrel's gallery to see Céline Dion with a full band.

The talented songstress smiles and launches into the first verse, singing in Leonie's native tongue. Since I'm fluent in French, my eyes well with tears when Céline sings about the woman belonging to the man and he takes her into his arms to whisper words of love.

I hold Leonie even tighter and do just that.

"Je t'aime tellement mon amour... Pour toujours... Never leave me again..." my voice breaks, and I bury my face in her hair.

Leonie gasps and wraps her arms tighter around my neck as she melts into me. Her body trembles as she too sobs, knowing how far we've come and the heartache we had to endure.

It all ends tonight. We're on a fresh path with no obstacles.

I cradle her face in my palms as I swipe her tears with my thumbs. Then I vow to her she will only see life in pink from this day forth. She nods vehemently and mouths I love you. I cock my eyebrow in return.

"Words, Pretty Kitty. I will have your words," I say.

"Oui, oui," she answers.

"Bien," I respond as I kiss her quivering lips.

Leonie sighs with contentment and melts into my embrace.

I also relax, knowing my woman loves me as much as I love her. Till the end of time.

When Céline finishes "La Vie en Rose," Leonie blows kisses and I bow to her. She offers us the best of everything in our lives together. Then she continues with her serenade.

Our parents join us on the dance floor with The Twins.

Happily, we scoop them into our arms and dance some more. Leonie partners with her father and I dance with my mother while my father twirls Josy into his arms. We continue until everyone dances as a pair while Céline performs more love songs and even her glorious renditions of Christmas carols. Then we return to our seats for Guy's welcome to the guests.

Between courses of our meal, Leonie excuses herself to feed The Twins. I rise to help. But she waves me back to my seat.

I'm chatting with Guy when his face lights up with a wide smile. A glance over my shoulder reveals a radiant Leonie in a shimmery platinum curve-hugging gown. My jaw drops at her beauty.

Leonie entered not from behind me where she left the room, rather from the screens passage. All heads turn as she sashays across the floor. The gown dazzles. But it's the sway of her hips that has me mesmerized.

She stops before the dais and lifts a microphone to her lips.

"Roger, you are the love I've always wished for. Each

day with you is the best day of my life. As exceptional as our wedding day is, I know that every tomorrow will be even more divine"—she takes a crystal flute of Taittinger Comtes de Champagne Blanc de Blancs from a server and raises it high—"To you *Mon Cœur*."

I rise and lift my flute without breaking eye contact.

Her little pink tongue slips out to skim across her lower lip before she sips. The glass hides her smirk barely as her heated eyes narrow.

My nostrils flare, and I dip my head to acknowledge her flirtatious act. Little does she realize if she keeps it up, I'm going to snatch her from the room and pound into her until she's hoarse from screams of intense passion.

Leonie spies my smirk and bites her plump lip as she shifts on her feet, more than likely feeling the same ache as me.

Yeah, Mrs. Steele… You're playing with a horny as fuck Alpha male.

Sebastian joins her on the floor and double kisses her cheeks after he takes the mic from her. She returns to my side, and I pull her into a tight embrace. She giggles when I tell her to be very careful. Then we listen to our family and friends regale us with fond memories and best wishes.

We cut the cake and toss Leonie's bouquet and garter. Funny enough, Starr catches the flowers, and Malcolm—despite Harris making a grab for it; he'll never learn—scoops the garter mid-air. We whoop and holler when Malcolm dips Starr and captures her mouth in a mind-blowing kiss. He brings her back on her feet, and she peers at him dazedly while he grins. They leave the dance floor with her tucked against his side and her head on his shoulder.

Check.

Leonie tells me she'll be right back, and I watch her and Lola slip through the crowd chatting with guests as they go.

"You finally got your girl, bro."

I glance to my left and see Sebastian chuckling. His gray eyes shine with mirth.

"About fucking time, I'd say!" Lucien adds. "If I had to watch you looking all pitiful another night at LEVELS Paris, I was going to revoke your Global All Access membership!"

I grimace at the reminder of the many nights I spent at his and Malcolm's BDSM/dance club.

Lucien came up with the idea since he figured the club would fill the void for safe, uninhibited sexual activities amongst the world's wealthiest and most influential people. They convinced Sebastian a global, luxury, members-only entertainment venue focused on hedonism would add to STEELE's bottom line. Baz, the net-net guy, saw the potential and gave them the green light.

Before Leonie, I would satisfy my sexual needs at LEVELS New York, London, or Paris. When we were together, we used the club frequently. However, during our time apart, I'd go, but never found solace with another woman. Instead, I'd just join the voyeurs and take pleasure in others' sexual satisfaction.

We haven't been in months. So I make a mental note to go once we're back from our honeymoon.

The wedding planner approaches to let me know they're ready for my surprise gift to Leonie. Just in time as I see her waltz back into the room.

This outfit change has her in a gold sheer vee-neck body suit with patterns of gold sequins and a matching open-front, floor-length skirt. Her long, toned legs go on for miles and end in fuck-me strappy heels.

I grin wolfishly and hold my hand out to her. Then I kiss her palm and twirl her to put her back to my front while I wrap my arms around her waist. We face a projector screen previously hidden behind the drapery. When the lights dim, the room goes silent.

A panoramic view of the snow-covered Swiss Alps fills the screen. The camera pans to Verbier Village, then to the exterior of the chalet I purchased for Leonie. The video continues to show me as I stand by the great room's massive fireplace.

"Hello, my love. We must be married, and you are all mine forever. I promised you the world and will begin with this chalet in Verbier as one of my wedding gifts to you. Tomorrow, after I fully claim you during our wedding night, we'll fly to Verbier with our families to celebrate Christmas and New Year's. Then, we'll boot them all out, except for our adorable sons of course, and enjoy our honeymoon. Two months of your favorite season, winter, and your favorite pastime, skiing. I love you with all my heart, Mrs. Roger Steele. Now, bid those fine guests adieu. It's time for us to say good night!"

The video pans to a mountain slope with golden rocks

forming the words I LOVE YOU, MRS. ROGER STEELE on the snow.

Leonie whirls around and throws her arms around my neck as she jumps into my arms. She plants kisses all over my face as she squeals in delight.

Leonie

I've never been so nervous in my life to get on a stage and stand before a crowd in skimpy lingerie. But my heart races since I'm as fuck right now.

It's Masquerade Night at LEVELS Paris and as my surprise to Roger, I booked the primary stage at Peepshow on the second level.

The seating alcoves are full of members in various stages of dress and sex. The mini-stages have demonstrations taking place. While others booked the performance rooms booked solid. Couples mingle at the bar that serves non-alcoholic mocktails or sit and watch the hedonistic displays before them.

He pinned me with an intense stare when he our driver Eric pulled up to the rear entrance. But I handed him a black leather half mask and donned a full one coated in gold and jewels. No one will recognize us.

It's been forever since we came, and I miss the thrill of the sex club. I'm not a sub and Roger isn't a Dom. We're into voyeurism, bondage, and plenty of toys. We well use all LEVELS Paris and all the other locations have to offer.

But me being on the primary stage in front of a crowd is a first.

For this little surprise, I had to persuade Malcolm and Lucien to help me. Initially they were adamant they would never let me get on stage without Roger knowing in advance. Once I told them I wouldn't strip completely and showed them my lingerie, they gave in. They arranged a Masquerade Night to take place the same night as my wedding with the insistence I wear a full mask.

Now it's showtime!

When the sounds of "Justify My Love" by Madonna start, my body automatically responds as it's used to the start of fashion shows with music. It's on.

I saunter onto the stage and the spotlight flicks on to reveal me in a floor-trailing red silk kimono. My mahogany mane is flowing down my back to below my ass. Roger doesn't want me to cut it since he likes to fist it when he takes me savagely from behind. I shiver at the memories as my pussy clenches.

The good thing is the spotlight is so bright, I can't make out the crowd. I only know where I left Roger standing and focus on the area.

Billie told me about a world-famous Las Vegas burlesque performer who offers private lessons via Skype. She helped me to choreograph my routine. When I performed it for her yesterday, she gave me a standing ovation.

I move to the music sensuously and disrobe one piece of specially designed Lola's Coterie lingerie at a time. The gold body sheen glows in the light and stresses my every curve and toned muscle.

The crowd quiets as they watch me perform, and the music grows louder.

I lose myself in the seductive rhythm and dance only for Roger. My hands become his as I cup and caress my heavy breasts, then pinch the turgid nipples through the lace. Turning from the crowd, I shimmy my hips as I bend at the waist to grab my ankles. My swollen, wet folds remain hidden behind the tiny briefs—I don't want Roger to have a coronary.

At the end, I widen my stance and slide to the floor in a straddle split. Then I press my torso flat to the floor as my hands reach in Roger's direction. The spotlight turns off.

The wild cries of the crowd bounce off the walls. I giggle giddily and rise. Hands grab me by the waist and hoist me in the air. I land over a shoulder in one swift movement.

Roger!

Wordlessly, he stalks off the stage and out the double doors straight to the elevator.

I hold on to his waist and squeeze my thighs together. The ache to have his ten-inch dick inside of me threatens to consume me in a fiery explosion. I whimper in sheer agony.

We exit the elevator and pad down the hallway to our private corner suite on the third level. Once inside, Roger deftly sits on the bed and places me across his lap, face down with one leg over mine.

WHAP… WHAP… WHAP… WHAP… WHAP

I jerk and yowl as Roger uses the palm of his hand to spank my ass. Each sharp blow hits my ass cheeks in rapid succession. I squirm to avoid the slaps. But Roger holds me firmly across his thick muscular thighs. The muscles bunch beneath me as the punishing blows continue.

WHAP... WHAP... WHAP... WHAP... WHAP

He adds in my upper thighs and the juncture under my ass where it meets my thighs.

Merde!

"Rrr... Roggerrr..." I wail, twisting as much as I can in his iron grip. "Whaaat... Pl—"

WHAP... WHAP... WHAP... WHAP... WHAP

The pain morphs into pleasure as my pussy contracts and my juices flow done my thighs to soak into his tuxedo pants. My squirms change into thrusts as I lift my hips to meet his palm. I mewl wantonly.

WHAP... WHAP... WHAP... WHAP... WHAP

"MINE! MINE! MINE! MINE! MINE!"

Roger's possessive growls make my nipples pebble into points, and my core vibrates with the need for his enormous girth to fill it.

I don't have long to wait.

He flips me to my hands and knees on the bed and stands behind me. The sound of his zipper opening makes me shudder.

YES! YES! YES! YES! YES!

Roger grips my hip with one hand and slides the other under my torso to wrap his fingers around my throat. The possessive hold renders me immobile.

I feel his bulbous tip touch my pussy opening. Then wham!

With one quick thrust of his hips, he plows deep inside until his balls hit my swollen clit and his pelvis smacks my redden ass. The force pushes me up the bed, but he tightens his grip. Then pounds into me with grunts and growls like a feral beast.

I keen and arch my back as my greedy pussy sucks him in deeper. I'm soaked and ready for penetration. My inner walls ripple as he pistons in and out. Each stroke more wild and out of control than the last.

A giggle bubbles past my kips.

Leonie *The Lion* once again causes Roger *The Responsible* to lose control!

Four quick spanks to my ass cheeks have me screaming.

"You think it is funny for me to see you in front of hundreds of men naked, Little Kitty?!" He growls as he increases his spine-jarring pumps.

I shake my head as I moan loudly.

"Words!" He commands.

I jolt forward from the impact of his pelvis and immediately respond, "*Non!* It was for yoouuu!"

Roger grunts in response. Then slides his hand from my hip to tweak my sensitive clit.

I scream as another orgasm crashes over me.

Roger is still hard and unrelenting in his claiming of me.

My eyes close and I twist the bedding in my fists as I give in to his dominance. He's all Alpha male and my lion bows before his wolf.

As if sensing acquiescence, I feel Roger's dick swells and pulsates. One last brutal thrust signals his impending release. Hot jets of his cum coat my pussy, burrowing deep to my cervix.

Roger lets off a bellowing roar that reverberates around us.

It triggers another orgasm for me, and I cry out in wild abandon.

"YEEESSS!!!"

ROGER

I stroke Leonie's soft, damp cheek as we lie in bed tangled in the sheets after hours of consummating our marriage. Without a doubt, we have fulfilled the requirement many times over.

She sighs in contentment as she snuggles her warm, naked body closer against my side. One of her long legs thrown over my thighs; Leonie's left hand sparkles in the moonlight with my rings on my chest. My arm loops under her to lock her in place with my hand on her rounded hip.

Undoubtedly Leonie's ass and pussy will be extremely sore for the next day or so. It's been three months since we last made love. And I haven't punished her since...

As much as I appreciate Leonie's surprise, I cannot abide others seeing her, even if she left on a skimpy lace bra and tiny as fuck panties. Nothing can contain her ample curves, and I know every man at Peepshow had a hard-on just looking at what is mine all MINE.

Not gonna fly!

Yes, I'm possessive by nature. But the caveman roared to the forefront and snatched his mate off the stage—albeit after he witnessed the entire cock-hardening performance —and claimed her fully.

Now my love sleeps wrapped in my embrace, and I can join her in a peaceful slumber.

LEONIE

"Good morning at last, Mr. and Mrs. Roger Steele! So nice of you to join us…"

The cabin explodes with a ruckus of wolf whistles, stomps, and laughter as Roger and I board one of STEELE's Gulfstream G700 private jets.

It's not quite my fault we had them waiting on the tarmac at Le Bourget Airport for twenty minutes. Blame it on the steamy shower sex scene we enacted before we left LEVELS Paris. Fortunately, we didn't have to take more time to get dressed since I had overnight bags packed with our clothes already at the suite.

Since Roger kept our honeymoon destination a secret, I picked simple outfits to keep us comfy during our travels. For him I chose a red vee-neck cashmere sweater, black cashmere joggers, and Adidas sneakers. I opted for a red oversized cashmere cardigan with black leggings and Loewe sneakers. Our mothers dressed The Twins in elf onesies. We have to stay true to our Merry Christmas theme after all!

As for the rest of our trip, Roger assured me he arranged for appropriate attire and belongings. Now that he revealed where we're going, I'm just bummed I didn't have a chance to buy new ski gear and sexy looks for après-ski.

"Leonie, I'm surprised you were on time to your wedding!"

Lola cracks up at her clever remark.

Sure, I'm just as famous for being perpetually late. But this time it's not my fault. Although I won't admit to why we're late. No need for the details, no matter how entertaining and juicy...

"Leave the newlyweds alone," Morgan says as he chuckles. "We added a buffer to the flight plan. So, we have plenty of time to spare."

Roger and I thank him and head for Rodolphe and Gaspard. Haley and Starr hold them playing with colorful rings on their laps. They're seated on the sofa near the center of the large jet.

"Hmmm interesting," Roger murmurs in my ear as he nods towards Starr.

I thought I was the only one amazed to see her on board. She and Malcolm must be coming out. They're worse than Roger and me!

"*Bonjour, mes beaux fils,*" I coo, lifting Rodolphe from Starr. "And to you too, *mon amie*. Nice to see you spending Christmas with us."

My eyebrows waggle as I purse my lips.

Starr unsuccessfully attempts to hold in a laugh. Her dimples deepen as a flush reddens her chestnut complexion.

"Well, the more the merrier. Right, Malcolm?" Roger adds as he scoops Gaspard in his arms.

Malcolm who sits at the table across from the sofa huffs.

Roger and I take the fifth living area behind them. We settle The Twins in their car seats, one next to each of us at the dining table. Then, sit back and enjoy the luxury of a custom-built seventy-five-million-dollar aircraft.

The ultra-plush G700 easily accommodates both our families and staff. The spacious interior boasts the tallest, widest, and longest cabin of all private jets. Its size suits the Steele men and my father whose large frames range from six feet, one inches to six feet, four inches.

I stretch my own long legs in front of me with a sigh.

Roger reaches across the table to grasp my hand and smiles. With his left sleeve pushed up his forearm, the sunlight coming through the panoramic oval window makes the platinum of his wedding band and Cartier Love bracelet gleam.

The bracelet was one of my wedding gifts to him. There will be no mistaking Roger is mine, even if he removes his band to box. It's my Back-Off-Bs message to all those women who still eye him after we announced our engagement. He's not the only possessive one in our relationship...

Funny enough, Roger gave me the Love bracelet diamond-paved in platinum for similar reasons!

We stare at one another and smile as only couples who are in tune can communicate without even speaking. Smiles that say, we made it, my love.

"WE WENT on a huge shopping spree for you! Roger gave us his AMEX Centurion Card. He asked us to get everything you'll need for a fabulous winter honeymoon—ski gear, après-ski, clubbing, even bikinis! Moncler, Bogner, Fusalp, only the most upscale for his blushing bride. Plus an entire wardrobe to leave here. Girl! We went all out!"

Haley's breathless by the time she finishes rattling off the clothes she and Lola picked out for me.

"Yeah, and Shelley and Josy bought everything for The Twins, too!" Lola adds. "We didn't leave the Little Pumpkins out."

Haley, Lola, Starr, and I are in the primary bedroom of my new Verbier chalet. I named her *Chalet de la Joie* since the home will bring us such joy to spend family holidays here.

As soon as we arrived and walked into the great room with its magnificent Christmas tree, my mother declared we'd spend every Christmas and New Year's here. "One big happy family," Shelley clapped in agreement.

Roger glanced at me and raised his eyebrows questioningly.

With a whoop, I gave my consent. Why wouldn't I want to surround myself with loved ones and The Twins have beautiful memories of their times here?

I peppered his face with hundreds of kisses until he couldn't hold me up from laughing too hard.

He gave us the grand tour. My face hurt from grinning so hard. I'm giddy with glee!

Now my girls and I stand in my dressing room with a custom closet filled to the brim. Lingerie, party dresses, Moon Boot snow boots, sky-high heels, ski suits, jeans— for a clotheshorse like me, this is absolute heaven.

"*Merci! Merci!*" I exclaim clapping while Lola and I do our happy shimmy dance. "I love it all! *Fantastique!*"

The rest of our bunch migrated to different areas of the chalet. Roger took the guys to the garage to check out the new snow toys he ordered. Our parents chose babysitting duties, or as they say, "important bonding time with their grandsons." So Nanny Grace acclimated herself with her suite of rooms above the garage.

We'll meet back up for an early dinner at home with a meal prepared by one of the chefs from STEELE Verbier. Roger left it to me to hire a permanent chef once I sampled a few dishes they'll make for us in the coming weeks. Yummy!

"How did your burlesque show go? I'm surprised Roger didn't lock you away in a tower for the rest of your life!" Haley quips.

Starr laughs and adds, "I know, right?! When Malcolm told me, I was like oh, boy…"

All heads spin to her. Realizing her mistake too late, Starr tries to backtrack. But we zoom in on her flub and demand answers on their relationship situation.

Too juicy for words!

Afterwards, the girls go to their suites, and I head to The Twins' suite through their dressing room passage connected to our primary bedroom. I find them fast asleep cuddled up in their cribs. I kiss my bundles of joy then chat with my parents and in-laws, still on duty in the nursery's anteroom.

My mobile beeps with a text message from Roger asking where I'm at in the massive house. Moments later, he strides into the room with his hair disheveled from the beanie and his olive-toned cheeks reddened by the icy mountain air. His dove gray eyes dance.

This is the most carefree I've seen him in a while. My heart swells with love for my husband.

He's had so much to deal with these past few months because of the pretrial that hussy caused. Then compounded by his concern for me having a healthy pregnancy with my mother's experience of multiple miscarriages scaring both of us. I say a silent prayer of thanks we made it over all hurdles.

"Hey, babe. How're my sons?" Roger asks as he bends over to kiss my lips. "Did you like your things? Are you all settled?"

I don't want him to get ramped up. So, I grab the sides of his face and pull him back to me for a full kiss to stop his rapid-fire questioning.

Roger sighs and opens up to my prodding tongue. I continue until he groans softly.

"All is good, *Mon Cœur*," I breathe against his full lips. "All is good."

* * *

"HA! CAN'T KEEP UP, SLOWPOKE?"

Roger shouts as he schusses past me on the black diamond piste, his Rossignol skis silent on the fresh powder.

The sunlight makes him shimmer as he zooms by in a black iridescent-effect Moncler Grenoble jacket with his eyes covered by orange Anon googles and matching helmet. Roger's long, muscular legs covered by black salopettes help him carve through the snow. He moves with ease and grace down the expert slope.

It's Christmas Eve morning and we're out en masse for an early morning run. The entire Steele clan and Beaulieus make our way from the top of the mountain piste to the base lodge. It's a popular time to come out, so other skiers bob and weave around us.

I've skied my entire life, so I catch up to Roger quickly.

He turns his head briefly to grin at me and blow a kiss before he zips ahead, his laughter trailing behind him.

"Last one down!" Malcolm yells as he, too, races towards the finish.

Another fine male specimen in his white and green Bogner ski suit. He bobs his head covered by a green helmet and mirrored googles over his eyes.

I laugh and tuck to bullet my way down the piste. My movements unrestricted by my new Bogner neon green stretch-ponte ski suit.

My outfit makes me feel like a racer, with black and white stripes on the upper arms and white strips along the outside of the legs. But the white KASK helmet with its silver eyes shield reminds me of an astronaut. Either way, I'm fast and overtake the others.

"That was incredible!" Starr exclaims when she reaches me.

One by one, everyone arrives. Our ski butlers help us remove our equipment and hand us our heated après-ski hats, sunglasses, and footwear.

Starr loops arms with me, and we follow the group inside for a hearty breakfast on the deck kept warm by heat lamps. As we walk through the great room of the lodge, I wave at friends who happen to be on holiday in Verbier, too. It's a popular destination for the low-key of the chichi crowd.

I stop to chat with a photographer I've worked with for years while Starr continues on. I don't realize how long I've been until a hand on my lower back and the press of a large body against mine draws my attention.

"Pardon. My wife's family requests her presence for breakfast," Roger says gruffly.

I make the introductions, and he leads me away to the deck, satisfied the photographer wasn't making a move on me. I tease Roger, and he zerbets my cheek.

"So sorry to keep everyone waiting! Let's eat!" I say when we arrive at the table laden with delicious food and steaming beverages.

"So what's the plan for the rest of the day?" Harris asks as he piles his plate high with eggs, bacon, sausages, and toast.

We turn to Roger and he claps his hands like a group

excursions guide. The thought of *National Lampoon's European Vacation* comes to mind. Just don't let private, sexy videos of Roger and me get out, I giggle to myself!

"Yes, my darling wife, we will have loads of fun! We'll go for another run, then return to the chalet. Shower and change to stroll through the village with The Twins. Take in the sights and do gift buying for those who are always last minute..."

Roger raises an eyebrow at Harris, who shrugs.

"That may be true. However, I always have the best presents. This year, you'll get coal in your stocking if you keep it up, big bro," he retorts as he takes another giant bite of his food.

Everyone laughs and digs in.

"IT'S JUST SO beautiful here! Usually, we go to Courchevel in France or Gstaad in Switzerland. What made STEELE open a ski resort here instead of somewhere else?" I ask Roger as we meander through Verbier Village.

He peers into the clear pane of the double stroller to check The Twins who ah-goo at the sights and sounds of the town's bustling Christmas market.

The cloves and spices of mulled wine mix with baked goods like bredele, semi-sweet cakes, pretzels, and macarons to scent the crisp air. Carolers dressed in costumes stroll through the aisles singing cheerfully and ringing bells. Vendors fill their stalls with handcrafted music boxes and toys, knit sweaters, scarves, and gloves, and candles and ornaments.

The festive atmosphere fills me with such joy!

"We have a resort in Gstaad. But wanted another one in a less congested location and less trafficked by tourists. Verbier has been popular with the jet set since the fifties but remains low-key with only those in the know spending time here. It also has the best off-piste trails, so more expert skiers choose Verbier. The après-ski partying is just as attractive as the slopes."

I grin up at Roger as I squeeze his arm.

"What?" He asks.

"You're just so passionate about STEELE," I respond.

He bends down to whisper in my ear, "Not as passionate as I am about getting you on the faux-fur blanket in front of our fireplace and making you beg to cum. It's the only spot we haven't christened in our bedroom."

My pussy clenches at the thought of Roger pounding into me from behind as our sweaty bodies bond in front of a roaring fire. Or me on my knees while he fucks my face; my nipples pebble and my juices drip between my thighs as sweat drips down my spine from the heat of the fire at my back.

Merde! I'm ready to go back home now…

Roger must sense my desire as he chuckles.

"But you will have to wait, Pretty Kitty, until our babies get their fill of the Christmas market," he says.

I pout and sigh dramatically.

"Oh, I will make it worth your wait. Don't you worry your pretty little head about it," Roger adds with a smirk, then kisses my lips.

"Get a room already!"

We glance up to see Sebastian and Lola striding towards us. Baz's hands filled with shopping bags brimming with presents. Lola beams at us, then squats in front of the stroller.

"Ciao, Little Pumpkins. How are you enjoying the Christmas market?" She asks The Twins in fluent French. "I know! It's something else... If you're good, Santa Claus will have lots of gifts for you!"

Roger gives Sebastian a look to say it won't be much longer. Baz grins and nods in agreement. Lola oblivious to their exchange finishes her conversation.

I smile knowingly. Yeah, my BFF's mind is changing definitely.

"Where's everyone else?"

Malcolm and Starr appear with him similarly laden with bags. Starr replaces Lola as she chats with Rodolphe and Gaspard.

Roger and Sebastian laugh out loud.

"To keep with French tradition, we'll open two presents each on Christmas Eve and the rest tomorrow," my father announces as he stands in front of the beautifully decorated eighteen-foot tree.

It even dwarfs him, and his brawny frame stands at six feet, four inches, still physically fit for a man in his sixties. He's studied jujutsu for decades and maintains a healthy lifestyle.

After returning from the market, we added our new

gifts to the already vast number beneath and around the tree's base. The colorful boxes of all shapes and sizes fill the space.

We're gathered in the great room with a blazing fire in the sizable stone hearth. Mariah Carey's "All I Want for Christmas Is You" plays in the background from my favorite Christmas playlist. The classic songs of Nat King Cole, Johnny Mathis, Céline Dion, Gladys Knight and the Pips, Frank Sinatra, and of course the Trans-Siberian Orchestra never get old.

The chef prepared steaming mugs of delicious hot chocolate and mulled wine for us to enjoy with the tasty morsels we bought. I asked her to make Roger's favorite Christmas treat—gingerbread cake with butter rum toffee sauce and fresh whipped cream.

When he saw it, he whispered how he intended to drizzle the warm, sticky sauce over my naked body and lick each delectable inch clean slowly. Then fill my pussy to the brim with the cream and eat it out.

Merde… I started to ooze my own cream right then and there.

Harris jumps up and rubs his hands together.

"Excellent idea, *Papa* Guy! I'll start with a gift for you," he says with a wide grin. "We give the best gifts first, you know!"

We spend the next hour exchanging presents and enjoying the goodies. I saved the painting I made of Roger for our return. I had it hung in our bedroom for our eyes only.

Instead, with Roger being an aficionado and collector

of fine watches, I give him the Assouline coffee-table book on Rolex and a watch. The hand-bound tome in a handsome presentation case offers a selection of the watchmaker's most exceptional timepieces in its history. He'll find it to be an interesting read.

Sebastian—another avid collector—told me about the rare Cosmograph Daytona Paul Newman "John Player Special" in eighteen-carat yellow gold going to auction. Its stunning black and gold livery makes it distinctive and eye-catching, just like my man. My bid of $1.54 million won. Without a doubt, I had to swoop it up for him!

"Leonie, babe, this is incredible… There are only ten known pieces in the world… *Merci, Mon Amour*," Roger says awestruck.

"The way you're ogling that watch makes me jealous!" I tease, laughing. "Should I worry, *Mon Cœur?*"

He smirks and says, "Well, she is an exquisite golden and black beauty, Caramel Bonbon…"

I giggle and swat his hands away as he reaches for my waist.

Undeterred Roger plucks me from the sofa and spins me around as he kisses me silly.

"Rest assured, no one and nothing compares to you, Mrs. Roger Steele."

I giggle and respond, "You had me worried for a minute there, Monsieur Steele!"

"Never," Roger replies gruffly. "Forever you."

Wolf whistles and applause fill the room. Even The Twins ah-goo from our mothers' laps.

Roger puts me on my feet, and we bow and curtsey to the enthusiastic crowd.

The chef announces dinner, and we troop to the dining room. She prepared another award-winning menu wait-staff from one of the STEELE Verbier restaurants serve.

In keeping with the French tradition of le *Réveillon de Noël* for the Christmas meal, the dishes include Beluga caviar, foie gras, oysters, lobster, scallops, fresh truffles, roast goose, venison, and cheeses. We end with the para-mount French Christmas dessert *la bûche de Noël*—the Yule log. All the while, a selection of wines and champagne please our palates.

We move to the cinema room to watch *It's a Wonderful Life*, Roger's favorite Christmas movie and a Steele clan tradition to watch it the night before. I adore the ringing of the bells and always add a new one to my tree every year.

Roger and I take a detour to feed Rodolphe and Gaspard in one of the nearby rooms. My new uniform of a comfy cardigan keeps it simple for me to feed The Twins. Roger also enjoys the easy access when he wants a little taste.

Once Roger helps me to get situated, he sits on the chair opposite with his elbows on his knees and his hands clasped in front of him. He shakes his head and smiles, then lifts his luminous gray eyes to me.

"What?" I ask as I shift Gaspard slightly. He gurgles, and I smile at him while I stroke his chubby cheek.

When Roger doesn't respond, I glance over at him and ask again with my eyebrow arched questioningly.

"When I heard the melodic sound of your laughter, then

saw your naked boobs two-and-a-half years ago, I never would have thought I'd see my sons feeding from them," he responds, shaking his head. "Damn, Leonie, can you believe how far we've come? It's amazing truly, babe."

I ponder his words, then shake my head, too. He's right. It hasn't been so long a period. Yet here we are, parents and married. Our blended families—my parents, Lola, the Steeles—enjoying time together during the holidays. It is amazing.

Never would I have imagined a meeting would end in marriages for my best friend and me. Particularly to brothers!

"I agree. And I'm so very thankful for it all"—I stare into his eyes intently—"How about you? Are you happy, *Mon Cœur*? Truly?"

Rodolphe chimes in with a loud laugh and waves his arms. His brother picks up on the sound and joins in.

Roger and I look at each other and crack up until tears roll down our reddened cheeks. I try to catch my breath, but with two babies it proves a challenge. He helps me by lifting Gaspard into his arms as he chuckles some more.

"Well, my sons took the words right out of my mouth!" Roger starts as he bends over to kiss me, "My love, I am beyond happy truly!"

My heart swells with joy.

LEONIE

"*H*ey. What are you doing up so early?"

Lola glances at me over her shoulder. She's curled up on a settee in the windowed walkway that connects the chef's kitchen and butler's pantry with a cluster of rooms. An oversized cashmere throw bundled around her, engulfs her petite body.

The sad expression on her face makes me pause.

"What's wrong?!" I ask urgently as I sit beside her hurriedly. "Why are you out here and not upstairs with Sebastian? Did something happen?"

My mind races with possibilities: she and Sebastian argued; she misses her parents, who died in a horrific car accident when she was a teenager; something happened with Lola's Coterie. The most important things in her life jump to the forefront of my guesses.

She sighs and wipes a hand over her heart-shaped face. With a smile, she shakes her head. The glossy raven tresses move about her head. "Sebastian and I—"

"I'll kick his ass! I don't care if he's Roger's brother! What did he do to you?!" I demand thinking how I warned him not to hurt my BFF when they first started dating.

Lola giggles and holds up her hands to stop me.

"No. It's not what you guess," she says. "He wants to have a baby for a while now. At first he only hinted at it, later mentioned it outright. Now, being around The Twins and seeing how happy you and Roger are and how you're making the family thing work, Baz brought it up again last night. I couldn't fall sleep. I stayed up thinking long after he fell asleep. So I came down here for some chamomile tea."

She twirls a strand of hair around her fingers. Her gaze goes back out the floor-to-ceiling windows and to the beauty of the snow-covered Swiss Alps beyond. Puffs of snow fall from a leaden sky.

It's Christmas morning and a picturesque wintry day. My best friend should enjoy a cuddle with her hubby instead of sitting down here all alone. I wait for her to continue.

Moments later, Lola shifts on the settee to face me.

"I do want children, and I know we can make it work, too," she starts. Again she looks away. "But I'm scared about them losing one of us like I lost my parents at seventeen. It's really so hard…"

Lola's voice cracks and tears fill her hazel eyes as her lower lip trembles.

I scoot closer and pull her into an embrace. The maternal instincts in me make my rock Lola and hum softly as I rub her back soothingly. I cannot imagine how she felt that night when the police came to her family's apartment on Manhattan's Upper East Side. Only a few hours before, she'd wished her parents a good time at dinner with their out-of-town friends.

Merde.

Lola gives me a squeeze before she sits up, drying her eyes with the back of her hand. She takes a deep cleansing breath like Starr taught us. On the exhale, Lola nods as though coming to a decision.

Again, I wait for her to speak, knowing my friend so well and how she likes to think things through uninterrupted.

"I can't not live because of a what may happen. I want what you and Roger have just as much as Sebastian. Hell, probably even more"—she chuckles and clasps my hands in hers—"What do you think? Am I being silly?"

I squeeze her hands and shake my head.

"Absolutely not! You had a traumatic experience that's not so easily overcome. Luc and I helped you and being around my parents did, too. But it still had to be hard"—I squeeze her hands again and continue—"But now, you have a man who loves you madly and an even bigger family with the entire Steele clan. You have the support of many loved ones. 'Live. Live. Live' as Auntie Mame says!"

Lola giggles at my reference to one of my favorite movies about the eccentric, carefree socialite who let nothing or anyone make her change course—much like me.

"There you are!"

"We've been looking all over for the two of you!"

Roger and Sebastian stride down the hallway, their long legs make quick work of the distance between us. Baz cocks his head to the side and narrows his eyes when he notices Lola's tear-stained face.

"What's wrong, baby? What happened? Are you sick?" He asks rapidly as he rushes to kneel before her.

I study his stricken face and determine he's more than the right partner for Lola as he's proven over the years. His love for her is limitless. I pat his shoulder and squeeze it. He glances at me, puzzled.

"Take her upstairs. Despite how nice it is for us to have some BFF alone time, I'm positive Lola would rather be with you than in this walkway with me," I say grinning.

Baz nods and scoops Lola in a bride-like hold. She wraps her arms around his neck as she nuzzles against him. Roger claps him on the back as they pass.

Once they're out of earshot, he turns to me and asks, "What happened?"

I pat the settee next to me and cover us with the throw. As I lean my head on his broad shoulder and he puts his arm around me, I recount Lola's concern and my response.

Roger agrees they're ready. Suddenly he laughs at how he bested his eldest brother for once.

He pulls me tighter to his side and lifts me onto his lap as we watch the snow continue to blanket the surrounding landscape. It's so beautiful and evokes a sense of calm.

Moments later, the sun breaks through the overcast gray and turns the sky fiery with shades of orange, gold, and blue. The clouds disperse for a glorious Christmas Day.

. . .

"How are you feeling now?" I whisper to Lola.

We, along with Haley and Starr, finished a few runs and kick back on chaises at the base lodge deck sipping hot cocoa.

Roger and his brothers went off-piste on Chassoure, as the locals call it, or Tortin to everyone else. It's one of the most challenging runs in Verbier and well-known in the ski world. The terrain and the level of difficulty concerned me. But he assured me they would take precautions with a trail guide, and each of them set with high-tech tracking devices and satellite phones.

In fact, all of us wear the gadgets and carry the mobiles whenever we're on the mountain slopes.

Still, I told Roger I'm not looking to become a widowed, single mother!

He promised me they'd be perfectly safe and would meet us back at the chalet later. After a scorching, knee-jellifying kiss, he slapped me on the ass and marched out the door. The carnal caveman...

But damn if my pussy didn't clench and heat permeate my core as my nipples hardened to points. Yeah, I can't wait for my virile Alpha male to get back home.

Our parents met up with friends who happened to be on holiday here, too. While The Twins stay with Nanny Grace.

All of which left time for a much-needed Girls' Day Out of good friends, laughter, and plain ole silliness!

Now a humongous smile breaks out on Lola's face, and

her eyes glitter more than the sun-kissed snow. She claps and shimmies before she shares their conversation. When she tells me Sebastian's reaction, I cover my ears and sing loudly. TMI!

"What's going on?" Starr leans forward from her chaise to ask.

Lola hesitates for only a moment. Smiling, she launches into the details once again. Afterwards, she stares pointedly at Starr and Haley.

"So, who's next? Hmmm? Lachlan... Malcolm... Do not consider for one second we haven't noticed signs and sexual tension between you guys!" Lola says, waggling her perfectly shaped eyebrows. "Don't even try to deny it."

"Yeah! Sparks were zipping amongst you at my wedding from the rehearsal dinner through the reception," I add, daring them to dispute the obvious.

Shy Haley flushes crimson while always-remain-balanced Starr gets flustered.

Lola and I rag on them some more, but all in good fun. We make a bet on who will come back next Christmas with whom. Included in the lineup are Luc and Blair and Billie and Patrick Rockett—her Scottish billionaire boyfriend and the CEO of STEELE International, Inc.'s biggest competitor Rockett Construction Company. Both couples showed their affection for one another openly during my nuptials.

"Well, Starr's already in this year and Malcolm is not one to bring women around at all," Lola says. "In over two years, I've never seen him with anyone seriously. But you had him disconcerted the morning after my wedding."

I agree with Lola in over the year Roger and I have been back together, I've only seen him occasionally with a sub at LEVELS New York or Paris. However, I don't mention that part to Starr. It's not as though they were dating at the time or even together as far as Roger and I can figure out. Both of them have been pretty mum about their situations.

"I know. But I'm not sure if I'm ready to get involved with anyone, and I've been putting him off for quite some time now," Starr admits. With a sigh, she tells us more.

We offer her words of advice and encouragement.

She's fast become a part of our inner circle since Lola met her at Starr's first international fitness retreat on Fijian Laucala Island. As the founder of Starr Light Fitness & Wellness Beverly Hills, she wanted to extend her yoga and meditation classes beyond Cali.

Lola raved about her experience and how cool Starr is as an instructor and friend. Later, she introduced her to Malcolm as he's the president of STEELE's Entertainment Properties Division, Malcolm oversees their casinos, hotels, and resorts. A partnership with STEELE gave her the access she wanted.

However, Malcolm wants more access, too…

"And you, miss?" I ask.

"Right… What's your story, morning glory?" Lola chimes in as we turn to Haley.

Normally she would push her glasses up her nose, but she's taken to wearing contact lenses recently. She says it's better for her peripheral vision. So instead, she pushes her mirrored Ray-Ban Aviators to rest better on the bridge. I think it's more of a nervous tell.

I also know not one of Haley's big brothers would appreciate Lachlan getting involved with their baby sister. Particularly Sebastian since he and Lachlan are best friends and Baz knows he's an Alpha Dom. Roger told me the idea of his little sister being a sub to Lachlan makes him want to knock him out.

Even though they refer to the Jackson siblings as their cousins, there's no blood relationship—only their mothers being BFFs for decades. So technically, the boys should stay out of it—if an it exists truly.

Lola and I think they'd make a cute couple—shy, curvy Haley and movie-star-looks, dominating Lachlan.

Roger and Baz would have conniptions if they even though Lola and I had a smidgen of interest in their cousin. I laugh out loud at the thought. Lachlan is as sexy as them, but Roger is it for me!

"What's so funny, Leonie?" Haley asks self-consciously.

I wave my hand and respond, "Thinking about your overbearing brothers. Better you than me!"

Haley shakes her head and purses her lips. She fills us in on her latest escapades with Cary Grant lookalike Lachlan.

"Speak of the devils... Look who shows up now. I thought they were meeting us at the chalet," Lola says, nodding towards the entrance.

As Haley finishes, and we were ready to dive deep with an analysis and strategic plan, the boys walk out onto the deck.

Every woman's head turns to gawk at them—young and old alike. I growl, feeling more possessive than my caveman. Back off, I want to snarl. Mine!

Yet, who can blame them?

As soon as Roger spots us, he smiles brightly and leads them our way. From his broad shoulders to his tapered waist and powerful thighs, he's the epitome of masculine beauty. He takes his Moncler Grenoble black skull cap off and runs his long fingers through his thick, collar-length ebony hair. His usually clean-shaven face covered by stubble he says keeps his cheeks and cleft chin warm while he skis.

To me, it adds to his sensuality. Mmmmmm.

Sebastian, Malcolm, and Harris don't differ from him at all. Baz and Malcolm could easily pass for twins being of the same stature and looks. Harris, who may be the shortest at six feet, one inch, is still cut from the same ultramasculine cloth as his elder brothers.

They're like a pack of Alpha males whose high testosterone levels call to every women's womb with an aching need to be pounded and filled by them. Funny enough, even some men glance their way in awe of their commanding presence.

The STEELE Quaternity live and in full effect.

In pairs, shoulder-to-shoulder, the boys glance neither left nor right as they stride past several tables and chaises to reach us.

All of us but Haley salivate at the sight of them. She groans and throws her head back against her chaise in annoyance at the interruption of her relationship advice session.

"Give me a fucking break already," she mutters.

Yup, and there goes our Girls' Day Out!

ROGER

"Fuck me, bro! How the hell are you sitting here all relaxed sipping Scotch while your sexy AF, new bride shakes her thing in a swishy mini dress on that center pedestal?"

Harris' disbelief at my outwardly stoic behavior makes me laugh.

In actuality an inferno burns within me, licking along my spine to my fill balls. A smirk curves my lips as I take another sip of the Jackson Reserve Scotch the fire in its bite matches the fire in my loins. Yeah, I appear at ease. However, I'm enjoying the show Leonie is putting on more than Harris can ever imagine.

We're at Farm Club Verbier, the dance and nightclub famous since the early 70s. It's maintained its popularity for decades, symbolized by its glamorous vibe and great reputation. It's like the Studio 54 of Verbier—if the walls could talk...

And with the way Leonie is doing her signature

shimmy—laughing with her arms thrown overhead, wriggling her curvy body while her hips sway to the beat—everyone is talking. The 20s flapper-style mini dress hugs her in all the right places as it rises to the tops of her toned thighs. Layers of white swishy beaded and sequined fringing atop white sheer chiffon glimmer on the dance floor.

The catch is Leonie wears my engagement ring, wedding band, and hand harness. The sizable jewels sparkle more than her dress. No one can miss she's taken. And by a man with the means to give her the world on a platinum platter.

So nah, I'm not worried in the least. Hence my relaxed stance as I partake of a fine Scotch.

"Leonie is dancing for me, little brother," I answer to put his mind at ease. "Watch closely."

No sooner do the words slip off my tongue than Leonie lifts her heated feline gaze to where I stand by our booth in the VIP section. When our gazes connect, a curl touches the corners of her full lips as she inclines her head slightly. Seconds later, she spins to put her back to me and jiggles her round ass. The plunging, glittery vee cut of the dress acts as a flashing pointer to the bullseye.

I accept the invitation, and with a nod to Harris, I go to claim my mate. Now everyone will see the man to whom she belongs. I lick my lips in anticipation of her lush curves against my hardness as my cock thickens and lengthens along my thigh inside of the black leather pants.

Harris' hearty chuckle follows me out onto the dance floor.

As I make my way through the throng of partiers, a small hand on my forearm slows me.

"Hi handsome," a buxom redhead murmurs in my ear. "Dance with me."

She presses her surgically enhanced tits against my side as she grinds her pelvis into my hip.

Uh, no.

As I shake my head and lift my left hand to show my wedding band, I extricate myself from her clutches. Just in time because over her head, I get a glimpse of *The Lion* stalking towards us. The dancers part like gazelles darting from the African Savanna's apex predator.

The expression on Leonie's face is deadly, more so than her namesake.

Oh shit.

Unfortunately, the redhead doesn't take the hint or chooses to ignore my ring because she loops her arms around my neck. She melds her body to my front.

"Wow! Oh my... Is that big ole thing all for little ole me?" She coos, gyrating her narrow hips.

Without delay, I pull back and grip her arms to unyoke myself. Leonie finishes the removal by grasping the woman by the waist and moving her aside.

I swear I can pick up a growl come from Leonie, but the sound of the music makes it hard to determine it clearly. However, she glares at the redhead with such ferocity the unlucky woman hastens away quickly, peeping over her shoulder to check she's not being chased by *The Lion*.

Leonie watches the redhead until she blends in with the

dancers. Then she tosses her glossy mane and rounds on me with an arched eyebrow and pursed lips.

My cock twitches at her possessiveness.

I grip Leonie's hips and crush her against me as I bend my knees to grind my engorged dick up against her clit.

The momentum forces Leonie's hands around my neck to maintain her balance in the five-inch fuck-me heels. Her pillowy tits press against my pecs; the pointed nipples poke through my thin cotton shirt.

We're eye to eye and chest to chest, connected intimately at our pelvises. I want Leonie to know just how much I want her and only her. No one else will ever do for me again.

Her nostrils flare as she scents the pheromones emanating from her mate. Slowly she traces the tip of her little pink tongue across her upper lip, then sucks her plump lower lip into her mouth.

I lose it and capture Leonie's mouth with mine.

Immediately her lips part, and my tongue surges inside to tangle with hers. I suck and nip at it until she whimpers and grips my shoulders to remain upright on wobbly legs. The savage kiss leaves her breathless as I plant open-mouthed kisses on the column of her slim neck.

She tilts her head to the side to give me better access.

Once I reach the sensitive juncture of Leonie's neck and shoulder, I suck a bit of the flesh into my mouth. Not until I'm satisfied my mark remains, I worry the skin.

Leonie cries out softly and squirms in my passionate embrace. My cock jumps from the pressure. She feels it and moans with her head thrown back. Her ample tits push towards my face.

I ache to bury my face between them and ram my swollen cock into her tight pussy. But settle with lifting her leg up to drape around my hip. With a tilt to my pelvis, I angle my bulge against her pussy lips through her thong when the hem of her mini dress rises higher.

We groan at the erotic contact and grind against one another steadily. When Leonie moans and shudders in my arms, I know she's reached her climax.

My mouth leaves her neck and I slant it over hers. My hips continue to move, but then still when Leonie slips her hand between us and unzips my fly. When I try to pull back, she winds her leg around the back of my thigh, locking me in place. A slight shift, and I'm balls deep inside of her warm, wet pussy.

Fuck. Me. Now.

With the lights dim and caught in the press of the partygoers, no one notices I'm fucking Leonie in the middle of the dance floor. I pound up into her repeatedly as both hands grip her firm ass, my fingers dig into her flesh beneath her mini dress. More marks for my mate.

The pressure mounts and my spine tingles with a frisson of electricity. A few more thrusts, and I jam my dick farther up her pussy, striking her cervix. My body stiffens and my thighs quiver as my release runs through my body from my heavy balls, through my dick, and out the bulbous tip.

Leonie's pussy walls flutter up and down my shaft, milking every drop of my cum deep into her womb. I cover her mouth with mine to muffle our cries of ecstasy as our bodies continue to pulse.

As I withdraw, my seed spills down the insides of her thighs. I collect some of it on my fingers and bring them to her mouth.

With a wanton gaze, she parts her lips for me to place my coated digits on her tongue. Purring contentedly, she laps them clean. I continue to swab her thighs with my fingers, and she licks them anew until not a bit remains.

Leonie lowers her cheek onto my shoulder as we sway to the seductive, throbbing beat of our racing hearts. The rhythm proves better than any music ever played.

And here's to another carnal story for the walls of Farm Club Verbier: Roger Steele took his new bride Leonie Steele higher than the Matterhorn in an explosion of fiery passion.

"DUDE, you need to open a LEVELS Verbier. Ski in, ski out style! A little action on the slopes and in the playrooms."

Harris says as we take shots of Oval Vodka at Public Verbier, the swanky spot and counterpart to Public London.

We hit all the hot spots leading up to New Year's Eve since we'll celebrate it at the chalet.

Leonie prefers to ring in the New Year as she would like the rest of the year to be—good times with family and friends at home for dinner and a party. It's a tradition for her and the Beaulieus. She gave me Christmas, so she can have her way.

Damn, look at me, a considerate hubby.

"You know, that's not a bad idea," Sebastian adds, slamming his glass down with a smile next to the Swarovski crystal bottle of vodka. "Of all the clubs we've partied at, none can compare to LEVELS. Bring the heat to the Alps!"

"Yeah, spoken like a true Alpha Dom," I chuckle.

Baz's laughter rings out.

He's been in an exceptional mood since we found Leonie and Lola in the walkway the other morning. I imagine getting his way adds to his happiness.

Good for them! I'm in favor of a family. Especially with a certified banger wife like Leonie. And Lola is no exception, the sexy petite firecracker.

"I can see that being a profitable possibility. Surprising how a tech geek can think beyond code," Malcolm ribs Harris good-naturedly.

He and Haley founded the subsidiary STEELE Technology and Cyber Security and jointly run it as co-heads. We tease the Dynamic Duo often for being nerds. But they're smart as hell and keep STEELE, other businesses, and high-net worth individuals up to date with their systems and well protected.

Yet, he's still an Alpha male, who like the rest of his brothers seeks release within the LEVELS clubs. Haley, not so much. We'll be damned if some schmo ties our baby sister to a St. Andrew's Cross and canes her ass.

Malcolm continues thoughtfully, "We can take over one

property near the hotel and close by the other clubs for accessibility. I'll run it by Lucien tomorrow, thanks."

They fist bump, and we down another round of shots.

Our server appears with an assortment of finger foods including Russian pancakes with Beluga caviar, marinated mushrooms, and cheddar olives. The leggy blonde bends over the table to reach for Malcolm's plate, nearly spilling her ample tits out her top.

He ignores her and carries on his conversation with Baz.

She lingers to throw a meaningful glance Harris' way, and he winks at her with a smirk. Taking his response as an invitation, she sidles up next to him to ask if he needs anything else.

A sly smile crosses his face, and he beckons her close. As he whispers in her ear, a crimson flush spreads across from the tops of her breasts to her cheeks. When she stands, she bites her lower lip and nods before she walks away. The exaggerated sway of her hips makes her skirt flutter around her thighs.

"Obviously you're doing all right without the play-rooms," I tell him, smirking.

Harris sits back and plants his feet wide on the floor, spreading his arms along the back of the booth.

With a smug expression he responds, "You could say so. I'll have some not so little action tonight."

Malcolm lifts his shot glass in a toast, "Here's to ski in and ski out, my brothers!"

"Hear, hear!"

"Abso-fucking-lutely!"

"You can say that again, bro!"

We raise our glasses and toss back the vodka shots.

Hands slide up my back, and slender arms wrap around me, pulling me into an embrace. The sultry scent of Dior's Pure Poison wafts in the air.

Leonie.

"Oh *Amoureux*, come dance with me," she purrs seductively in my ear.

I grin at our new code phrase for fucking. My cock pulsates knowing I'll be balls deep within her always ready for me pussy. I turn to my brothers and bid them a good night.

Time for my action to start.

LEONIE

$\mathcal{W}$hat a way to end the year with my legs thrown over Roger's broad shoulders and his head between my trembling thighs. He laps from my back hole past my pussy lips to my sensitive clit.

"Aaaahhh... Fuck... ah..."

A gasp falls from my slack mouth when Roger nips my nubbin. He worries the distended tip with his teeth and the flat of his tongue to draw another toe-curling climax from the depths of my being.

I arc off the bed, screaming his name, clamping my legs against the sides of his tousled ebony head. My hands push and pull at the long strands, undecided to accept the pleasure or the pain.

It's been hours of lovemaking with only moments of rest between bouts.

Roger insists upon completing a marathon representing each month we've been back together before midnight New Year's Day. Every opportunity he gets, he seeks to achieve his goal. With a total of seventeen months, that's a hell of a of fucking in a few days...

The sex-driven man chuckles darkly against my pussy lips as he kisses them. After he readjusts his grip on my ass, Roger spreads me wider and presses my body back onto the tangled sheets.

Now my most private places are super-exposed to his onslaught. I try to squirm, but to no avail.

"No getting away from me this morning, Pretty Kitty," he hums against my seam. "I will have my fill of my succulent, pink pussy."

The vibrations roll through my core; my wrecked pussy weeps.

"Merde... Tu te sens si bien, Amoureux... Aaahhh... S'il te pla" t..." I wail as my inner walls clench then spasm with another massive orgasm. No longer able to think clearly, I lapse into my native tongue to tell my lover how good he feels and to plead for relief.

Roger responds to me in fluent French to deny my request and continues his ministrations.

His molten-platinum eyes stare intently as I writhe and shake my head from side to side. His tongue flicks lazily over my swollen clit.

Unable to look away from him, I watch helplessly as Roger settles deeper between my legs. His wide shoulders push my achy thighs further apart.

"Give me one more, Pretty Kitty," he growls before he spears me with his tongue.

Rapid strokes to my G-spot send me over the edge once again. I yowl as another wave of pleasure swallows me.

"Good girl," Roger croons as he slides over my sweat-soaked body, trailing open-mouthed kisses on the heated flesh.

I shiver and mumble incoherently, too spent for any other response.

However, my mind snaps to when Roger's plunges his ginormous dick past my soaked folds to plunder my dripping pussy.

Each powerful thrust rocks the bed and shifts me upwards

"Hold on to the headboard," he growls. "And keep your knees separated, thighs on the bed."

Straightening out over the length of me, Roger widens his legs and rises to his toes with his hands on either side of my head.

Locked in place, I can only take the force of the impact. My breasts bounce with each powerful thrust. The intense pleasure like nothing I've ever known. I cry out repeatedly and beg for more, harder, deeper.

Roger with precision focus gives me exactly what I crave. His grunts and groans as savage as his brutal pummeling.

"Whose is it? Who do you belong to?" He demands.

My pussy contracts around his thick length in response to his caveman possessiveness. I mewl and toss my head, tilting my hips to take him deeper.

"FUUUCK!" Roger roars. "MINE... MINE... MINE!"

He slams home each word battering my wet heat, triggering another orgasm for me as I follow his.

"ROGEEERRR!" I keen.

"Say it!" He rumbles in my ear, the weight of his much larger body pressing me into the mattress as we remain tied in our erotic embrace.

"Tout à toi, Mon Amour..." I murmur, twining our limbs before bliss envelops me.

* * *

"GOOD THING each of the bedrooms are soundproof," Roger says, smirking. "Or else everyone would know how well I pleasure you, Pretty Kitty."

I awake in a state of sheer euphoria. Languidly, I stretch my sore limbs as I blink at my demanding lover.

Roger kisses the peaks of my nipples, then leans on his elbow. He traces patterns on my skin while he stares back at me.

"How very true, and I thank you for your inimitable foresight," I reply cheekily, my voice low and throaty from screams of ecstasy.

I hiss when Roger pinches my nipples. He arches his eyebrow and cocks his head in response.

Merde.

When I refuse to give in, he straddles me and tickles me nonstop.

Laughter bubbles up, then snorts as I squirm to keep the upper hand. I toss my head to deny him again and again.

My Alpha male has none of it. Roger ups the ante with zerbets wherever his lips reach.

The combination proves too much, and my resistance crumbles. Hands raised up; I call a truce. But a truce is not enough. Roger wants it all as he does with our lovemaking. Relentlessly he tickles me until I give in fully.

"Fine! Fine! I apologize for being snarky!" I shout breathlessly.

Roger nuzzles my neck and rolls onto his back, pulling me along with him. He rubs my flanks to soothe me as my body calms.

"Bully," I mutter against his muscular chest, only to get swatted on my ass.

Roger laughs as I yelp.

"*Bonjour, mes beaux fils*," I coo as I walk into their nursery through their dressing room passage.

Nanny Grace lifts her head from dressing Rodolphe to glance my way and smiles brightly.

"*Bonjour*, Madame Steele," she greets me.

"*Bonjour* to you, too! It's a glorious day, *non?*"

We chat for a bit as we get The Twins ready.

Roger wants to go to the village for breakfast at one of the quaint restaurants. Followed by a stroll while we shop. He wants some family time with only the four of us before the year ends.

A knock on the door calls my attention from bundling Gaspard in his navy blue Moncler snowsuit. I pop the hood on his head as I call for the person to come in.

"Bonjour! How are my darling nephews?" Haley asks.

She swoops Rodolphe from Nanny Grace and cuddles

him to her chest. Then she strides over to me and kisses Gaspard on his chubby cheek, the only part not covered.

"Where are you going?" Haley asks as she bounces Rodolphe, who laughs. "Bouncy, bouncy, baby!"

Everyone's enthralled by The Twins, I laugh to myself.

"Into the village for some family time."

Roger's booming voice makes us turn around. He greets Nanny Grace and takes Rodolphe from Haley.

A disheartened expression crosses her lovely face. She nods and heads for the door.

I glance at Roger. He rolls his eyes, but shrugs, albeit reluctantly.

"Hey! Why don't you come with us? We can have breakfast and see what's going on," I ask Haley.

She declines. But I know it's only because she doesn't want to intrude.

No such thing. We're family and families make time for one another. Besides, she and Harris are the only ones unattached. Well… Harris had some dalliances. But those don't count.

In the end, we climb into one of the Mercedes-Benz G-Wagen and head to Place Centrale. We drop the SUV with the STEELE Verbier valet, then walk along the main street checking out the options.

The delicious scent of cinnamon and nutmeg escapes the warm confines of a restaurant as a couple with a toddler exit. They smile at us, and the husband holds the door. We thank him and ask if the restaurant is kid friendly. They laugh—understanding some patrons prefer a peaceful meal—and nod.

The Twins fully fed and fast asleep in their carriers won't disturb anyone. Even if they wake, they're not likely to make noise. They're new things are to stare at their surroundings and to vocalize.

Roger slips his beanie off, and his hair falls around his stubble-covered cheeks. The light streaming through the oversized windows makes his eyes sparkle as he smiles at the hostesses.

They nearly swoon.

Haley and I glance at each other, then roll our eyes. A baby in his hand and two women with him don't deter women. Good grief.

One of them seats us and grins at Roger the entire time. Shortly after we settle The Twins, a server takes our orders.

"So, you're the new DILF on the scene?" I tease Roger.

Haley cracks up, and we come up with jokes about hot dads until he growls at us. Which only adds to our humor. We laugh louder.

"Haley?"

We turn to find a handsome Scotsman towering over her chair. His emerald green eyes darken when she smiles at him. She introduces us to him as Callum Graham—a duke she met while attending Harvard Business School.

He explains he was just leaving since his friend never showed up because of a hangover.

Haley looks to Roger, and he offers Callum to join us. He accepts happily.

While we make room for him, I peep how his eyes never leave Haley. Then I notice how Roger's eyes never leave Callum. *The Responsible One*'s signature intense stare on full alert. Undoubtedly he'll arrange a comprehensive background check. Not even a duke is good enough for their baby sister.

I giggle, and Roger glances at me. With a shake of my head, I busy myself with adjusting my linen napkin.

We enjoy a tasty breakfast during which Callum regales us with royal tales. The Twins wake to gaze around themselves ah-gooing at the sights and sounds.

After the meal ends, Callum asks Haley to go for a stroll around the village. She agrees and they leave us with a promise by Callum to return her to the chalet.

"The four of us at last!" Roger huffs as we bundle The Twins in their gear.

I laugh, "Everyone will leave in two days and you'll have us all to yourself for two months!"

Roger leans down to kiss my lips, then responds, "Exactly how I want it, my love."

"WHAT DID you and Sebastian get up to today?"

Lola, Haley, Starr, and I stretch out in the chalet's spa sauna before our deep-tissue massages start. Ninety-minute of pure decadence.

As a treat, Malcolm arranged for a Girls' Spa Day with masseuses and aestheticians from the hotel's facility to pamper us prior to our New Year's Eve dinner and party. He said we were good girls and deserved special goodies.

Haley and I rolled our eyes at the "good girls" part. But

Lola and Starr grinned from ear-to-ear. I knew Lola was a sub, yet Starr...

Whatever the situation, I appreciate the treats. Between Roger's marathon lovemaking and the rigors of skiing, tobogganing, and ice skating, my muscles need a rubdown.

I lift my hands to consider my mani/pedi color as I wait for Lola's response—a matte silver would do nicely with my jewelry. I'll never get over the exceptional pieces!

"Oh, a little bit of this and a little bit of that," she hedges.

Starr shakes her head, causing long, curly tendrils to escape her messy topknot. As she tucks them back in to the Scünci, she laughs.

"What kind of evasive answer is that?" She asks. "What exactly does that entail?"

Lola giggles and waggles her eyebrows.

"Well, if you'd prefer all the details... Sebastian bound my arms and legs to the four bedposts with red silk cords—"

"Uh, no, thank you!"

"TMI!"

"Girl! Not all of those details! Please!"

Lola's giggles turn into snorts as she doubles over, cracking up. Her eyes twinkle with mischief when she lifts her gaze.

"Okay, okay! I mean, you did ask for it!" She starts. "After a morning of multiple orgasms, we went ice skating. Boy, when I tell you my legs were wobbly—"

Haley throws a towel at Lola's head and she ducks, laughing hysterically.

"Lola!! I do not care to hear of my brother's sex life!"

Haley shouts. "And that goes for the two of you, too. Not interested in the least."

Starr and I exchange looks, then throw towels at her. Lola grabs the one Haley threw and tosses it back at her. We end up laughing and exchanging our tales for the day, minus the sex scenes. From the broad smile on Starr's face, I conclude Malcolm put it on her real good!

A gentle knock on the sauna's door draws our attention. A masseuse reminds us it's time, so we troop out to rinse off.

Aside from the sauna and showers, the spa accommodates a steam room, plunge pools for hot and cold therapies, a tranquility lounge, and four of each manicure stations, pedicure chairs, and treatment rooms. We settle in the rooms for our sessions.

The rejuvenating massages put us in even higher spirits when we reemerge. They added a body polish treatment, so our skin glows and feels like satin. The warm oil soothed my achy body and added to the softness.

The aestheticians help us into the pedicure chairs first. We gab some more while they set to our feet and hands. The start of a new year excites everyone. We're ready to leave all the drama behind and to begin anew!

BEFORE THE FULL-LENGTH MIRROR, I take a final spin in my 70s disco era style white chiffon party dress. The white and blue sequins glisten from the plunging vee neckline to the nipped-in waist to the hem at the top of my thighs. I love how the voluminous bracelet sleeves showcase my wedding jewelry. I paired it with shiny silver leather high platform chunky heels with straps around my toes and ankles to round out the 70s glam.

My hair cascades down my back in waves, skimming the middle of my ass. The glow from our spa day remains, so I leave my face bare except for glossy lips and extra mascara on my eyelashes.

The party girl is ready!

A wolf whistle cuts through the air.

I pivot to find Roger leaning against the doorframe. He's debonair in a black tuxedo with a black dress shirt open at the neck. His patent leather shoes gleam as much as his jet-black hair. His hooded gaze takes me in from the tips of my toes to the top of my head, lingering around my hips and décolletage.

He licks his lower lip and peers at me through his thick lashes.

"*Bonne soirée, Mon Amour,*" he croons.

I bite my lower lip as I smile. My body thrums from the sound of his seductive purr. Will we make it out of the dressing room, I wonder.

Merde...

"We're missing one," he says as he strides towards me.

I cock my head in question.

A devilish grin spreads across Roger's gorgeous face. His nostrils flare.

Continuing to walk forward, he drives me back against the mirror. A quick kiss, and he spins me around as he places my hands on the glass with his on top, twining our fingers. His nose runs along the side of my neck, eliciting shivers down my spine and sparks in my pussy.

Boxed in by the press of his massive frame against my smaller one, I melt into his embrace.

"One last fuck before Midnight. Or did you forget, Pretty Kitty?" He growls.

That answers my questions. *Merde.*

Roger slips hips hand beneath my mini dress to cup my mons. His middle finger strokes the crotch of my silk thong.

My pussy juices flow and moisten the material.

Roger purrs in my ear as he plunges his finger inside my core. He grinds his hips forward, wedging his thick dick between my ass cheeks, driving me to my tiptoes with each thrust.

My forehead drops to the mirror's steamy surface, hot from my pants.

The sound of his zipper is music to my ears. I delight in it and relish the first pistoning stroke.

Roger doesn't delay my satisfaction. He grunts as he slams into me, and I squeal.

He's rough and fast. We grunt and groan with the effort. The raw, primal fucking brings us to climax quickly. Copious ropes of his cum shoot deep within my pulsating, dripping pussy.

"Happy Early New Year, Baby."

Roger chuckles darkly as he withdraws and watches me slump against the mirror, breathless and spent.

. . .

"So, who's the bonnie Scotsman with Haley?"

Starr appears at my elbow and nods towards the other side of the wine cellar.

I glance at Starr before I turn to the cuddled-up couple.

She looks fantastic in a slinky metallic lamé brown and gold wrap-effect mini dress. Her long, toned legs end in brown sky-high sandals with gold serpentine metal straps wrapped around her ankles. The long curls of her chocolate-colored hair frame her heart-shaped face, the dimples pop with her giggle. She reminds me of Christie Doll, Barbie's friend.

"Well, don't you look fabulous, darling!" I tell Starr.

"Why thank you! We're hot babes, huh?" She laughs.

"Very hot indeed."

Starr and I startle at the unexpected gruff voice of Malcolm. He chuckles and strokes the five o'clock stubble on his chin. His eyes rove up and down Starr as she shifts from one foot to the other.

All righty then…

I laugh and pat his shoulder as I make a fast exit, their erotic energy too hot for me to handle.

We're enjoying pre-dinner cocktails with our families and friends, including some we met up with on holiday. The bartender and sommelier for STEELE Verbier crafted a selection of drinks and wines for our dinner and party.

I head over to my parents, who chat with a couple I recognize from their social club. A pair whose son would like to have me on his arm.

"*Bonsoir*, welcome. It's good to see you," I greet them with a smile politely.

"Congratulations on your marriage, my dear," the wife responds. "And your beautiful sons. Your mother showed us their photos."

"Thank you very much."

I glance up to Roger, smiling warmly as he extends his hand to the couple and places the other on the small of my back. I lean into him and rest my head on his shoulder.

"Ah. You did well for yourself, Monsieur Steele. We've tried unsuccessfully to match our son with Leonie for years!" The husband adds.

My father sputters as he sips his drink. While my mother and the man's wife look aghast.

Roger stiffens, and his fingers slip around to grip my waist, pinning me to his side firmly.

"That's because it always meant Leonie to be mine forever," he replies. "*C'est la vie*! Excuse us."

He nods and draws me away. I smile and wave.

"What the fuck?!" Roger huffs. "He comes into my house as a guest and tells me some bullshit about hooking my wife and the mother of my children up with their son. *Bof*!"

I giggle, and Roger glares down at me.

"I'm wearing off on you! *Bof*!" I explain.

It's in reference to my "arrogant Gallic shrug" as Lola says where I stick out my lower lip; raise my eyebrows and shoulders simultaneously; followed by a patronizing, *Bof*.

Roger leans close and murmurs, "Well, they say couples begin to take on the other's attributes. So like I told him, MINE!"

He swats my ass for emphasis.

I yelp as the butler enters the wine cellar to announce dinner is being served.

Roger returns his hand to my lower back and guides me to the dining room. We chat with others as we make our way upstairs.

Fortunately, the delicious meal goes off as planned with no more graceless comments. Roger keeps our family and guests entertained. His mood much improved after he reminded me it's his seed buried deep within my womb right now, not some sod.

I shiver when I recall Roger's declaration I couldn't wash his essence from my pussy, only what dripped down my legs. He wanted his mark to remain on me.

Mmmm... *Merde...*

The DJ from Farm Club spins a range of music perfect for everyone.

We party it up in the disco next to the wine cellar. The set up works well with people moving seamlessly from the bar to the dance floor or the banquettes along the walls. A gigantic screen shows scenes of countries around the world celebrating the start of the New Year with Sydney, Australia first.

Roger twirls me, then pulls me close. He buries his nose in my hair as I drape my arms around his neck. We move in sync, letting the stress of the past dissipate with each bump and grind. Finally carefree with no drama!

A piercing whistle blasts, and we turn to see Sebastian on a raised platform with one arm around Lola and the other beckoning to Roger and me. Then he raises his champagne flute.

"Before midnight strikes, I want to congratulate my brother on his new bride and darling Twins, my new sister and nephews. We love you all. Steeles for life!"

Everyone claps and stomps with more wolf whistles.

Roger picks me up and swings me around before dipping me and kissing me silly.

The DJ calls for more champagne with five minutes to go.

Earlier, Harris angled the exterior cameras toward Verbier Village and relayed the footage to the screen. Now, he switches the feed, and the live view appears for the countdown clock and fireworks display.

Nanny Grace emerges through the cluster in the cellar to bring Rodolphe and Gaspard to Roger and me. We thank her and kiss their sleepy faces. Mini noise-canceling headsets cover their sensitive ears.

Roger hands me a flute from a passing server, then slips his arm around my waist, pulling me close. I smile up at him and whisper I love you. He kisses the tip of my nose and tells me the same.

The lights dim as the countdown begins.

The screen is so large, we might as well be front row in the village.

I'm so ecstatic and say a silent pray of thanks.

We chant the countdown, then cheer as midnight strikes and glittery silver, gold, and white balloons fall from the ceiling.

Roger leans over and whispers in my ear, "Round two begins for month seventeen and seven days…"

ROGER

*I*t's been two weeks of pure bliss at *Chalet de la Joie*. We've had our home to ourselves since our family and friends left after New Year's Day. I love them all, but need some private time with my wife and my sons.

We've spent enough time with others, having lived at *Le Beaulieu Manoir* for six months initially because of the reconstruction of our penthouse duplex into a triplex. Then, by necessity, because of the rabid media and the frenzy behind the pretrial, we stayed through to our wedding day.

Even there, the media pestered us with drones and hanging outside of the front gates. We increased security patrols and upgraded the surveillance systems under Harris' supervision.

After being harassed by a photographer while out shopping for The Twins, I hired a security detail to protect Leonie. The paparazzo didn't give a damn she was pregnant. I promised to destroy him and the rag he worked for. Pain in my ass.

I sent Nanny Grace to stay at the hotel, not wanting anyone else on the property with us. She'll come as we need her help. We're hands-on parents and can take care of The Twins with ease.

Now, we're alone for six more weeks. No distractions; no work; no news or the Internet. Leonie insisted we give up our mobiles, too. Our family can reach us on the chalet's landline. Otherwise, we're untouchable. Period.

Sebastian and Malcolm volunteered to manage my division in the interim. The same as Malcolm and I did for Baz when he and Lola took a two-month honeymoon yachting to private islands in the South Pacific. He only had two satellite phones. Talk about untouchable...

Hell, I don't blame him in the least, I chuckle to myself.

Leonie stirs in bed next to me. She reaches out for me and murmurs my name.

My heart swells at her wanting me while she's still asleep. I gather her outstretched hand to press a kiss to the knuckles.

She sighs and settles back to sleep.

The sound of one Twin—I hazard a guess it's Gaspard as he's more vocal, like his *Maman*—comes through the baby monitor on the nightstand.

I grab and turn it down before his cries wake Leonie. She needs her sleep since I had her up all night revering her luscious body. It's amazing how flexible she's become with her regular yoga sessions. Pretty Kitty is a sexy contortionist.

On my way to their dressing room passageway, I cover my nakedness with a pair of sweatpants. No need for them to see the family's jewels.

"Good morning, Rodolphe! Good morning, Gaspard!" I greet them.

As expected, my younger son fusses in his crib, waving his arms in frustration. I imagine he's saying, "Feed me!"

"Okay, okay. Breakfast coming right up, boss! Kindly forgive my tardiness," I chuckle as I stride over to check on each of them.

Rodolphe gazes back at me and offers a gummy smile as he lifts his hands up. I collect them for a good morning hug and quick diaper change.

"So what's the plan for today? Shall we go to the village or take a sleigh ride?" I ask as I feed them in their chairs.

Leonie and I thought it best to speak to The Twins in French and English to encourage their multilingualism. And those are just the beginnings of their languages. Both of us are fluent in Italian, and Leonie adds German and Spanish. Since we live in Europe with different countries, it's best to understand as many languages as possible.

"Let's ask *Maman* what she'd like to do, too. She's still asleep. Let's give her a rest for now, yes?"

With his belly filling up, Gaspard laughs around the bottle. Yeah, like Leonie, who also gets hangry. It's intriguing to watch their personalities develop along with the growth.

"Happy now?" I tease.

"*Non*. I reached for you, but the sheets were cold, *Mon Cœur*."

My cock jumps when I glance over my shoulder to see Leonie leaning against the doorjamb in nothing but my cashmere sweater she ripped off me last night.

She's tall, but it still falls to the tops of her bare thighs— thighs I forever want to nestle between, cock or mouth. Her disheveled hair hangs past her round ass. The memory of the silky strands wrapped around my fist as I bow her back to spank her from behind makes me diamond hard. Her nipples poke into the soft material, standing in bas-relief from my vigorous suckling.

Leonie's full lips pout tantalizingly as she toys with the hem.

"You should have woken me to help you," she says, then pushes off the doorjamb.

The unintended seductive sway of her hips mesmerizes me. I want to grip them as I pull her beneath my body and drive my dick deep inside her warm, wet pussy.

The desire raging through me must reach my face because Leonie smirks.

"I would have fed them," she says, cupping her bountiful breasts. "I'm full."

A growl slips out of my mouth as I lick my lips, "No worries. I'll ease your ache."

Leonie nods her head and tweaks her nipples.

Fuck. Me.

"I'll get their bath ready," she says sashaying into The Twins' en suite bathroom and heisting the hem at her ass up for a peek at her globes.

Cushion for the pushin'.

Another growl, and Leonie shimmies as she raises her

arms overhead to slide the long sleeves past her elbows. Her giggle makes my balls tighten.

This woman will be the death of me.

The Twins finish breakfast, and I carry them into the bathroom. Leonie puts my waxed apron on me. We've learned the hard way; The Twins enjoy splashing the water everywhere. Bath time is full of fun with squeaky rubber ducks and bubbles.

And anytime with water is sexy with Leonie.

Once our sons are nice and clean—and Leonie and I are dry—we carry them into our bedroom. Leonie plays with them on the bed while I shower, then we switch.

When she comes out, I've made the bed, and she kisses me silly in appreciation.

Any man who doesn't help his woman with their children and domestic tasks misses out on their exuberant thanks. I love my sons and will care for them for life, but I love how Leonie thanks me just as much!

We head downstairs for our adult breakfast. Although not a cook, Leonie made certain the chef prepped a variety of meals for us before I threw everyone out.

I felt like Martin Lawrence: "Get to steppin'!" I would have added the jump kick as I held the front door open, but it would have proven too much.

"What should we do today?" Leonie asks as she adds yogurt to her granola.

"How about a sleigh ride? The Twins liked the tinkling of the bells and laughed at the horses," I respond. "It's colder today, but we can bundle up under the blankets."

Leonie agrees it's a good idea.

144

Gaspard laughs while Rodolphe ah-goos in support of our planned family activity. Leonie's giggle joins The Twins.

"THIS IS SO MUCH FUN! The Twins love it!"

Leonie exclaims as the horses pick up their pace to a trot and the red sleigh with brass bells zips along the snowy trail.

We just left the bustling streets of Verbier Village, and the driver cracked the whip in the air above the horses' rumps. They tossed their heads and neighed in response as they forged ahead.

A light snowfall drifts around us as we cuddle beneath the heavy wool blankets—Leonie insists we use our own and not the ones from the sleigh ride company. With the blanket up against The Twins' faces, she doesn't want one used by countless others on our sons. I agree whole-heartedly.

The breathtaking scenery of the Swiss Alps depicts the awesomeness of nature. Majestic snowcapped mountains rise skyward to incredible heights. The sheer beauty of the pristine peaks makes my heart soar.

"I love it, too!" I respond, laughing as the wind whips around us.

Slipping my arm around Leonie's waist, I snuggle her closer to my side, and she leans her head on my shoulder. The Twins bounce on our laps, thrilled with the action.

Yup, this is the idyllic family life for me!

LEONIE

"*H*appy One Month Anniversary, *Mon Cœur*. I love you from the depths of my soul."

I raise my flute of Taittinger Comtes de Champagne Blanc de Blancs—my favorite thanks to James Bond in *Casino Royale*—to toast Roger.

We're sitting in a private dining room at STEELE Verbier's STEAKhouse restaurant run by Lucien through one of their many Jackson Corporation partnerships. A reservation at the three Michelin star restaurant is the most sought-after in this part of Switzerland.

Lucien created a special menu of Roger's favorite foods, including lobster bisque and steak frites. Then he sent it to the chef to prepare. The sommelier paired the dishes with the most choice wines. I planned it shortly after we arrived, determined Roger would have a scrumptious meal for our celebration.

It pays to be the owner's wife!

Time flies by within a blink of an eye. One minute

we're engaged and the next we're celebrating our first month as a married couple. I'm beyond blissed-out.

Roger's such an attentive, caring, and loving husband. Many a morning he wakes up early to feed The Twins and to get them ready for our day so I can rest. He says I carried them for thirty-six weeks, so he can share the load now. Or he'll pretend to be a masseuse who offers happy endings in the chalet's spa. All much to my delight.

But most of all, he's my one true heart. No man has ever loved me the way Roger does. Or put me above all else. Our time apart almost ended me. But our time together makes me whole. Thankfully, our *coupe de foudre* proves its determination to be long lasting.

"Happy One Month Anniversary, baby. I love you more than you can ever imagine," Roger replies with a broad grin.

His eyes sparkle in the light put forth by hundreds of candles positioned throughout the room. Their warmth heightens the scent of his Tom Ford Noir cologne—a heady, sensual blend of Bulgarian rose, clary sage, and patchouli.

For tonight, Roger shaved his temporary beard, so his cleft chin looks lickable. I like the sexy five o'clock shadow, but I prefer the velvety smoothness of his skin. The cut of his bespoke three-piece charcoal gray suit with a custom white dress shirt opened at the neck emphasize his muscular physique. The width of his shoulders, the column of his throat, and the thickness of his thighs call out to me.

My man looks as tasty as our dinner. I can't wait for the decadent dessert I have planned back home...

"You're in for a delightful treat," I say, beaming. "A much-deserved one, or is it two?"

Roger smirks and drags his fingertip around the rim of his flute while pinning me with his intense stare.

"And what must I do to receive the second treat, Mrs. Steele?" He asks huskily, eyes hooded.

I bite my lower lip between the front teeth as my gaze darts between his thick finger and his luscious smug mouth.

Merde... I was supposed to be the seductive one.

"Be a good little boy, of course," I purr.

"As you know, Mrs. Steele, nothing is 'little' about me nor am I a 'boy.' A robust man is more like it," Roger starts. "However, I am very, very good. *Ne suis-je pas*, Pretty Kitty?"

Indeed, he is more than very, very good, I think as my core clenches and leaks juices into the silk of my thong. My body concurs with his assessment wholeheartedly.

Roger's nostrils flare, and he chuckles alluringly.

Yeah, he took the power back... And I happily hand the reins to him. Ride me till I sweat, baby!

"Monsieur et Madame Steele."

We glance up to find the servers hovering at the room's door with our first course in their hands.

As I smile in thanks, beneath the linen-covered table, a silken touch glides up my calf along my inner thigh. My eyes fly to Roger, who chats with his server regarding the dish.

An insistent push to my leg makes me widen my knees

to allow Roger's toes access to my upper thigh. His long leg makes it easy for him to tease my mons.

He thanks the servers, and they leave us alone once again. Then turns to me with his hand outstretched, palm up.

"Give me your thong," Roger commands.

Immediately, I comply and rise from my chair. I saunter to his side, slip my hands beneath my mini dress, and shimmy my thong down. Then I lean forward to give him an unobstructed view of my heavy boobs while I step out of the thong and place it in his hand.

Roger brings the damp scrap of material to his nose to inhale deeply, then puts them in his suit jacket pocket. He smacks my ass when I pivot to return to my chair and chuckles when I yelp.

"Fuck your ass is delicious," he says.

I give it an extra shake before easing into my chair while I maintain eye contact with him. The expression of an undisguised desire on Roger's face adds another tick in my power of seduction column. Gotcha!

Automatically, I part my thighs when the touch of Roger's big toe glides up my calf.

"Wider," he demands, prodding my upper leg.

I oblige and am rewarded with pressure to my throbbing clit. Sliding down in my seat, I open my legs even more, wantonly offering my pussy to Roger's propping digit.

"Eat," he commands.

Is this man mad?

How the hell can I eat when he's toying with my sensitive clit and stroking my pussy lips? Better yet, how can he sit there all cool, calm, and collected polishing off his lobster bisque while his toe gets soaked by my wetness?

GRRR!

"What was that?" he asks nonchalantly.

I mutter nothing and tuck into my soup as best as I'm able. When my hips begin to move to match his rhythm, Roger tsks and removes his big toe.

My eyes narrow as I shoot golden daggers at him.

"Patience," he states.

The servers return to remove the soup tureens and replace them with the next course.

But does Roger stop?

No! He keeps up his ministrations despite me being on the edge of an orgasm. Whenever he senses I'm close to exploding, he backs away with a smirk.

I hope to take advantage of his distraction. So I shift in the seat to angle my pussy for better penetration.

Roger swings his intense stare to me.

"Something not to your liking, Mrs. Steele?" He asks with a raised eyebrow.

The servers panic and ask if the food meets my expectations or do I prefer another dish.

I blush, embarrassed they believe it's somehow their fault. I assure them the meal is superb and smile until they leave. Then, I glare at Roger; he smirks.

"Argh! You're being a beast!" I declare.

"So behave," he responds. "I will give you pleasure. Do not attempt to force it."

I mutter how he's the one behaving unfairly. It's

our anniversary, for goodness' sake! How can he taunt me?

Roger chuckles. Then he crooks his finger at me.

I scowl and shake my head no. Now I'll behave like a petulant child. I let my hair fall in a curtain to cover my face and tuck into my food.

"Here, Pretty Kitty, Kitty," he croons. "Let me make it better."

My ears perk up, and I cock my head. Hmmm… That's more like it. With a peppier attitude, I rise hurriedly and sashay over to Roger's side.

"There, there, now. Tell me where it aches," he says gruffly.

I point to my pussy and whimper as I shift from foot to foot. The ache unbearable.

"Let me see," he purrs as he lifts the hem of my mini dress. "Show me."

I widen my stance and point to my bare swollen lower lips. My arousal amped up by the possibility of us being caught by the waitstaff.

"Aaawww. My sweet little pussy needs a release?" He asks, stroking my folds with the tip of his finger.

I mewl and rock my hips as I grasp his strong shoulders.

WHAP. WHAP. WHAP.

Sharp slaps strike my pussy, and I squeal from the unexpected pain on my sensitive flesh.

"What did I tell you, Pretty Kitty?" Roger demands as he narrows his darkened eyes at me.

I mumble a response, and he spanks my ass.

"Words, Pretty Kitty. I will have your words," Roger commands.

"You... You will give me pleasure..." I whine.

"Exactly," he responds. "Will you behave, or will you remain unsatisfied on our anniversary night?"

"*Oui! Oui!!* I'll behave, *Amoureux!*" I cry without hesitation.

Roger nods and drapes my leg over his shoulder. He buries his face between my thighs and gorges on my dripping pussy. His fingers dig into the fleshiest parts of my ass to lock me in place, also preventing me from humping his mouth.

His grunts of pleasure intensify as my body ramps up for a mind-blowing orgasm. Roger tightens his hold as his feast continues. Then presses his thumb against my bottom hole. The tight rings of muscle give way, and his thumb plunges inside, twisting and thrusting,

My pussy flutters as my legs quiver. Fuck! This is going to be massive...

Not giving a damn who hears, I throw my head back and roar Roger's name as wave after glorious wave crashes over me. My body jolts from the white heat he built.

Roger doesn't let up, drawing two additional orgasms from my shook pussy. He ignores my cries of no more to relish in the aftereffects of my release. Gently, he laps at my swollen folds to eat every drop of my juices.

He hums in delight.

I fold over his shoulder and sob.

Fuck! That was indescribable.

"Better?" Roger purrs as he kisses my clit and inner thighs.

I jump, much too delicate for even the slightest touch.

Roger chuckles, and the warm air makes me shiver and my nipples pebble to painful points. He settles me on his lap and strokes my back soothingly.

"So, do I deserve my second treat, Mrs. Steele?"

LEONIE

"*Bonjour, Maman et Papa!* It's so good to see you! How are you doing? Is all well?"

Even though we decided no outside connections, I have an urge to reach out to my parents. It's been weeks since we last spoke. I need to make sure they're all right. So I sent a text message earlier to let them know I'd FaceTime and wanted to get both of them.

"*Bonjour, Mon Trésor!*" My father booms, then continues in French. "You look so happy! Roger must treat you well."

"Leonie! We miss you, honey!" My mother exclaims.

The smiles on their faces warm my heart.

"Oh, I miss you, too… We're wonderful!" I respond. "Wow, The Twins are excited to call you, too."

I angle my iPad to show them in their chairs waving their arms and ah-gooing attracted to our cheerful cries. Granted, their joy also comes from full tummies. My greedy little monsters.

"Aaww. We're glad to hear from you, too," my mother

laughs as she wiggles her fingers at The Twins. "Oh, my! They've grown so much, Leonie!"

We chat some more about their new milestones at five-months old. They crack up over peek-a-boo and hide and seek, watching Roger pop in and out of their view with delight. Another new favorite is playing with their toys. We've noticed they prefer to grab the more colorful toys like their shiny cherry red rings. Their chubby cheeks match the hue of their toys and widen with their smiles.

My parents ask after Roger, and I tell them he's terrific. In fact, he's in the gym working out via Skype with Norman.

"So tell me. Is everything okay? I just had a sense to check in on you," I ask as a worried sensation hovers around the edge of my thoughts.

They exchange glances and communicate as only couples who have been together for years can. My father gives a slight shake to his head, then smiles at me.

"*Mon Trésor*, you focus on your new husband and babies. Enjoy your honeymoon. It's time for you to relax and bond," he says.

I glance at my mother, and she smiles quickly as she nods in agreement.

"Listen to your father, *Mon Cœur*. He knows best," she adds. "Now tell me, which chef did you select? I'm partial to the third one. She has knowledge of various cuisines good for entertaining. Plus, she shared her secrets for the perfect Gateau St. Honoré with me."

I laugh when my mother's eyes widen. She's a pastry

aficionado. So anyone who can impress her with their skills goes to the top of my list.

"Well, in that case, *Maman*, she's the winner!" I declare.

"Shall I tell her, or would you prefer to let her know? She gave me her mobile so we can chat now and then," she replies clapping her hands.

Sometimes I feel terrible I hate to cook and didn't learn our Tunisian family's recipes passed down through the generations. I took after my father's Parisian side with travel and the love of beautiful things. So I tell my mother she can share the good news with the chef. Not quite my substitute, rather someone my mother can offer her knowledge to as she did with Lucien.

Perhaps they'll open another restaurant together in Verbier like they did in Paris! I make a note to ask Malcolm and Lucien when Roger and I return home.

We catch up on other happenings before we end our video call with a promise to connect next week.

I feel better. But I still get a sense they're holding something back from me.

Seemingly it's not my parents. I ignore the tons of text messages highlighted on the banner for my Messages app and shoot a quick text to Lola.

Hey! How's everything? I miss you!

Immediately, the three dots appear as Lola types her response.

OMG! I was just thinking about you!! :D
All good, I hope!
LOL Yes! I miss you, too :(We're in Paris this week. Baz has

some things to take care of. Hey! Aren't you supposed to not have your mobile???

I know! But I have a weird sense and want to check in. My parents are well, but evasive. So I wanted to ask you...

A minute passes, and Lola hasn't typed. Huh. I wonder if she's busy or dodging my question like my parents did.

Helloooo...

She's taking forever. *Merde.* Finally, the dots show up on my screen.

Sorry about that. Baz just came in and you know how he kisses me breathless when he

Errrr! TMI Lola!

;D Look, I've gotta fly! TTYL Kiss my Little Pumpkins XOXOXOXO.

Well, perhaps I'm going crazy, I mutter to myself.

The sound of clangs draws me from my musings. Rodolphe discovered slamming his rings onto the tray in front of him makes a loud noise. Gaspard follows suit. Soon the room is full of cymbal sounds.

I giggle and join in, clapping my hands and singing. The Twins go wild. Soon my thoughts drift from concern to bonding with my sons like my father suggested.

Whatever may brew, it will take care of itself for now.

"WHAT HAVE you been up to, babe?"

With The Twins napping after their orchestral performance wore them out, I sat in the window seat of our bedroom to sketch. Some ideas for playrooms come to mind as The Twins grow and become more active. The peacefulness of the pristine scenery clears my head to let the images form.

I glance at the door to spot Roger striding in, oozing sex appeal without even trying.

A warm flush from his boxing session covers his cheeks —he's kept the stubble to a minimum for me—and his eyes shine like liquid platinum. The long-sleeved t-shirt clings to his powerful chest and biceps while the gray sweatpants hang low on his narrow hips. His flaccid dick runs down the length of his thigh; its head outlined through the material.

My man is hung, honey! Yum.

Roger runs his fingers through his hair. It's grown longer since we've been here. The glossy ebony waves frame his chiseled face.

I can never get enough of looking at him. He's like a Renaissance masterpiece sculpture come to life.

"Hey there, handsome," I purr. "Yearning for you."

He grins as he heads towards me and bends down to kiss my proffered lips.

"Mmmmmm chocolaty," he says, smacking his lips together.

I nod at the cup of cocoa on the side table.

Roger takes a sip, then kisses me again.

"Tasty, Caramel Bonbon," he says. "Shall we discover what other decadent uses the whipped cream has for us?"

Roger hums as he places a dollop on my lips and licks it off.

"*Absolument, Amoureux*," I purr, sucking his finger clean.

Children's playrooms give way to adult fun in a flash of

fiery heat. The blast sizzles enough to melt the glaciers of the Swiss Alps.

Roger removes the cashmere blanket from my lap and folds it neatly as his intense gaze heats my skin. His deliberate delay makes me want more. Right. Now. He snickers as he senses my instant need for his carnal touch.

"Anxious, Pretty Kitty?" He asks as his eyes spark brightly with desire. "Patience, my dear wife. Know I will always satisfy your every need, when you need it most."

I watch his tight ass muscles flex beneath his sweats as he strolls over to place the blanket on the foot of our bed. The power of his ass and thighs when he pistons inside of me drives me insane with pleasure. My pussy walls clench on air just thinking about the pounding Roger gives to it.

Merde…

When he turns, he catches me staring at his lower half, and he chuckles darkly. With a glint in his eyes, he stands still. One hand grips the back of his shirt and yanks it over his head, then pulls the sleeves off to reveal his thick biceps. They bunch and flex along with his eight-pack abs when he tosses the garment to the side.

Roger glides his fingertips down the chiseled chest of his beautifully ripped torso, slowly reaching for the drawstring of his sweatpants. A tug, and the waistband loosens to show the mouthwatering v-cuts of his Adonis belt.

I lick my lips and swallow hard.

A smirk appears on his face. He bends at the waist, never taking his wolfish eyes off of me as he pushes the pants down his thick, muscular thighs and calves. Then he steps out of the sweats to stand to his impressive height of six feet, three inches. His giant dick—in all its ten-inch glory—stands tall and proud to reach above his navel while his sac hangs heavy below.

Did I say my man looks like a Renaissance masterpiece sculpture come to life, or what?

HOT DIGGITY DAYUMMM!

Sizzling doesn't describe Roger. But he has me burning up inside.

My face heats with a flush to my cheeks and chest. Pricks to my underarms tingle as my nipples harden to points. My chest rises and falls with an increase in my breath, just shy of panting with my mouth hanging open and my tongue lolling out the side. My pussy weeps at the sight of his splendid form, knowing the power of his dick will stretch and fill it to the maximum capacity.

I ache for his dominant possession.

Roger cocks his head to the side to survey my wanton reaction. Lazily, his fist strokes his turgid length. He's back to that slow burn.

The anticipation builds until I want to scream as I press my thighs together for some semblance of relief.

Then an idea strikes... Meet him where he stands...

With a smirk of my own, I pin him with my predatory feline stare as I rise from the window seat. Ever so slowly, I slide my fingers in the waistband of my leggings, bend at the waist, and shimmy my hips to slide the clingy material down my long legs. Then fold them neatly before I put them on the seat behind me.

I glance over my shoulder as I start to unbutton my cardigan. Letting it fall down one shoulder, then the other until it slips to the floor in a heap. The tips of my hair brush my bare ass cheeks, and I shiver. Folding in half, I slip my thong off, ensuring my most private parts show.

Roger isn't the only one with enticing bits.

He growls and rushes me.

"You want to poke the bear, Pretty Kitty?" He rumbles in my ear as he pins my back to his front with his knees bent to align our centers. "Because I can poke back with something much larger."

He punctuates each word with a thrust of his hips, poking the crack of my ass.

I moan with indescribable need.

"Well, then... What are you waiting for?" I ask cheekily.

Roger's lips curl into a grin against my neck as his grip tightens on my upper arms. He starts a slow, circular grind of his hips. One hand glides down my arm to slip around my hip to land on my lower belly, pressing me in place.

His erotic dance enthralls me, and my head lolls onto his broad shoulder.

Roger takes advantage to the access to suck the flesh of my neck into his fiery mouth. Like a caveman, he marks his mate. Then growls and licks the sensitive area to soothe the delicious bite of pain.

I groan and press back against his thick dick.

More, my mind shouts.

Roger kicks my feet apart to open me to his probing fingers as they glide along my belly to my damp folds. Two fingers plunge inside my pussy, stretching me as they flex and curl to stroke the rough textured mound just inside.

The palm of his hand grinds against my mons, adding more pressure to my throbbing, aching clit.

I mewl and ride his hand as he fucks me with his talented fingers.

"Uh… Uh… Uh… Uh…" I moan, closing my eyes tightly to give in to the carnal sensations my lover inflicts upon me.

My orgasm rocks me on my feet as I cry out in wild abandon, bucking against Roger's hand.

He continues to finger fuck me. Then he takes his claim on my body even further when with his other hand, he cups my heavy breast and pinches my beaded nipple.

"Aaaahhh… *Amoureux*!!" I wail, writhing in his firm embrace. "*S'il te plait*… I need you inside of me!"

Roger rumbles in my ear, "Ready for the larger poke now, Pretty Kitty?"

I plead again, and he satisfies my desire by forcefully thrusting his massive dick deep in my dripping pussy with one demanding stroke, driving me to my toes with an anguished wail.

The sound of his balls slapping at my ass mingled with the sounds of our grunts and groans fill the room.

Roger adjusts his grip on my hip and urges me forward to rest my hands on the window seat. The muscles in front of his thighs strike the back of mine. I revel in his primitive mounting of me!

His punishing strokes continue as he wrings climax after climax from my quivering pussy. Roger is a demanding lover who seeks to draw out my pleasure before he seeks his own.

"Rogeeerrr... Oooh... Oooh... No more... Please!" I wail as another orgasm replaces the snowflakes outside the window with dazzling stars before my eyes.

"Yes? Your teasing is over, Naughty Kitty?" He growls, still jackhammering through my earth-shattering release.

"*Oui, oui!*" I cry pitifully, no longer able to take another mind-blowing climax. "*Je promets!*"

"You promise, do you? Remember who's in control in our bedroom, Naughty Kitty," Roger rumbles in my ear as he increases his steady rhythm.

My head drops to my chest, and I give in to my Alpha male's dominance. He knows exactly what I need and when I need it. My caveman, my husband, my lover.

Roger's pummeling picks up as his massive dick grows impossibly larger and harder inside of my pussy. His release is near.

I tighten my inner muscles and clamp down on his cock with a groan. I'm rewarded with three successive smacks to my ass—again I tried to take control—and a roar from Roger as his dick pulses and pumps his hot, thick seed deep within my greedy pussy.

"Yaaasssss!!!!" I scream, undulating my hips as his release triggers another one of mine.

My hand slaps the window seat, and I toss my head back. So. Fucking. Good.

Roger's legs shake, and he huffs as he collapses against me. His powerful arm braces him from crushing me with his sizable weight. The other arm winds around my waist, locking us together.

He nuzzles my neck as his sultry breath sends goosebumps along my sweat-soaked, feverish skin.

"We forgot the whipped cream. Naughty Kitty, you distracted me with your wily ways," Roger chuckles against my neck.

"Well, *Amoureux*, there's always round two..." I taunt.

Roger nips my shoulder and shakes his head.

"You will never learn will you, Naughty, Naughty Kitty?" He laughs.

I giggle and turn my head to meld our lips in a passionate kiss.

Non, I never will, and he loves it.

ROGER

"*T*his is just so incredible. Words cannot describe it. *Merci, Mon Cœur.*"

Leonie whispers in awe of the impressive Corbassière Glacier.

The panorama from the glacier to the majestic Grand Combin mountain massif is breathtaking to say the least. The snow-covered terrain glistens from the rays of the sun as it rises for the day. The backdrop of the inky sky morphing to varying shades of pink, orange, and gold makes it all seem surreal.

The location is easily accessible since it's in the same Valais Canton as Verbier. The concierge at the hotel arranged our sunrise visit via helicopter with a guide to top off our honeymoon.

I want to give Leonie one more unforgettable experience before we head back to the real world tomorrow morning. And this surpasses all my expectations.

Leonie isn't the only one entranced by the beauty of nature. I'm rendered speechless.

We stand with her back to my front, my arms wind around to hold her firmly to my body. I rest my chin on the top of her hood-covered head.

She places her mittened hands over mine and leans into my embrace.

No more words pass between us as we're captivated by the stunning sunrise. The next ten minutes provide a kaleidoscopic display of naturally colored lights. Their dazzling glow demands no competition from any sound.

When the last traces of the night disappear in the face of the rising sun, I give Leonie a squeeze.

"Let's take a selfie, baby. I want you to have a keepsake," I tell her.

She nods, and we shift so the glacier and the mountain are behind our backs. The view is further depicted in the reflections on our silver mirrored ski goggles. Oversized to protect our eyes from the intense glare, they emphasize the enormity of the scenery.

The guide comes over and takes more photos for us. Then he points out some sights. By the time we're ready to leave, Leonie has more than enough keepsakes.

Once on board the helicopter, the guide continues to explain highlights along the way we couldn't see in the pre-dawn. With the sun up, the view is more impactful.

Leonie swings her head from one side of the helicopter to the other, not wanting to miss a thing. Her enthusiasm is contagious. Neither of us can believe how awesome are the sights.

When we arrive on the edge of the village, Leonie and I thank the crew before we head to the G-Wagen. The concierge also arranged for the hotel's restaurant that serves breakfast to open early for Leonie and me.

"How did you like the glacier, baby?" I ask as I drive the short distance.

Not surprisingly, the streets bustle with early risers eager to hit the ski slopes for the fresh powder.

"Oh, Roger! It was amazing! I've seen nothing like it before," Leonie exclaims as she claps her hands.

I lean over and kiss her lips. Fuck! I want to devour her.

She giggles at my growl of longing.

"Where are we headed?"—Leonie's amber eyes widen when she spots STEELE Verbier—"You're taking me to the hotel to ravage me??"

I bust out laughing. Not a bad idea. One that should have occurred to me. Instead of sitting in a restaurant, I could dine on Leonie in the palatial Matterhorn Suite and take her to heights unknown.

My guffaws die out as I consider the possibility.

"Dial STEELE Verbier concierge," I voice command the SUV's mobile system.

Leonie's mouth drops, and I chuckle.

"You asked for it, Pretty Kitty," I smirk. "We were having an early breakfast at the hotel's restaurant only. But since you insist…"

Leonie squirms in the plush leather seat as she bites her lower lip.

"I do," she breathes huskily.

My cock throbs.

"Dial Nanny Grace…"

HOURS after we end our honeymoon with an unforgettable bang—more like five or six—I stare at my wife and sons on board my Gulfstream G650 headed back to Paris. We flew out of Verbier on my Sikorsky S-92 Executive Helicopter to Geneva, then switched to the jet for the seventy-five-minute flight.

They're my precious cargo I vow to love, care for, and protect with my life. I will allow no one to bring them harm or heartache. Leonie is a fierce *Lion*, but I'm a feral wolf whose pack is his top priority. Don't fuck with me.

Especially after the bullshit ordeal with Delia Shaw. The stress caused Leonie to go into labor early. We made it through with healthy, beautiful sons. But no repeat of outside interference to my family.

Leonie must sense my intense stare and glances over at me. She tilts her head to the side and arches her eyebrow in question to the scowl on my face.

"Nothing, babe," I respond. "Just thinking about the real world popping our bubble after eight, well nine if we include the holidays, weeks off the grid."

Leonie's laugh lights the cabin as she throws her head back in glee.

"If you consider being in a multimillion-dollar, ginormous chalet in a bustling Swiss ski village 'off the grid.' Roger, you crack me up!" She whoops.

I roll my eyes.

"Semantics. You know what I mean, smart aleck," I

retort. "You do realize what happens to sassy pants? Do you not, Pretty Kitty?"

Leonie glances at the door that separates us from the flight crew where Nanny Grace also sits.

It's closed and soundproof. No one will enter our section of the jet once the Do Not Disturb light turns on.

Her gaze returns to mine and she juts her chin out in defiance.

"*Non*, I do not 'realize what happens to sassy pants,' Monsieur Steele," Leonie states using her fingers for air quotes.

Slowly I rise to my full height of six feet, three inches, and stalk over to her.

Leonie's eyes track my movement as she licks her lips. Once I near, she glances at The Twins asleep in their seats.

"Well, you better be quiet so as not to wake them," I say as I indicate their peaceful sleepy forms with a nod.

Leonie shivers and her amber eyes darken as her pupils dilate, driven by lust.

"Well, I guess so," she replies.

"Ah, still so cheeky are you now, Pretty Kitty?" I ask with a smirk. "Hmmm. Let us see how much your cheeks appreciate your mouth."

Abruptly, I lift her to her feet and crush her body to mine as I slant my lips over hers in a scorching kiss.

Leonie's moan morphs into a squeal when I smack that ass, alternating cheeks several times through the thin material of her leggings. She squirms in my arms.

But I hold her firm, not breaking our kiss. A nip to her plump bottom lip, and I pull her to the bedroom at the back of the jet. She whimpers and trails behind me, easily keeping pace with my long strides.

I urge Leonie through the door ahead of me, then leave it open so we can hear The Twins should they awaken.

She peeks at me over her shoulder and watches as I walk past her to sit on the bed with my feet planted wide.

"Strip," I demand.

A flush blooms on Leonie's cheeks, and I smirk thinking how it will soon appear on her ass. Through my jeans, I stroke my cock, lengthening in anticipation.

She unbuttons her cardigan and lets it slip off her shoulders, then shimmies out of her leggings and thong. Her ample tits jiggle with her movements and almost spill over the tops of the bra cups.

When she stands, Leonie runs her hands over her breasts and moans when she pinches the nipples through the lace. She unhooks the front clasp, and the bra slides down her arms to the puddle of clothes at her feet.

Splendidly naked before me, I lean back on my hands and marvel at her beauty. I'm reminded of our first encounter when I walked in on Leonie topless in the conference room at STEELE New York. Her plump brown nipples were just as succulent.

My cock strains against the zipper of my jeans. I shift my hips for some relief.

Leonie smirks as her gaze lands on my impressive bulge.

"Come," I command.

She swallows when I pat my thighs. Her curvy hips sway as she sashays to stand before me.

I grip them and pull her forward to press my open mouth against her bare mons. A deep inhale fills my nostrils with the succulent aroma of her arousal. My tongue darts out to prod her seam, laving her juices in one slow swipe.

"Ohhh, Roger," Leonie moans as she grips my shoulders, widening her stance.

I swat her ass, relishing in the jiggle the spank evokes. Then I drape her torso over my thighs. Her hip rests against my engorged cock.

She wiggles. But I hold her in place with one hand clasping hers on her lower back and one leg over hers.

Whap. Whap. Whap. Whap.

My palm connects with her round cheeks—left, right, left, crease of her ass and thigh, right, left.

The steady rhythm has Leonie dancing on my lap. With each spank, she gasps.

A brilliant crimson bloom spreads with the heat. Her cries become mewls as her heady arousal fills the bedroom.

"Now do you realize what happens to sassy pants, Pretty Kitty?" I purr in her ear. "Or do you need a further reminder?"

Leonie shakes her head, and the curtain of her mahogany waves undulates.

WHAP. WHAP. WHAP.

Another quick volley to her cheeks—left, right, left, crease of her ass and thigh, right, left—reminds her to use her voice.

"Nnooon... Non... I mean OUI!" She cries as she slumps over my thighs in surrender.

I purr against her neck as my middle finger slips between her ass cheeks. A swipe from her puckered hole to her soaked seam makes Leonie judder with a strangled cry.

Slowly I pump my thick digit in and out of her slick pussy, adding another pointer finger as my thumb presses her swollen clit. All the while I purr, nuzzling her damp neck.

The flutter of her pussy walls vibrates along my fingers, announcing the arrival of her release.

"Cum for me, Pretty Kitty. Cum undone for me," I command in a voice rough with desire.

Leonie's pussy contracts as my pumps increase in tempo, plunging deeper within her dripping core. A strangled scream falls from her slack mouth. She arches her back like a cat and grinds her pelvis into my thigh, adding pressure to my thumb on her clit.

"Give it to me, now!" I growl.

Leonie stiffens, then wails as her entire body ignites from the erotic energy coursing through every cell of her being.

Soothingly, I pet her and croon in her ear as she returns from a state of sheer euphoria. When she stretches languidly in my arms, I nip her ear.

"My turn."

In one swift move, I rise, place Leonie on her hands and knees at the edge of the bed, and tear open my jeans. My painfully swollen cock bobs free and hits my abs, the bulbous tip an angry red and shiny with pre-cum.

I grip the base with one hand and Leonie's hip with the other before I ram home.

"Fuuuck... You feel so good," I groan balls deep within her warm, silken pussy.

Leonie keens. She digs her nails into the bedding as she drops her head, panting. My long and lean strokes grow wild, and she slides forward.

I grip the top of her shoulder to hold her in place, leaning my torso over hers as our lower bodies slap against the other. My heavy balls hit her clit with each strike.

We buck and grunt.

Leonie cries out from another orgasm.

I'm relentless and demand two more from her before I give in to my own spine-tingling release with a roar.

We collapse onto the bed in a sweaty heap, still intimately connected. Moments later Leonie peers at me over her shoulder, her feline eyes glow.

"*Amoureux...* I change my mind. I need a further reminder after all..." she purrs as she wiggles her hips.

LEONIE

$\mathcal{M}$y body still thrums from our lovemaking as we ride in the private elevator up to our newly renovated triplex penthouse. I cannot wait to move in to our family home officially.

My mother assured me all is ready and my big surprise for Roger hangs in our bedroom still covered by the tarp. I didn't want the movers and the installation crew to see Roger's nude body.

It's for my eyes only—mine!

It's just the four of us tonight. Tomorrow, Nanny Grace will move into her suite of rooms on the first floor. Although Grace will have rooms at each of our residences, she'll only stay until Roger gets home or when we go out. But we plan to be hands-on parents who have the help of a nanny.

The porters took the service elevator to bring our luggage to the service entrance of our penthouse. So when the elevator doors open to the foyer and Roger sets The

Twins down in their car seats beside the front door, I glance at him.

He grins and swoops me from my feet in a bride hold against his powerful chest. Then he places his hand on the plate to unlock the door before carrying me inside.

"Welcome home, my love," Roger says.

The open expression of emotion on his face makes my heart soar.

I clasp his cheeks and pull his mouth to mine. The electricity that roars between us is undeniable. We will never be apart again. Over and over we justify our love.

Ga-ga-gas from the foyer remind us of our little ones, and our passionate kiss ends in laughter. Lovers, yes. But parenthood calls.

Roger places me on my feet, kisses my lips, and brings our sons inside.

"Welcome home to you, too, Rodolphe and Gaspard!" I tell them.

Smiles widen their chubby cheeks and drool slips down their chins. Roger and I exchange glances and laugh some more.

"Yes, my sons, welcome home," he chuckles.

We make quick work of settling them in their nursery. I'm eager to show Roger his wedding present. He must sense my excitement and asks what I'm up to. I giggle and pull him from the room.

We race holding hands to our suite of rooms, laughing along the way. Our mood is light and carefree. Once we pass the lounge, I pause at the double doors to the bedroom and en suite bathroom.

"I have a surprise for you, *Mon Cœur*. Close your eyes," I tell him.

Roger grins and rubs his hands together, "In the bedroom? Give it to me, baby!"

I lead him inside and position him at the foot of our massive, four-poster canopy bed. As I move away, he grabs for me, but I swat his hands.

"Behave! Or I won't give your wedding present to you, naughty boy!" I reprimand.

"We've had this conversation before, babe," he says, motioning towards his sizable crotch and thrusting his hips.

"You are impossible, Roger Steele! Give me a minute," I laugh as I remove the tarp and stand back at his side. "Surprise!"

Roger opens his eyes, and they widen when he sees the life-sized painting of his nude body as he sleeps. My eyes follow his as they roam over his beautiful form. His likeness is unmistakable and lifelike.

So peaceful and at rest. No concerns worry him in his slumber.

One chiseled arm thrown over his face to block the morning sun coming through the windows. Its rays of light slant across his powerful chest and eight-pack abs, highlighting the happy trail of dark hair. Even lying flaccid and against his thigh, his massive dick with its bulbous head, veins, and heavy balls makes my mouth water. His thick thighs and muscular calves stretch out beneath the silk sheet.

The five o'clock shadow along with his mussed, collar-length hair emphasize his sex appeal. His sensuous full lips and long eyelashes make any woman jealous. Balanced out by his sculpted cheeks and jaw add a decidedly masculine edge to his features. No mistaking Roger is anything but all man.

I captured his beauty. My Adonis.

"Leonie, this is magnificent, thank you," he murmurs in awe. "When did you paint me? Where are we? Wait a minute who hung it?"

I cover my mouth and giggle. Roger *The Responsible* on full alert.

"First, it remained covered by a tarp I sealed around the frame. So no one but me has ever seen you in all of your glory!

"I'm so happy that you like it. It was eight months ago at *Le Beaulieu Manoir*. A moment in time while you were so peaceful and undisturbed… Before the pretrial began."

My voice trails off at the unwanted memory. But I let go of the negativity and offer Roger my most seductive smile.

"So, how are you going to thank me, Monsieur Steele?" I purr, gazing at him from beneath my eyelashes. "This portrait always makes me so hot and achy for you."

Roger bites his lip and lowers his head before he charges and tosses me onto our bed. He pounces and thanks me repeatedly.

* * *

"Joyeux Anniversaire!"

"Happy Birthday!"

My parents, the Steeles, and Luc celebrate The Twins' six-month birthday the day after we return from Verbier.

We're gathered around the dining room table with Rodolphe and Gaspard sitting in their high chairs. They're bedazzled by the flickering candles on the identical cakes before them.

As everyone sings, The Twins bounce and wave their arms in amusement. Each has one little tooth that gleams in the light. All the drooling and tears led to their first tooth. Every day, they surprise us with their growth.

I still can't believe it's been half a year already.

Roger and I bend over to blow out the candles. When we lean in to kiss their chubby cheeks, Gaspard says, "Dada, dada!"

My eyes fly to Roger, who looks stunned.

"Dada, dada."

We look over to Rodolphe, and he waves his arms, repeating the words.

Roger has tears in his eyes as he lifts first Gaspard, then Rodolphe into his arms. He kisses their cheeks and holds them close.

I wrap my arms around the three of them. Roger buries his face in my hair. It's an unexpected, momentous occasion that overwhelms us.

The room is silent save The Twins and their baby sounds.

"Well, Dada, don't get all sappy on us!"

Roger and I lift our heads as Harris laughs.

"I'm ready for some cake, bro!"

Everyone laughs at the jokester.

While Roger continues to hold The Twins and chats with Sebastian, Lola helps me cut the Gateau St. Honoré cakes. With the recipe tips the chef shared, my mother made them. The Twins' birthday gave her the perfect excuse to try the recent version.

I glance up to see her nervously watching Lola and I cut into the flaky confections. My mother looks relieved after Harris takes a bite and raves about the delicious factor being off the charts.

She smiles at me, and I hug her, whispering congratulations and my thanks for such thoughtful goodies. I take a bite of my piece and swoon from the delicious flavor. Harris is right!

We spend the next half an hour opening presents. With The Twins' development in mind, the gifts include stacking toys with different-sized rings and multi-colored cubes; cars, trains, and balls that roll, light up, and make music to encourage crawling; roly-poly toys; sturdy toys that encourage pulling up to standing; to keep them entertained, colorful board books.

The Dynamic Duo give them some gadgets claiming one is never too young for technology.

Luc bought them their first stock portfolios. The men were more impressed and had a lengthy discussion about the growth potential.

Afterwards, we go to the cinema room with aperitifs.

Haley surprises us with a compilation movie of our first family Christmas and New Year's. No one even realized she was taking footage while we were together. Some scenes from us skiing, the angle straight on as though we were still on the piste; making s'mores at the outside firepit; The Twins first snowfall; the New Year's Eve fireworks in the village.

She has it set to some of my favorite Christmas songs, including "Christmas Canon" and Andrea Bocelli and Céline Dion's "The Prayer."

I give her an enormous hug as tears well in my eyes.

Haley impresses everyone, and we request copies. Always prepared, she hands out artfully packaged copies to each of us.

Later, as Roger wraps around me with my back to his front in bed, I think about how tomorrow we'll return to reality. Roger has a full schedule of meetings set up at STEELE and site visits already. I plan to finish my sketches and proposal on my new division for Sebastian. Then present them to him, Roger, and Morgan at the end of the week.

I sigh and snuggle closer to the warmth and solidness of Roger. The strength he exudes is more than enough to sustain us both. I smile when I correct myself, the four of us.

Yes, I'm an Independent Woman. But I value all that my Alpha male provides. So with him, I have no doubt we can emerge from our bubble and face the real world head on—

"Stop thinking, my love. Sleep. I've got you," Roger whispers.

ROGER

"What the fuck?! I thought this bullshit was over already! What do you mean another lawsuit?!"

My mind blows through the roof at STEELE Paris. I am so pissed my body vibrates.

Today is my first day back. When Sebastian mentioned we had meetings this morning, I presumed they were project status updates. I found it odd he insisted I wasn't late—not that I am late to a meeting, ever.

My angry eyes move from one face to the next at the conference table in my suite of offices. My father and my siblings along with Albert Perry STEELE Paris' General Counsel stare back at me.

"Roger, it is understandable it upsets you. Sit back down. We have mush to discuss," my father states.

I run my hands through my hair, tugging at the roots to ground myself.

"Leonie. She has to be here. I promised her I wouldn't

keep anything from here again," the words tumble from my mouth as I reach into my trousers pocket for my mobile.

No way can I speak. She'd hear anger in my voice and question me. Questions for which I do not have answers.

Hey, I need you to come to my offices now.

A moment passes, and my mobile rings. I have no choice but to accept.

"What happened?" Leonie asks without preamble.

I sigh, then respond, "We're having a meeting about some unexpected developments. You need to be here. Just come now. Please."

Dropping into my seat, I toss my mobile onto the table's shiny wooden surface. I watch it slide until it rests against a leather pen holder.

"She's on her way," I say unnecessarily since they picked up my side of the conversation. "We'll continue once she arrives."

I swivel my chair to face the wall of floor-to-ceiling windows. The city stretches out before me with unobstructed views from the twentieth floor. The Seine below with the Eiffel Tower in the distance serve as the notable landmarks in the area. On a clear, sunny day like this morning, the panoramas are riveting.

Today, not so much.

My mind is in turmoil. Thoughts bounce around as I try to wrap my brain around this news.

FUCK!

No one speaks loudly; inaudible murmurs and the shuffling of papers fill the void.

"What happened?"

Leonie burst into the room. Her amber eyes glow as her gaze seeks me out.

When we connect, she rushes forward. Concern covers her beautiful face. I did not want her to worry so soon after we return. Now this.

I stand to meet her, and she implores me again. Instead of responding, I gesture to the chairs and we sit.

Leonie looks around the table expectantly. Morgan nods at Albert.

"Delia Shaw filed a lawsuit in New York City against STEELE International and Roger. The allegations differ slightly from those in the previous claims. The Paris legal team has been working with the New York general counsel for the past few weeks—"

"Few weeks?" I explode. "Why am I hearing about it now and not when it started?"

Morgan holds up his hand for silence.

"You were on your honeymoon. I left you to enjoy time with your new wife and sons. The baseless claim did not need your attention," he starts. "Allow Albert to finish. He will explain."

I glare at Sebastian and spit out, "I should have been told."

Leonie takes my hand in hers and shakes her head.

"Roger, our anger is not for our family. They did what they thought was best," she pauses, then continues as she rubs her thumb over my hand. "I agree. That woman inflicted enough pain. We deserved to enjoy our honeymoon. Please, *Mon Cœur.*"

Leonie's heartfelt plea and her soothing presence refocuses me.

I cup her face and stare into her eyes deeply.

"Okay, my love. Okay," I comply.

The smile she rewards me with could light the Eiffel Tower more brilliantly than any extravagant light show. She turns her head and kisses my fingertips.

I beam at her, then nod at those gathered.

"Give me the net net. This ends now."

"Now there's the Roger *The Responsible* we all know and love," Sebastian smirks. "And for the record, I voted to tell you, that is after Lola threatened to deny me the pleasures of—"

Haley throws her hands up and screams at the ceiling, "I've had enough of my brothers' sex lives already!"

The tension in the room dissipates after shy Haley erupts. Everyone laughs, including me. As always, my family has my back. I'm sure I would have done the same for them.

Our father clears his throat, and Albert continues.

Leonie and I learn Delia Fucking Shaw has been extremely busy these past seven months. The shit starter left France shortly after the pretrial ended to return to the United States. But instead of going home to West Bumfuck, she went to New York City.

In an attempt to divulge STEELE information, Delia applied for a position at Rockett Construction Company.

Sebastian says he received an urgent call from Patrick. His head of human resources flagged Delia's resume as a former STEELE employee. Immediately he brought her application to Patrick's attention. He recognized her name from Billie mentioning the trouble she was causing me and the company—not to mention how she wanted to strangle Delia for upsetting Leonie.

Patrick and Baz devised a scheme for Delia to interview with him under the pretense he wanted information on their top competitor from the source directly. She agreed to the videotaping, and he captured her disclosing confidential plans. Hell, she even flirted with him and offered to tell him more over dinner.

From one multibillionaire to another...

Patrick turned her down for the position and the offer.

Delia does not know STEELE and Rockett are on better terms since Billie started dating Patrick. So he gave the footage to us—and signed an ironclad nondisclosure agreement. Now we have an ace in the hole.

Not one to give up easily, Delia sold her story to some gossip rag, and a bottom-of-the-barrel book publisher had a ghostwriter fabricate her tragic tale. Some low-level legal firm accepted her case with more bullshit claims. She has a smear campaign leading up to her book tour, including appearances on less than stellar talk shows.

My personal assistant Françoise video conferences the STEELE New York legal team on the big screen. They provide an update and answer the questions Leonie and I ask. The judge scheduled a meeting with the teams in two weeks. However, the general counsel assures us the case won't make it to court. The fact the French pretrial judge threw out the case adds to our favor. Their confidence puts us at ease.

Next the global head of communications joins us with

her New York lead via video conference as her Paris lead enters my office. They discuss protocols to handle the media—they're already circling like vultures—and next steps. They drafted a press release for our review and scheduled some good-feeling stories to run for STEELE and me.

I'm a proponent for community improvement and volunteer through STEELE Foundation regularly. My mother runs our family's foundation that builds and manages attractive, affordable housing for urban, lower-income families. The name is a play on the house foundation, being strong and supportive like steel. So it's not a tough sell for our philanthropic efforts.

The communications team forwards a list of interviews and events they encourage Leonie and me to take part in together. They want to present a united front and highlight our newlywed status and family life.

Leonie agrees immediately and offers valuable suggestions. Her experience being in the world's spotlight as a megamodel makes her accustomed to handling all kinds of media coverage with ease. She impresses everyone with her knowledge.

After further discussion, the communications team signs off.

The room grows quiet as everyone absorbs what we discussed. I know my mind is mulling it over, so I don't doubt they're cogitating it. too.

My father turns to me and scans my face. Then his gaze falls on Leonie. He makes a decisive nod before he speaks.

"Roger, do not stew over these latest developments. We

defeated that woman's baseless claims once. These circumstances do not differ," he says before shifting back to her.

Morgan continues, "Leonie, you settle my son and provide support for hum. However, you must take care of yourself, too. We cannot allow you to stress over this nonsense, again. The Twins need their mother healthy and happy."

"We are a family and as such everyone takes on the mantle of tending to each other's needs. Everyone here, your parents, Shelley, and Lola stand as one," he concludes, as he spreads his arms wide to indicate all, including those not around us.

"*Merci, Papa* Steele, family is extremely important to me, and I appreciate your kind words," Leonie says, her voice thick with emotion before she clears her throat and a fierce look brightens her eyes. "I agree with you completely. She who shall not be named will not hurt our family again."

"Hear, hear!"

"Well said!"

"Absolutely agree!"

"Oh, she'll get what's coming to her. I guarantee."

Every head spins towards Haley. The determined expression on her face belies her shy nature. Rarely does she speak so adamantly. She's the most soft-spoken one of us all.

Haley meets our surprised gazes with a steely glint to her gray eyes.

"If that is all, I have work to do," she says, then rises when our father confirms we're done. "Roger and Leonie, no need to worry."

A nod and she's out the door.

"Well, all righty then... Was Haley enigmatic or what?" Harris laughs, pushing back from the table. "Leave it to me to solve the mystery of my twin. Leonie, Roger, I'm here for the next week or so. Holla at your boy."

I chuckle as Harris salutes and about-faces before following in his twin's footsteps.

"Thanks, everyone"—I squeeze Leonie's hand and smile at her. Then glance around the table at our family—"We appreciate your support. And I'm not mad you left us to enjoy our honeymoon. This news would have put a damper on it without a doubt."

Sebastian smirks, knowing the fun had during two months of uninterrupted time with a new bride. He nods and claps his hands.

"Well, now that's over... We have a company to run, revenue to generate, profits to increase. You know the really important matters," he says. "Leonie, my lovely sister, we must bid you adieu. It's time for business updates since Romeo has been otherwise engaged."

She laughs, then rises to salute the STEELE CEO à la Harris.

"Yes, Sir!"

Baz busts out laughing when he spies my reaction to "Sir." The Alpha Dom finds it hilarious my wife referred to him by the title.

Leonie winks as she leans over to kiss me.

"Oops... Did I say something wrong?" She purrs against my lips, audible to me only. "See you later, *Amoureux*..."

My cock jumps.

LEONIE

"Why, Monsieur Steele, don't you look scrumptious? My own James Bond oozing sexiness in a bespoke tuxedo. Rawr..."

The sight of my man oh so debonair makes me wet my lace thong.

We're heading to a charity gala for the girls and teens center I mentor at twice a month. It's a passion of mine I've done for over eleven years now. My mentees trust me and find the center a safe space to open up. Even those I've mentored before often come back to meet with me and to talk to the new girls. It's so good to watch them grow up.

Besides their concerns about life and the state of the world, we discuss their goals and what they want to do after they graduate from school. Just as important, they share their thoughts on body image and stereotypical misperceptions about women.

As someone who has worked hard my entire career to dispel models as dumb; only clothes hangers; only good enough to stand there and pose prettily, not think, I can relate. I've encouraged my peers to do the same.

My mentees and I also have fun doing makeovers and spa days. Several times a year, they attend my photoshoots and fashion shows. Several photographers and designers have joined our sessions and become mentors.

This is the first year I didn't chair the gala committee because of my wedding. However, Roger and I donated the use of the rooftop ballroom at STEELE Montaigne. Funny enough, the city named the street for Luc's family.

In the *huitième* arrondissement the five-star hotel has extraordinary views of the Champs-Élysées, Arc de Triomphe, and the Place de la Concorde, not to mention the Seine. At night, with the lights of Paris shining brightly, will prove a spectacular venue for the gala.

But nothing compares to the sight before me of sexy Roger Steele in his tux. Yum.

He chuckles and adjusts the sleeves over his cuffs. The platinum and diamond cuff links glint in the light—along with his wedding band.

Mine!

"Pleased with my appearance, Mrs. Steele?" He asks in a husky voice with his eyebrow raised.

I step into his personal space. The air between us charges with erotic energy. Immediate tightness in my nipples and pussy makes me lightheaded with desire.

Skimming my hands over the lapels of his jacket, up his muscular chest to wrap around his neck makes my fingertips tingle.

"Absolument, Amoureux," I purr, my lips brush against the sensitive shell of his ear.

The sensation of Roger's sizable frame shuddering with need resonates through my smaller body. He grips my hips possessively and grinds his burgeoning erection against my mons. Pressure to my clit sends a zing down my legs to curl my toes in the sky-high strappy sandals.

"You are even more delectable in this sexy as fuck gown, Mrs. Steele," he murmurs against the side of my neck. His warm breath and seductive growl cause goosebumps to surface on my heated skin.

When Roger cups my ass, I purr in contentment as I melt into his embrace.

The crotch-high slit in the floor-length, silver silk-satin gown allows me to wrap my long leg around Roger's hip. I rise onto the ball of my standing foot to align our centers.

Simultaneous growls fall from our mouths as Roger ups the ante by bending his knees to prod from below. The increase in contact rocks my mind.

"Do you want something from me, Mrs. Steele?" He murmurs between hot, open-mouthed kisses to my collarbone and the tops of my breasts along the sweetheart neckline.

"Make me cum," I respond breathlessly in need of release from his massive dick.

Roger chuckles, squeezes my ass, and unhooks my leg.

"Duly noted, Mrs. Steele," he says as he holds my hips to steady me.

The sudden loss of his solid body and heat leaves me on wobbly legs. Like a newborn foal, my footing is unstable.

I clutch his wide shoulders and scowl.

"We can't be late, slowpoke," he teases me for my time flaw. "They expect the gala hostess on the red carpet as scheduled."

My lips form a pout, and Roger nips at them as he murmurs, "Be a good girl, and I will make it up to you, Pretty Kitty."

With a pat to my ass, he strides to the wall of drawers.

"Oh, so I See, Monsieur Ste—"

My words stop at this new sight dangling from Roger's hands: a diamond necklace crafted like a zipper. The Van Cleef & Arpels Zip necklace stuns me speechless.

Roger smirks as he lays the couture zipper with filigree lacework and sumptuous tassels around my neck. The cool platinum heats as the zipper dips into my décolletage, the diamonds on the tassels tickle the delicate skin.

"You were saying, Mrs. Steele?" Roger prompts as he toys with the tassels, setting the zipper to just the right closure. The tips of his fingers brush against my skin.

My nipples pucker from his touch.

He chuckles and returns to the drawer. When he stands before me, he opens his left hand, gesturing towards my ears.

Quickly, I remove the antique diamond and sapphire chandelier earrings and place them in his outstretched palm.

Roger nods and opens his right hand. Light sparks as a pair of matching diamond tassels shimmer.

With an eagerness a woman who receives such magnificent jewels can muster, I nearly snatch the baubles from his hand. Set in my ears, I grin from ear to ear as I swing my head from side to side, loving the feel of the tassels tickling my jaw.

"*Merci, Mon Cœur!*" I exclaim as I kiss his luscious lips curled into a smile. "You're so good to me!"

"Yes, and you will be even better for me later in your diamonds only, Pretty Kitty," Roger growls into my kisses.

I purr in delight.

"ROGER! THIS WAY!"

"*The Lion*! Here, here!"

No sooner do we step out of our Rolls-Royce Phantom Extended at the STEELE Montaigne, then the photographers go wild. Their flashes put spots before our eyes.

Roger tightens his grip on my hand, the only sign of the tension in his body. He's bracing for their questions. The smile on his face as he pulls me into his side to pose for their cameras gives no clue.

My modeling instincts kick in. A tilt to my head, the angle of my hips, a purposeful kick of my bare leg with my wedding jewelry on my upper thigh. Not to mention the dazzling smile made blinding by the diamonds framing my face.

The photogs go wild.

Gotcha!

I rule this land, not some wannabe trollop seeking her fortune at the expense of others. *The Lion* is ferocious. Don't fuck with my family or me.

A subtle squeeze to my hip, and Roger encourages us to

continue down the gauntlet of the red carpet as the STEELE Paris communications lead joins us. When we near the center, another roar from the crowd harkens Lola and Sebastian.

Roger and I watch as they play to the cameras.

Lola looks radiant in a black strapless Swarovski crystal-embellished gown with a slit as high as mine. The red silk lining of her gown draws the photogs like a bull by a matador. Rubies adorn her ears, neck, and fingers. Baz—as dashing as my Roger—smirks with his hand possessively on her waist as the flashes go into overdrive.

The center's public relations manager approaches Roger and me with a request for an on-carpet interview with an American magazine. He confers with the STEELE lead, and they decide she will shut down the interview should it go left with questions about she who shall not be named.

"Ready?" I ask Roger, stroking his back as I gaze up at him.

"Yes, my love," he responds, then brushes his lips over mine.

The female reporter and her male photographer eagerly watch us approach. She begins the questions directed at me regarding my involvement with the center —basic. Then she swings her gaze to Roger and her eyes gleam.

"Mr. Steele, how supportive are you of your wife's endeavors with young women?" She asks.

Roger smiles down at me before he responds with praise and admiration.

"What are your thoughts on women having the right to say no?" She asks glaring at him.

"Thank you for your questions," the STEELE Paris communications lead cuts in as she opens her arm to separate us from the interviewer. She moves us away.

"Oh, so no answer, Mr. Steele?" The magazine writer persists. "Don't women have—"

"Women have every right to say no. And men have every right to not fall victim to someone who falsely accuses them under the guise of sexual assault. That tactic does a disservice to women, and men, who have been victims of actual sexual assault. Not fabrications for monetary gain. Thank you for your questions."

Roger's response silences the woman, and her photographer nods in agreement.

Sebastian and Lola stand behind us, along with Luc and Blair—who Roger and I hadn't seen arrive. The interviewer glances at them and back to us. Daunted by their show of support, she turns away without further comment.

"Well said, bro," Sebastian says when we move away from the row of media reps. "You handled the situation perfectly."

The STEELE Paris communications lead agrees and tells us she will contact the magazine publisher to follow up on the piece. She takes us along the line to media reps she vetted in advance. Fortunately, we don't encounter another ridiculous question.

We pose for more photos in front of the step and repeat highlighting the event sponsors including STEELE International, Inc., Lola's Coterie, Banque Montaigne,

Jackson Corporation, Elie Saab, Van Cleef & Arpels, and other high-profile companies.

Lola and I joke about our leg-baring gowns while Roger and Sebastian chuckle. The photogs eat it up.

"Hey, Hot Mama! I love your necklace!" Lola exclaims. "It's beyond gorgeous!"

I run my fingers over the handcrafted piece and grin.

"My latest present from my husband," I respond.

"I'm glad you like it. Monsieur Steele commissioned it especially for you, Madame."

Lola and I turn to the alluring French voice to find the President and CEO of Van Cleef & Arpels smiling at me.

His cornflower blue eyes shine.

"In fact, Madame Steele, we would love to discuss a spokesmodel opportunity with you," he continues. "It would honor us to have *The Lion* represent our Maison."

I smile at him as I extend my hand, "The honor would be all mine, Monsieur."

"My office will reach out to your agent next week," he replies then turns to smile at Lola. "Madame Steele, the Maison's Flowers look lovely on you."

She grins and touches her fingers to her ears as she thanks him. "Roses are my favorites."

A palm on the small of my back draws my attention to Roger, who also extends his hand to the head of the jewelry house. They chat along with Baz before we make our way to the cocktail hour with signature libations crafted by Lachlan using the Jackson portfolio. *The Sexy Chef* Lucien created the tantalizing hors d'oeuvres.

"The decorations are fantastic! I love how they incorporated the rubies and diamonds theme," Blair says.

She dazzles in the Van Cleef & Arpels Snowflake Collarette with earrings that match the pendant. Her red mikado-piqué strapless mermaid gown skims her curves and sweeps the floor in the back. With her chestnut brown hair swept up, her wide cerulean blue eyes stand out in her heart-shaped face.

"*Oui*, Leonie, tonight's gala is spectacular, even better than last year. Are you ready to host?" Luc asks.

I smile at *Le Renard Argenté*. Lola and I are so happy he's found a partner in Blair. Who would have thought he'd give in to her flirtations?

"So are you saying this year is better since I was less involved?" I tease.

Luc chuckles and his sapphire blue eyes shine.

"Of course not, *chérie*. You are an essential part of this center and have helped to involve many others, including me. Few would be here tonight, or any in the last few years, had you not been a mentee to the young women," he responds.

His words make me proud of the impact I've accomplished with the center. Luc is correct it wasn't widely known when I started and their donations were not as abundant. What I care about the most are the girls and teens who keep coming back and being certain they have a facility with staff worthy of them.

"How kind of you! *Oui*. I'm excited and cannot wait to get started," I say. "We have a great surprise for the young ladies."

For the rest of the cocktail hour, we mingle and place bids on the silent auction.

Normally, I would offer a date night with me or a chance to have backstage passes at one of my fashion shows. The high numbers would generate incredible donations for the center.

This year, to avoid Roger going buck wild, my offer is a mock cover shoot with a famous fashion photographer, designer clothes, and a glam squad makeover. The pictures compiled in a portfolio as a unique coffee-table book.

As Roger and I stroll past the displays, we check out the other offers. The week aboard a vintage steam yacht in the Mediterranean Sea catches my attention. Its design fascinates me. I place a significant bid since it would make for a fun getaway.

I notice a pair of prints for offer. Intrigued by the tableau of a spring day in Bois de Boulogne, I take a closer look. The artistry is superb. But it's the sponsor that offers them that makes my eyes widen.

Mattei Art Galleries!

Of course. My ex-paramour Giovanni Mattei supports the center—at my request—and provides a piece from his collection for the gala every year.

Gio is a wealthy nobleman from an Italian aristocratic family dating back to the Middle Ages. And was nowhere near being ready to settle down when we dated for a few years. The billion-dollar playboy, who races cars professionally to boot, attracts women with no effort. They throw themselves at him—one reason I ended our affair. He believes he's *God's Gift* truly.

I glance around. But it's a pointless endeavor since the alcove with the auction doesn't allow a view of the primary room. Nonetheless, I don't want Roger to spot them. He'd likely rip Gio's head off. They do not get along. At all.

"*Mon Cœur*, let's take our seats at the table," I say as I all but tug Roger out of the alcove and surreptitiously shift my gaze about us.

We make it without incident to the dining area. The view is spectacular with three of the walls comprising floor-to-ceiling windows that lead out to an enormous terrace. Paris stretches out before us with the beauty of its lights aglow.

"This is lovely, Leonie!" Lola exclaims as I settle in my chair beside her. "Who's the event planner? I'd like to use them."

We chat through dinner with Roger and Sebastian and Luc and Blair, along with Lucien and Lachlan and their dates. The meal as expected tastes divine. We congratulate Lucien on another delectable menu.

Before they serve dessert, the head of the center and public relations manager come to our table. They escort me to the stage for my welcome speech and the presentations.

I quip to Lucien to save a dessert for me. The chocolate torte with mocha ice cream sounds irresistible.

As I make my way through the tables—stopping to chat with guests—a hand on my arm stops me. I glance over my shoulder into the warm chocolate brown eyes of Gio.

From the table next to me he stands to his full height of six feet, three inches. His muscular frame emphasizes his commanding presence. With a charming smile, he runs his fingers through his collar-length, curly brown hair.

"*Ciao bellissima. Come stai?*" He asks, double kissing my cheeks with an enormous hand on my waist.

Too taken aback to speak, I stare at him with my lips parted. I'm not sure how I'm doing.

Fortunately, the head of the center interrupts to usher me along to the stage.

I'm shook at seeing him so unexpectedly. But by no means sense any desire for him. Roger claims my heart completely. With that thought in mind, I take the stage and deliver my impassioned speech and appeal for donations.

The guests show their appreciation with a record-breaking total of €750,000. The silent auction generates an additional €250,000. The young women share their gratitude with touching speeches and a video montage of the past year's activities and highlights.

At the end of the presentations, Roger joins me on the stage for the last speech.

I watch him approach and marvel at his sex appeal. *Non*, Gio's name may mean *God's Gift*, but Roger is my heart. No comparison and no competition. At all.

He slips his arm around my waist, possessively pulling me into his side as he thanks the guests for their generosity. Then he adds on behalf of STEELE International, Inc. he presents a check to match the total €1 million raised.

The guests applaud with a standing ovation as the head of the center accepts the check and the photographers capture the moment.

I beam at Roger, completely off guard by his gift.

The Zip necklace and earrings are beyond. But the money to support the young women's center tops it.

As we step off the stage, Roger bends down to murmur in my ear.

"Do not think I did not see that slimy dick kiss you, Pretty Kitty. You wear my rings. You bore my sons and will give me more. You are mine. I am not concerned. However, you will atone for his actions in only your diamonds when we return home. *Tu me comprends?*"

Merde...

ROGER

"Well, that's a fucking relief!"

I say as I slap my palms on the conference table in my office and jump to my feet.

The chair slides backwards and spins at the force. The bang of it colliding with another piece of furniture doesn't faze me in the least bit. I'm in a state of impenetrable euphoria.

The New York City judge threw out the case after two months of talks.

Hell. Yeah.

Leonie leaps into my arms, wrapping her legs around my waist, and grabs my face, planting kisses all over it between words of joy and gratitude.

I cup her round ass and hold her tight to my chest. Our hearts beat wildly with excitement. Six months of marriage and this will never get old.

"Excellent work! Now we can put that woman behind us permanently," my father proclaims at the other end of the table to Albert and the New York legal team present via video conference.

Sebastian slaps me on the back and says, "Absolutely. Keep that bullshit in the past. However, we'll continue to monitor her activities. We can never be too sure with the likes of that conniving woman."

"I'm already on it. My top guy in surveillance at STEELE Cyber Security and I have the situation well in hand," Haley adds with a confident nod.

Harris also nods and returns his gaze to his tablet. His focus had been on it all along.

What is the Dynamic Duo up to now? I wonder.

"That's fantastic news!" Malcolm says as he bro hugs me. "She's one annoying ass broad. Don't even look at the rearview mirror when you zoom past that one. Leave her in the dust."

Everyone laughs when he shudders in revulsion.

"This calls for a celebratory dinner tonight!" Leonie exclaims as she claps her hands and shimmies her shapely hips. "Let's go to Alléno Paris au Pavillon Ledoyen."

"Great idea. Invite Françoise, Luc, Blair, and Lucien. I want to thank my entire support team," I respond, then turn to Albert as I extend my hand. "You and your lead must come, too. Your team did a stellar job."

We shake with claps to the backs, and he agrees.

Leonie makes the call to her friend, who's the chef of the seventh-century restaurant.

Set in the *huitième* arrondissement amongst the gardens of the Champs-Élysées, the three Michelin star eatery is a favorite of ours. Besides the quality dishes, we love the architecture and design, not to mention the views.

Leonie confirms the reservation for the upstairs private dining room that still boasts some original features. Then calls everyone not present.

I pop my head out of my door to ask Françoise to join us now for a champagne toast—who cares if it's only three in the afternoon—and dinner at eight.

"Monsieur Steele, I am so happy for you. That woman deserves to punishment for her incessant lies," Françoise says as she enters the room.

"That is the absolute truth!" Malcolm *The Enforcer* adds as he rubs his hands together. His eyes gleam devilishly with his smirk.

Once again we laugh at his comment.

Baz pops the bottle of Dom Pérignon Vintage 2002 and pours the elixir in Lalique Crystal flutes. Haley hands them out, then takes hers as my father raises his glass in a toast.

"To the power of family unity. The Steele clan forever!"

Amen to that, I muse as I lift the flute to my lips and squeeze Leonie's waist.

LEONIE and I arrive early at the restaurant—unbelievable for Ms. Tardy—and sit at the bar for a drink. The mixologist recognizes us and waves while he makes our preferred cocktails.

When he brings the drinks to us, we chat for a moment. Then he's off to work his craft for other patrons.

"*Mon Cœur*, I am so thrilled for you and STEELE,"

Leonie says as she lifts her Kir Royale. "Here's to a fresh start so rightly deserved!"

I raise my Rocks Glass of Jackson Reserve Scotch on ice and stare intently into her eyes, the same color as the liquid. I'd much rather wrap my lips around her clit than around the tumbler's rim. But when I tried to ravage her earlier, she promised me later.

"I'll make it worth your wait, Amoureux. I promise you," Leonie purred as she stroked my thick length when I crept up behind her in the shower.

Now, watching her little pink tongue lick the edge of the crystal flute, I regret not pressing the issue.

Sensing my thoughts, the wily seductress winks at me as she sips the champagne and Chambord Liqueur cocktail. Her thumb and index finger glide up and down the stem when she sets the flute on the bar top. Leonie glances at me sideways beneath her full eyelashes and smiles.

"What's on your mind, Monsieur Steele?" She purrs softly.

Without hesitation, I lean towards her, place my lips against the shell of her ear, and murmur, "Your swollen clit lapped by my tongue. I know you are wet for me, Pretty Kitty. I can scent your arousal since we left the shower."

I nip her earlobe, then lick the sensitive flesh when she jumps. A dark chuckle falls from my lips as I sit back in my chair.

"Well, well, well, don't let us interrupt your love affair."

Leonie and I tear our eyes away from the other and glance up to find Lola and Baz smirking at us.

"I mean, we only came here to celebrate with you,

Roger. But if you'd rather take your party to LEVELS Paris… Well, let me get my collar," Lola continues deadpan.

Baz chuckles and whispers in Lola's ear as he tucks her into his side. Her reddening cheeks and giggles prove whatever he said was encouraging and well received.

"Honey! I'm so glad it all ended as we knew it would!" My mother gushes as she hugs me and kisses my face. "And Leonie, sweetheart, what a relief for you!"

They double kiss and embrace.

When the rest of the group arrives, we head upstairs to the private dining room. The waitstaff have more flutes of Dom Pérignon Vintage 2002 and bottles in ice baths ready to pour. They also have trays of Beluga caviar on toast points and foie gras on toasted brioche to complement the champagne.

The waitstaff leave us to enjoy ourselves and only return to serve our food or to replenish our drinks.

Alone in the separate room, not encumbered by other diners, we relax and unwind. The atmosphere is jovial as we chitchat and laugh.

Harris cracks jokes, and Lucien quips how he's insulted we didn't choose one of his eateries for the impromptu party. Josy concurs with Lucien, and we laugh some more.

At the end of our meal, the chef enters. He greets Leonie with double kisses and grins when he spies Lucien, who nods in acknowledgment. We thank the chef for accommodating us on such brief notice and for the delicious meal, particularly since he included some of my favorite dishes.

As we part, my mother hugs me tightly and whispers

how glad she is it's over. Then my father—followed by Guy —claps me on the shoulder and shakes my hand.

Leonie and I bid everyone good night and slip into my Aston Martin DB7 Vantage. She mimics the purr of the engine as she glides her thumb and index finger along my cock through my trousers. It's quick to swell along my thigh.

When she tweaks the tip, I growl.

"You are playing with fire, Pretty Kitty. If you keep this up, we will not make it home before I take you," I rumble.

Leonie leans over and coos in my ear. Her warm breath and the brush of her full tits and pointed nipples against my arm further ignite my desire.

I pull into a space on a side street and cut the engine. The power seat slides back and reclines.

"Here, Kitty, Kitty, Kitty," I tell her as I pat my muscular thighs.

Leonie's amber eyes glow in the dim light from a lamp-post on the corner. She lifts her midi skirt over her long, toned legs to straddle me.

Although Aston Martin did not design the interior of the sports car for fucking in the driver's seat, we intend to make it work.

I grip Leonie's hips and lower her exposed, wet pussy— she's no longer allowed to wear panties with dresses and skirts—onto my crotch. We groan as she undulates her hips, rubbing her slick folds against my hard cock.

"Oh, *Amoureux*, I want you deep inside of me now," she mewls, biting her plump lower lip.

"You will have my thick dick how and when I say," I respond with a growl. "First, you will ride my fingers—"

Eagerly Leonie rises onto her knees, her back brushing the roof of the car, to give me access.

"But, you will not cum until I say."

She whimpers in frustration, then moans when two of my thick fingers plunge inside of her pussy. Leonie's breathing increases to pants as I drive my fingers in and out of her slippery channel. The flutters of her inner walls foreshadow her orgasm.

I withdraw and she growls until my fingers press against her upper lips, demanding entrance for her to lick them clean.

"Mmmmmm," Leonie hums as she delights in the taste of her sweet pussy juices.

The vibration on my fingers and her moans of pleasure make my cock jump.

"Unzip my pants and take out my dick," I command.

Leonie scrambles to move her hands from my shoulders to my fly while my fingers remain in her hot, wet mouth.

My head falls back against the seat with a thump when her fingers wrap around my achy cock. As she spreads the pre-cum over the fat head, a groan falls from my parted lips. When Leonie rises to her knees again and strokes her wet folds with my sensitive tip, my hips jerk up as my hands tighten on her waist to pin her in place.

She gasps when I slam into her pussy in one long thrust. Leonie recovers posthaste and grinds her pelvis into mine.

Our erotic connection scorches us.

I grasp her buttocks in my generous hands to hold and to steady her. Then piston my hips to slam my cock to the very end of her channel. Through the vee-neck of her silk blouse, I latch onto her turgid nipple covered by sheer mesh.

She rides me as my brutal thrusts rock her to her core. Each time she's close to her climax, I slow the pace and depth of my strokes. I wet her tits from my suckling and laving. She's ready to break beautifully for me.

I pull her ass cheeks apart and press my thumb against her back hole. The rings of muscle give way as she babbles incoherently. The sensation of her pussy walls clenching through the thin membrane that separates it from her back hole precedes her plea for release.

"Come undone for me, Pretty Kitty," I command in a voice rough with desire.

Her entire body tenses. My fingers nearly break when her pussy walls clamp down on them. A keen starts from her toes to rise to her slack mouth.

As it fills the car with the guttural sound, simultaneously a jolt runs up the backs of my legs and down my spine to meet at the base as my heavy balls fill.

A roar rips from my mouth as I jackhammer into Leonie, chasing my climax. Three plundering thrusts, and my hot seed spews from my pulsating cock to fill her wrecked pussy.

I possess Leonie fully.

And she possesses me.

LEONIE

"*O*h *mes beaux fils*, you like your New York City nursery? ... Really? Is that so? ... Well, your *Papa* had to go downstairs to his offices for loads of meetings."

At ten months old, I adore their jibber-jabber as they speak actual words, and their new thing of blowing kisses makes me laugh. Roger got a kick out of them when we escorted him to the Steele family private elevator.

We're in The STEELE Tower's luxury, modern, gray-tinted glass fifty-seven story mixed-use skyscraper on the southwest corner of Fifty-Seventh Street and Fifth Avenue. The area known worldwide as Billionaires' Row.

The residential portion of The Tower runs from the thirtieth through the fifty-seventh floors. Our penthouse on the fifty-second floor is one of the Steele residences. Morgan and Shelley occupy the top two floors with the penthouse duplex. Sebastian and Lola live below in their duplex. Malcolm, Harris, and Haley live in penthouses on the fifty-third, fifty-first, and fiftieth floors, respectively.

The elevator Roger rode down to the executive offices on the twenty-ninth floor links the Steele penthouses to the floors occupied by their divisions.

We came to the city for work at the STEELE headquarters on the nineteenth through twenty-ninth floors of The Tower. Other businesses take up the eight through the eighteenth floors with a luxury retail mall on the street level through the seventh floor. Lola's Coterie has a prime spot as one of the anchor stores.

We'll be in town for the next three weeks leading up to Labor Day weekend.

Roger's tasks include some potential residential sites, visits to current construction projects, and overall meetings. He also has to attend the quarterly board meeting.

Morgan has the role of Chairman Emeritus since he retired, making Sebastian Chairman. Malcolm moved up to First Vice President, replacing Baz as Roger moved to Second Vice President. Harris and Haley serve as members.

I also have a full schedule of meetings with the Residential Properties Division's Interior Design Team and the Entertainment Properties Division's Amenities Team. We're set to review plans for my newly created STEELE Children and Young Adults Division to incorporate for residential nurseries, bedrooms, playrooms, and playhouses and for hospitality kids clubs and play areas. As the head of the division, I report to Roger and Malcolm, respectively.

While I'm in town, I'll take care of some Lola's Coterie business. We scheduled some photo shoots and marketing activities. Plus, I have the latest designs for the pre- and postnatal collections.

Our hectic schedules called for Nanny Grace to join us for the next couple of weeks.

We'll take one of the company's Sikorsky helicopters out to Steele Southampton Village before Labor Day weekend for the annual party. Shelley and Morgan use it as a fundraiser for STEELE Foundation. The family's magnificent beachfront compound comprising a massive main mansion and three smaller—but no less impressive —mansions.

Roger explained they purchased the adjacent properties over the decades. The elder siblings occupy the three smaller homes while the twins stay in separate wings of the main house. All the residences share the similar style of weathered shingles on the exterior and beach-chic interiors.

He told me I could redo our home, however I preferred. But I told him not this summer since I have a lot on my agenda.

My parents and Luc will fly over to join us for the weekend festivities. Billie and Blair are already in town working with Lola. While Starr plans to come in from Beverly Hills. Baz even invited Patrick—although he's still skeptical...

I love how well our families and friends blend seamlessly.

Tonight, however, Roger and I have plans for LEVELS New York. It's been forever since we last played at one of the clubs. And I cannot wait!

. . .

"YOU ARE DRIPPING, Pretty Kitty. Obviously you take pleasure in watching others in the throes of passion, little voyeur. Tell me. What do you want? Do you want me to fuck my pussy until you lie boneless beneath me? Or do you want me to plunder your dirty little hole while I spank that luscious ass?"

I can only widen my hooded eyes and moan in response.

Roger stuck three of his thick fingers coated with my arousal inside of my mouth.

I do my best to lick them clean while I balance reverse cowgirl on his lap, enjoying the view before me as much as my taste.

We arrived at LEVELS New York forty-five minutes ago. After we selected the black enamel bracelets reserved for voyeurs, we entered Peepshow on the 2nd level—my absolute favorite spot with the multilevel dance club next. Both allow me to get my groove on.

To avoid unwanted interactions amongst club participants, the system requires partnered subs to wear collars given to them by their Dom; partnered Doms wear gold bracelets; available subs wear red; available Doms wear white; voyeurs wear black.

All LEVELS locations mandate consensual interactions.

They enforce strict protocols members, their guests, and applicants must follow. From nondisclosure agreements to no-names given unless provided by the person to super tight ongoing background checks and other security measures.

Besides being luxurious and catering to the elite, LEVELS clubs provide safe, judgement-free zones where all sexy fantasies can come true.

Right now, my sexy fantasy is to just cum!

My teasing husband has kept me on edge the entire time we've been in this darkened alcove, not to mention on the ride over. His fingers toyed with my puckered nipples and swollen clit as my Lola's Coterie Swarovski crystal-embellished black sheer tulle chemise and matching sheer stretch-tulle thong mesmerized him.

This time we didn't wear masks—although Roger will never let me walk around stark naked…

And boy is he right. The sight of the carnality all around us makes my pussy juices drip down the crease of my ass to puddle on his massive bulge covered by his black leather pants.

The Peepshow atmosphere is all about bacchanalia with the melodic thrum of sensual music and the moans and groans of men and women as the backdrop to intense sexual play. Some show off their punishment or bondage skills on the demonstration platforms, while others fill the seating alcoves in various stages of intercourse. The air is heavy with the scent of perfume, cologne, and sex.

I grind down on Roger's dick, seeking enough friction to rub my aching clit. My mouth works his fingers like cherry-flavored Popsicles. It's my way of pleading for a reward.

"Words, Pretty Kitty. I will have your words," he demands.

I gasp when he plucks his fingers from my swollen lips. Then glance at him over my shoulder, swinging the curtain of my hair out of my line of sight.

"*S'il te plait, Amoureux*," I plead. "Fuck me with your big dick, please!"

A smirk spreads across Roger's handsome face. In one yank, he tears my thong from my body. The crotch pinches my wet folds, and I yelp.

He rasps in my ear, "Poor, Pretty Kitty. I will make it all better."

Roger grips my hips and lifts me in the air. My fuck-me mules slip from my feet and clatter to the tile floor. He steadies me on the banquette with my feet on either side of his hips. Then he places my hands on the tops of his sturdy thighs.

My bare pussy and bottom hole sit within tongue distance to his face.

Merde!

One long, sinful swipe from the top hole through my slit to my clit, and my knees turn to jelly. Roger wraps his powerful arms around my thighs and delves into his feast.

That skillful tongue of his makes my body quiver in ecstasy. My cries of passion mingle with those of the other members surrounding us.

I ride Roger's face. Then freeze when my pussy clenches and my toes curl from my orgasm as it rips through my body. My back bows, and I scream his name as wave after wave washes over me to the point of light-headedness.

The pounding of my back against polished wood wakes me from my carnal stupor. I open my eyes to Roger's blackened, focused stare.

My gaze skitters away from the intensity of his eyes to take in my milieu.

We're in one of Peepshow's performance rooms with the curtains drawn over the viewing window. I'm naked and bound by my arms to a St. Andrew's Cross.

Roger holds under my thighs to cup my ass. His forceful thrusts drive me into the cross repeatedly. His grunts and groans fill the room.

Fully awake, my moans join his passionate growls.

"Uh. Uh. Uh. Uh."

I follow each pistoning stroke with a strangled cry as my head tosses side to side and my fingers ball into fists.

"Tell me... Is this how you want my big dick to fuck you... Pretty Kitty?" Roger demands, without faltering in his rhythm.

"YEEESSS..." I scream, then hiss when he shifts the angle, and his tip hits my G-spot.

Electricity races along the surface of my heated skin. I squeeze my eyes shut to revel in the sensations bombarding me.

The scent of our sex floats around us. Wet suctioning sounds as my pussy captures and releases the thick invasion of Roger's ribbed and veiny cock. The smooth texture of the wood against my sweaty back. His firm grip bordering on painful, sure to leave his mark.

Once again, I'm on sensory overload.

"Take it... Take every single inch, Pretty Kitty," Roger demands.

I mewl because it feels so fucking good. I just can't take anymore.

Roger clutches my chin to tilt my face back down. When our eyes meet, he growls, "Cum on my cock. Cum for me now!"

My body fractures and floats away.

"Hi, my love. How do you feel?"

My eyes flutter open to find Roger peering down at me as we lie in the bed.

No longer driven by lust, his gray eyes return to their liquid platinum state. His tender look caresses me more deeply than his fingers skimming my cheek.

"I love you, Mrs. Steele," Roger murmurs before his lips meet mine in a sweet kiss.

When his mouth slides to my neck, I whisper, "I love you, too, Monsieur Steele."

LEONIE

"*I* love the different shades of ocean blues around the Hamptons. Mixed with the warm tones of caramel and orange and a base of eggshell white, it's the perfect palette for a beachfront home."

Roger smirks, "Really? Well, you told me you're not interested in redecorating our home at the compound. So, what's with 'the perfect palette'?"

I nudge his side with my elbow and roll my eyes.

"Just a comment, smarty pants," I respond. "Is that all right with you?"

"*Just* saying…" He quips. "You declined the opportunity, babe."

We along with The Twins, Nanny Grace, Sebastian, Lola, and Blair are on board the STEELE Sikorsky helicopter heading to the Southampton Village Heliport. Billie will fly in with Patrick on his helicopter later this afternoon and stay at his beachfront property.

Already at the beachfront compound are Morgan, Shelley, Malcolm, Starr, and Harris. Haley and her "we're just friends" Callum also left early. They're prepping for tonight's sunset dinner on the beach—a traditional New England Clambake. And I cannot wait, yum!

My parents and Luc should have landed by now at the private airport for the Hamptons. They flew in on Luc's new Gulfstream G700. He heard how much we enjoyed our flights for Verbier in the STEELE jet, so he ordered one even though he has a plush G650. This trip his excuse to try his new toy. I teased he's a spoiled *duc*!

"Bro, it's been eight months. You haven't learned, yet?" Sebastian chuckles. "Sometimes you have to not say a word!"

"Yeah. Happy wife, happy life and all that," Lola says, glancing up from her laptop.

Then she turns to The Twins in their car seats and adds, "Learn that lesson now, Little Pumpkins, and you'll be all right."

Rodolphe waves his car in the air while Gaspard claps and says, "Dada, Dada!"

"Yeah, Dada," I laugh and point to Roger as I clap.

Everyone joins in, and The Twins' laughter is the sweetest of all.

Malcolm, Harris, and Haley meet us at the heliport with two Black Badge Rolls-Royce Cullinans and a Suburban. The guys load up the Suburban with our luggage while Lola and Blair hop into the back of Malcolm's SUV.

Nanny Grace and I secure The Twins in the middle row of the SUV Haley drove. Then Nanny Grace slips onto the third row, and I sit between The Twins.

When Roger opens the driver's door, Haley crosses her arms over her chest and cocks her head to the side, peering up at him.

"Oh, so you think you're just going to bogart my ride, Big Brother?" She asks.

Roger pinches her cheeks and grins.

"You're so cute when you're annoyed, Baby Sister," he says wiggling her face. "I love you with all my heart. But I will drive any vehicle with my wife and sons in it."

Reluctantly, Haley relinquishing the SUV to her brother. But not without giving him the stink eye as she walks around to climb into the passenger seat.

"Don't feel bad, *Chérie*," I tell her. "Roger does the same thing to me. He refuses to let me drive The Twins anywhere. Either he drives or Eric. *C'est la vie.*"

Haley nods, then says, "Only because of my nephews did I give in to you, Roger..."

He winks at her and starts the engine. His chuckle blends with the purr of the premium engine.

We pull up to the compound's private road. A security guard in a gatehouse triggers the oversized wooden gates set between stone pillars with wrought iron lanterns to swing open. A long driveway of pressed oil and natural stone rolls out before us like the yellow brick road.

We're not in Kansas! This is Southampton luxury living at its finest.

Once past the impressive gates, it's another world. The property rests on ten acres all beachfront. Its incredible surroundings include native trees, grassy areas, and closer to the ocean sandy dunes. The briny scent of the ocean through the open windows fills my lungs. The calls of seagulls ring out.

On either side of the primary driveway, secondary ones appear as we drive along. Malcolm pulls off to one on the right. Roger turns onto one of them to our left and Harris follows.

A shorter driveway ends in a circle before a classic Hamptons-style three-story mansion. Robin egg blue shutters lean against gray weathered shingles. Beneath the windowsills flower boxes filled with white blossoms add to the beauty of the home.

"Here we are," Roger says as he pulls to a stop at the front door behind a golf cart and cuts the engine.

We hop out, and I wrap my arm around his waist as I gaze at the house. Atop the widow's walk, an antique weathervane idly switches direction with the breeze. The top half of the navy blue Dutch door stands open. It's absolutely picturesque.

I glance up at Roger to find him staring at me with a soft smile. His aviator sunglasses reflect mine. He drops his head to kiss me sweetly.

"You're here!"

"*Mon Trésor!*"

We look to the front door to see Shelley unlatching the bottom and my parents behind her. They wave and walk over to us. We exchange greetings, and The Twins pulled into hugs.

The interior doesn't disappoint. It's a center hall with a double staircase rising along the walls. The cream, pale blue, and dusty yellow hues complement the stone floors.

Canvas covered furniture with the accent colors fill the great room. It's comfy and elegant.

But the view of the ocean out of the wall of windows takes my breath away.

Drawn to the endless expanse of the Atlantic Ocean, I walk over to step onto the deck. Out on the private beach, caterers prepare for the clambake. They dug the pit and lined it with large stones and wood. The fragrant scent fills the air.

"Come, let's get settled then meet up with everyone at the main house," Roger says as he bounces Gaspard on his hip.

I nod and follow him back inside.

We spend the next hour getting our personal things in situated. I ordered clothing and essentials for me and The Twins to leave at this home. The staff put everything away before we arrived. After a tour, we follow Shelley's golf cart with ours and we give Nanny Grace the rest of the day off. The Twins will be well taken care of amongst the entire Steele clan.

The day turns into evening, and we go to the beach for a seafood feast with the backdrop of a spectacular sunset. The perfectly steamed clams, lobsters, potatoes, and corn on the cob topped with melted butter and paired with local beer and white wine make for a scrumptious meal. Dessert options include warm blueberry and apple pies with vanilla ice cream. Afterwards, we sit around the bonfire chatting.

Rodolphe and Gaspard sleep in their mesh beach cots, Blair found online. They enjoyed their first taste of seafood. The greedy little monsters wanted more! So with full bellies, they doze during the rest of our beach time.

"Time to go to bed, Mrs. Steele," Roger murmurs against my windblown hair as I sit between his legs and lean my back against his broad chest.

Wrapped in the warm cocoon of Roger and an over-sized blanket, I don't want to move. But nod, and we gather The Twins and bid everyone a goodnight.

"Don't forget beach yoga at seven tomorrow morning!" Starr calls out to me, as she sits huddled up with Malcolm.

I give her the thumbs up and place my hand on Roger's back as he walks ahead of me with The Twins asleep in his muscular arms. I carry their cots and bag.

When we get home, we give them a bath before we put them to bed. Then Roger and I take a steamy shower where we make love beneath the steady flow of warm water from the rain shower head. Roger dries me tenderly, and we collapse in the bed, his body spooning mine.

We whisper I love you and fall into a restful slumber.

* * *

"WHAT A GORGEOUS START to the day! I'm so glad the summer weather continued into September."

"It could stay summer year-round as far as I'm concerned."

The girls and I spread our yoga mats out on the sand at the beach in front of the Shelley and Morgan's house. Originally, Starr wanted us to gather for a sunrise meditation at six-thirty, but after the long night we convinced her to start later—if only by half an hour.

I fold into Child's Pose to release tension and to prepare my mind and body for our session.

After the mediation, Starr undoubtedly has a vigorous flow planned with a dharma talk during Savasana. My consistent Skype sessions with Starr and in-person with Anita over the last two years increased my endurance and ability to handle more advanced asanas. I look forward to today's practice.

"Let us begin. Come to a comfortable sitting position with your palms face up on your knees, fingers in Gyan Mudra. Center your mind…"

Starr takes us from a reflective guided meditation through a sequence of asanas that build up to the challenging peak pose of Scorpion Handstand.

In practicing asanas, the point isn't to twist oneself into a pretzel and the more you can bend, the better. Rather, the focus on the breath and releasing the mind to move the body.

Starr loves to push our ability to focus, and Scorpion Handstand requires lots of it.

I'm beyond grateful for Savasana as we settle onto our backs. With our eyes closed and our minds open, Starr speaks to us about surrender. Despite the purpose of her dharma talk, I can't help but wonder if she surrenders to Malcolm's Alpha Dom as his sub!

Just as we stand to take a dip in the ocean, here they come…

"Rats, did we miss the yoga?" Patrick jokes in his Scottish accent.

It turns out he and Callum know each other, and it surprised them to find the other with us.

Last night at the clambake, Billie teased how she and Haley are into bangers and mash. The visual of the double entendre made her blush and Callum sputter his ale.

"Of course it's over since I left you snoring almost two hours ago!" Billie replies, her Granny Smith apple green eyes sparkling in the bright sunlight.

With her wavy, medium-blonde balayage hair and pecan-colored skin, everyone says she's Tyra's doppelgänger. Billie is curvy like the megamodel, but a petite version at five feet, four inches. Patrick towers over her by eleven inches.

He scoops Billie into his arms and carries her off to the water as she giggles.

"I saw you with your pussy in the air holding the position for me to come over, grab your thighs, and fuck you until you saw stars in the daytime."

A gasp slips past my lips as my pussy clenches and my nipples pebble beneath my white bandeau bikini. I sway in Roger's sudden embrace as he presses his front into my back with his hands on my lower belly.

He makes his arousal known with his lengthening dick sandwiched between us.

"Can you back up your claim, Monsieur Steele?" I purr.

Roger chuckles, his warm breath tickles my neck. "Absolutely, Pretty Kitty. Come back to our house, and I will show you."

"Bye, guys! See you later!" I tell the others.

* * *

THE NEXT FEW days are so relaxing. We do more yoga, lounge around the pool, swim in the ocean, or hang out on the entertainment level of the primary house to bowl, play in the arcade, or watch movies.

It's good to unwind with everyone since it's the first time we've all been together after the judge threw the New York City case out.

Roger's laughter comes easily, and he jokes with his siblings. They along with Patrick and Callum played a rowdy game of touch football on the beach.

Between drooling over the gleaming muscles, the girls and I cheered them on. Our parents, Luc, and The Twins watched from the sidelines.

Patrick and Callum told them American football sucks and isn't even football since the ball stays in the players' hands more often than not. They insisted on a round of rugby—"the real man's sport."

We couldn't care less as long as the guys remained sweaty.

I giggle about it as I tie the strings on the halter-top of my white silk maxi dress. The soft caress of the material swirls around my body as it falls to the tips of my crystal-embellished gladiator sandals.

"You look like my new bride all over again."

A glance over my shoulder reveals Roger in the doorway of my dressing room.

He's delectable in an untucked white linen button-down shirt with the sleeves rolled midway up his muscular forearms and white linen pants with a pair of white leather slides. The Rolex watch I gave to him for Christmas on his wrist and his wedding band puts a smile on my face.

His sun-kissed skin makes his gray eyes even more translucent. Two-day stubble covers his cheeks and cleft chin. With his hair combed back, his bone structure stands out. Roger can outdo any male supermodel.

Yum!

The corners of my mouth lift in a grin, and I twirl for him. As I stop, my hair swings over my shoulder to cascade past my hip in glossy waves. My eyes shine with love for my man.

"Beautiful," Roger says.

I blush under the intensity of his stare and bow my head. He makes my heart race uncontrollably.

"Come. Let's get to the party," Roger continues. "Later we'll make our own fireworks."

Now, my pussy throbs. We have hours before the party ends.

Merde.

Roger smirks at me knowingly and takes my hand to lead me to the nursery, where we say goodnight to The Twins and Nanny Grace.

A quick ride in the golf cart along a path separate from the driveway—that's lined with cars waiting to reach the party's valets—and we arrive at Morgan and Shelley's house.

The giant side lawn, aglow by thousands of fairy lights

and lanterns, has two sumptuous pavilions, one for dinner and the other for dessert and dancing. Beyond it, on the beach, several bonfires burn. Waitstaff mill about with trays of champagne and wines or hors d'oeuvres. To one side a band plays lively music piped through speakers, also out on the sand.

Guests mingle, sipping drinks in the different areas, all dressed in the theme of the annual STEELE White Party.

It's already bustling since it's the party of the season and everyone wants a ticket for a chance to see and be seen amongst the world's elite. Not to mention raising funds for STEELE Foundation.

As soon as we're spotted, people approach to get a word with Roger or to take a photo with *The Lion*—"I've been a fan forever!" "You're even more stunning in person!"

Automatically, I smile for the cameras and snicker inside. Oh boy...

When they congratulate us on our marriage, Roger's chest puffs up visibly. Every time, he slips his arm around my side right below my braless boob so his fingers brush underneath it and hugs me close. Caveman.

Finally, we spot people we know and make our way to Luc and Blair.

"Hey! I love your dress!" I gush to her.

She has on a goddess dress that falls to the floor. Her cerulean blue eyes stand out against her tanned skin and twinkle when she smiles.

"Thanks, you look phenomenal, too!" Blair responds.

Luc smiles at her. His hand on the back of her neck slides down as he strokes her possessively.

"Hi! You're finally here!"

I turn to see Lola and Baz striding over. A giggle escapes when I notice Lola wears a diamond and platinum choker—at least that's what those unfamiliar with BDSM would think. Tonight she wears one of the collars Sebastian gave to her as his sub.

Okay… So the guys need to prove we're theirs, huh?

We chat for a few minutes, then return to mingle before the waitstaff serves dinner.

I catch sight of Haley and Lachlan talking off to the side. It appears serious, so I don't interrupt them with a greeting.

The Jacksons, who also have a compound nearby, came over for the party. Laurent, the playboy, flirts shamelessly with three female guests. Lydie who seems to have a new boyfriend laughs with some industry titans—she's a killer in the boardroom. Lucien, whose Southampton restaurant caters the event, holds court in the dining pavilion for last-minute preparations.

A quick scan of the crowd reveals my parents in conversation with Connor and Lucie while Morgan and Shelley stand next to them chatting with other guests. The couples make a powerful trio and became fast friends over the past two years.

Roger and I visit a third tent for the silent auction.

Luc offered two weeks at his family's ancestral seat. In his case, it's a magnificent chateau on one hundred acres of park-like grounds and forests once used as royal hunting grounds. Excursions for cooking and wine lessons and tours of the countryside round out the visit.

STEELE went further with a six-week-long trip around the South Pacific. Two-week stays at three five-star hotels and resorts in Fiji, Tahiti, and Hawaii make for a memorable holiday. Plus, use of a STEELE private jet and helicopter to transport the lucky couple. The imagery for the display is so vibrant and romantic, I want to put a bid on it!

The gong rings to announce dinner.

We follow the guests to the dining pavilion and take our seats. The Steele clan disperses across the room, sitting at tables with guests to make everyone feel welcome and included.

Shelley makes her speech, and the emcee keeps the party going through dinner and on to the dessert and dancing. A DJ famous for his skills on the turntables spins popular music that gets the guests on their feet.

The fireworks display from a barge offshore lights up the inky night sky with vivid sparklers, crowns, glitter, and crosettes. We cheer with each round, delighted by the glitziness.

"I have an explosive pistil with your name on it, Pretty Kitty. Shall we?"

For the rest of the night and well into the early morning, Roger makes me oh and ah in erotic, toe-curling delight.

* * *

"I CAN'T BELIEVE *Mr. Responsible* let you take The Twins and drive into the village without him."

I bite my lip and raise my eyebrows at Lola's comment.

We're heading back to our Cullinan after a couple of hours shopping on Main Street. Roger and the guys went to play golf. So I took advantage of his absence to prove I can handle driving us around—alone.

"Wait a minute. Do you mean to tell me you did not let Roger know?" She asks incredulously, stopping in the middle of the sidewalk.

I shrug and press the key fob to unlock the doors.

"Leonie! He's going to be so pissed off with you!" Lola says as she buckles Rodolphe in his car seat. "And do not give me that *Bof* shrug!"

I laugh and respond, "Don't worry! We'll return before them. So stop yammering and get in the car already."

Lola shakes her head and steps up to the passenger seat.

Along the way, we chat about our final dinner tonight before we leave in the morning. We spent an extra week after Labor Day because it was just so nice to hang out.

"It's amazing how time flies! I cannot believe The Twins will be one year old in a couple of weeks—"

WHAM!

The SUV veers off the road and crashes head-on into a tree. Lola and I jerk forward as the front end smashes, then bounce back when the airbags deploy. The Twins' cries fill the car along with Lola's pained moans.

My ears ring as my head pounds. I try to turn to see my sons, but can't see, blinded partially by the airbag dust.

Relief sweeps through me when the back doors open. *Dieu merci*, someone helps us.

"Ar— Are... they okay?" I ask. Still unable to move, I lift my restricted gaze to the rearview mirror.

The chilling tendrils of horror close in when two masked faces stare at me and without a sound take Rodolphe and Gaspard from their car seats.

"*Noooooooon*," I yell, now frantic and forcing my body to move despite the pain in my chest and head. "*Ne prends pas mes bébés!!!*"

Unable to think in English, I scream at them to not take my babies.

In my haste and limited eyesight, I misgauge the height and fall out of the SUV. Adrenaline pumps through me, and I leap to my feet to run after the kidnappers. Screaming, I pound after them, fueled by the cries of The Twins.

As if in a dream, the kidnappers leap into the back of an unmarked white van and peel away. The tires kick up gravel from the side of the road. Black rubber marks trail in their wake. The dust and caustic smell clog my nostrils.

I give chase until they're too far away.

When the van turns a bend in the road, I fall to my knees screaming.

ROGER

"*R*oger! We have to go. NOW!!"

I freeze in the middle of my swing at Harris' words.

Leonie!

I drop the club and race after him. He's already running to the golf cart. Luc and Callum close in on us.

My mobile rings, and I snatch it out of my pocket, praying it's Leonie. It's Sebastian.

"What the fuck's going on?" He demands, the sound going in and out as though he's running, too.

In the background, Malcolm and Patrick shout questions.

"Harris! What the fuck is going on?!" I yell as I jump into the cart.

Without taking his eyes from the path, he shakes his head and says, "Your Cullinan crashed."

The world tilts.

Leonie!

Frantically, I end Baz's call and dial her mobile. No answer. I dial Nanny Grace.

"Where are Leonie and my sons?" I yell.

She sucks in a shocked breath, then responds, "Mrs. Steele went into the village with her sister-in-law and The Tw—"

I hang up and kick the front panel of the cart with enough force it cracks, and we lurch forward.

FUCK!

From the back bench, I hear Luc speaking about Lola. More than likely he's on with Baz. Sure enough, yelling comes over the line.

I try Leonie's number again, then the SUV's phone. No answer.

Callum's talking to Haley filters into my brain.

"Where?" I ask Harris.

He tells me it's the road from Main Street toward our compound. His app alerted him to the crash along with the STEELE Cyber Security emergency team. First responders are en route to the scene.

"The scene." My nightmare. Bile rises in my throat as my stomach clenches. I pray they're not injured.

When we get to the country club's parking lot, we abandon the cart and race to the Suburban just as Baz, Malcolm, and Patrick jump from their cart. All of them are on their mobiles.

I go for the driver's door, but Harris stops me.

"You're too keyed up, bro," he starts, then continues when I interrupt. "I got this, get in."

By the time we get to the car crash, the police cordoned

off the area. Fire engines and ambulances line the road. Cars backed up prevent us from getting any closer.

We leave the SUV and rush to the yellow caution tape.

An officer stops us, but Sebastian and I yell it involves our wives and my sons. When he reaches for his radio and doesn't lift the tape to give us access, I duck under and run to the first ambulance.

My stomach clenches again when I catch sight of the Cullinan's crushed hood. The force of the impact decimated it.

FUCK!

I step up on the back of the ambulance and see Lola on a stretcher.

Her eyes widen when she sees me. Mine widen when I see the bloody gash on her forehead.

"Leonie? The Twins?" I ask.

Lola bursts into tears, and I nearly die.

Baz pulls me out of the way and climbs on board.

Adrenaline pumps through me, and I race to the next ambulance, screaming Leonie's name.

A paramedic pops her head out the back and waves me over.

Inside, Leonie is hysterical. Her wild eyes dart from the police officer's face to the paramedic as she yells in French, *"Ils ont kidnappé mes fils!"*

My heart stops.

The world falls off its axis.

Leonie turns in my direction when she hears my sharp intake of air. Fresh tears roll down her cheeks, and she covers her mouth with shaky hands.

The officer shifts his position to face me.

"Mr. Steele?" He asks.

I can only nod since my mouth is too dry to form words.

"Please come with me, sir" he says.

My eyes never leave Leonie's. In French, she whispers she's so sorry, and it's all her fault. I open my mouth to speak, but nothing comes out.

The officer takes me to the side of the ambulance as Harris and Sebastian run over.

"We know where they are!!" My brothers yell simultaneously.

Officers come running, and Harris shows them another of his apps.

Two dots blink green on a map with heat signatures of four other individuals in various locations. The coordinates place The Twins near to where we stand. The street view shows a secluded house on a private lane.

Just then my mobile rings with a call from my father.

"A person contacted me with a ransom demand of $10 million," he says without preamble. "Each."

"We've got The Twins via their trackers, and—"

"*Quelle? Veux-tu dire??*"

Leonie stands behind the officers with Lola. They clutch each other. At that moment, I notice the bruising on Leonie's face, too.

I stride over to her and pull her into my arms as Baz embraces Lola.

Leonie peers up at me and asks again, what do I mean.

Tightly holding her, I explain so only she can hear that

every member of our family has a tracker in case we get lost or kidnapped. She questions why I didn't tell her about The Twins having them, and I tell her it slipped my mind.

Then Leonie frowns and asks if she has one, too. I nod and tell her I'll explain after we get them home. She whispers it's all her fault again.

Unlike last time, I find my voice and tell her not to think such nonsense. Then kiss her head and nod to the paramedic to take her back inside the ambulance.

Meanwhile, the officers plan an extraction and send a unit to the compound to monitor the communications from the kidnappers.

Sebastian, Harris, and I insist upon accompanying the extraction team.

The officers see we won't let them deny us, so they give in on the condition we remain in the patrol car. No one knows whether the kidnappers have weapons.

We agree.

Luc promises to take care of Leonie and Lola. Since he's known them longer than Baz and I combined, we trust he won't allow any harm to come to them.

Malcolm drives them and Callum back to the compound.

"More people arrived at the house!" Harris exclaims as he monitors his app's feed. "What the fuck?! Haley is there now!!"

Baz and I swing our gazes to the front seat where Harris sits beside the sheriff.

"Whaaat?!?!" We yell at the same time.

Then we tell the sheriff to drive faster.

Shortly thereafter, we arrive at the house. According to the app, The Twins still blink green in the same room with a heat signature next to them. However, ten heat signatures surround three others in another room while four appear in a third one beside The Twins.

The STEELE's security team lead for our compound flags us down.

"Mr. Steele," he says to me. "We have the situation under control. Ms. Steele alerted us to the kidnapping, and we used the tracking app to locate your sons. They're with the team medic. The kidnappers are being held by other members of the team. Come with me, sirs."

Just as he said, we see our team with three men who sit handcuffed in the middle of the floor. One is jabbering on about not being a part of the kidnapping. His voice gives me pause. It's Antonio Velasquez.

What. The. Fuck!

If Delia is behind this, I'm going to finish the psycho bitch once and for all!

Raised voices draw my attention from the asshole Antonio.

Baz, our security lead, and I rush into the next room. Two of our team members stand aside, but at the ready. Delia runs screaming like a banshee with her arms outstretched and long nails ready to claw at Haley.

Surprisingly, Haley stands her ground in a defensive posture. No one is prepared for what happens next.

"You BITCH!"

WHAM!

"You fucked with my brother."

WHAM! WHAM!

"You tried to steal my nephews!"

WHAM! WHAM! WHAM!

"Stay. The. Fuck. Away. From. My. FAMILY!!!"

Haley whales on Delia.

"I've got your number, bitch, and it's all legit. You're going away for the rest of your miserable fucking life," Haley ends in a deadly tone made more terrifying after her shouts and thrashing.

Delia—whose face already shows signs of swelling—stares with one open eye up at Haley. Delia's busted lip trembles as she mumbles how sorry she is for all she's done.

Haley refuses to give in and tells her it's too fucking late.

The officers rush in, and we explain what happened. They proceed to arrest Delia, who starts crying assault. When they ignore her and read the Miranda warning, she doesn't have the sense to shut the fuck up.

Instead, she slings more baseless claims against me and curses while they take her away.

Bye, bitch!

"Mr. Steele, your sons are safe and sound."

I turn to face the door and see the security medic as noted by the word on the front of his uniform's bullet-proof vest. He and another team member hold Rodolphe and Gaspard, who wear black adult-size t-shirts.

When they see me, they call out Dada and reach their arms out.

Tears fill my eyes, and my breath escapes me at the

sight of their reddened faces puffy from crying. Two strides and they're in my arms. I squeeze them so tightly to my chest they squirm and cry some more.

Never in my life have I been so terrified. All sorts of crazy thoughts ran through my head. Nightmarish and ghastly things are done to children, and I would end anyone who would harm what's mine.

Arms enfold me and I open my eyes to see Baz, Harris, and Haley hugging The Twins and me. We're a tight-knit clan, and I feel the love flowing from them to us. Even The Twins calm, hiccups replace their sorrowful sobs.

We take a moment to absorb the intensity of the situation.

Then Baz squeezes us and looks at each of our faces. His, like ours, streaked with tears. But the steely glint in his eyes shows he's back to business. As our eldest sibling, he's always taken on the responsibility of his brothers and sister—no matter our ages.

"Let us go. Haley, call Leonie. Harris, you get Dad on the line. He needs to prep for our arrival"—Baz turns to the security lead—"I want a full briefing with the team, the police, and the FBI. We will meet in my father's office in an hour."

Big brother, CEO, Alpha Dom, all in one takes charge.

I'm grateful, as I can only think of my wife and sons.

When we reach the compound's perimeter fence, armed security members stand spaced in intervals along its full length. At the front gates, two of their armored Suburbans block the entry and dozens more armed members stand around them. We are on full lockdown.

"ROGEEERRR!!!"

Leonie roars as she runs out of the house.

She throws her arms wide, pulling The Twins and me into her embrace. She trembles as sobs rack her body. I murmur words of love and let her know they're fine to soothe her anguish.

Josy and Guy join us, and we hug in a unit as I did with my siblings. The pile on continues when we make room for my mother and father.

I notice the others hovering, not wanting to interrupt. So I give them a nod and suggest we move inside.

We settle in the living room where Leonie and I hold The Twins on our laps. She checks them over one at a time, rubbing her hands over their bodies and holding their faces to look into their eyes. I tell her they're fine since the medic did an examination, and I assessed them on the ride over.

But *Maman Lionne* ignores me.

The silence broken by Malcolm.

"That bitch is going to pay," *The Enforcer* declares. "No way will she get away with this shit. I want answers now!"

Everyone shares his sentiment, and we decide to have the briefing here instead of in the office for more space.

Before they arrive, Leonie and I take The Twins upstairs to bathe and redress them. The forensics team took their clothes for evidence, thus the t-shirts.

"I'm so sorry, Roger. This is all my fault..." She whispers sadly.

No way am I going to allow Delia to hurt the love of my life... again. It's not Leonie's fault. Delia is a conniving monster who would stoop so low as to kidnap babies to get revenge and money.

"Leonie… No, look at me," I say when she lowers her head as tears slip down her reddened cheeks. The defeat in her lackluster eyes breaks my heart. "Oh baby, listen to me. This is not your fault in any way—"

"I drove without telling you—"

"True, but… *But*," I repeat when she interrupts. I silence her with my finger pressed to her lips. "That does not give Delia the right to crash into you and kidnap The Twins."

I pause to take a deep breath when the horrific thoughts swirl in my mind once more.

"They could have killed you, our sons, and Lola. All for that monster's selfish gain. She's put our family through enough already. Do not give her power over us," I say adamantly.

"Remember when you told me 'we will move forward from this moment on with only positive thoughts and words of love' almost two years ago?" I ask. "Well, you're 'the most responsible person *I* know.' Sweetheart, you would never put our sons in harm's way."

Leonie leans into me, and I wrap her in my comforting embrace. I have more than enough strength for both of us. I vow we will get beyond this nightmare and come out even stronger.

It turns out Haley is absolutely correct—it is too fucking late for Delia Fucking Shaw.

When the FBI agents question him, Antonio flips immediately.

He admits it was Delia's idea to claim sexual assault and harassment since I gave him a sum of money in recompense for the fight we had at Leonie's Paris American Academy end-of-the-semester reception. Delia was jealous of Leonie and hoped she would leave me because of the accusations. That plus Delia wanting to get money was payback for me rebuffing her advances.

He also admitted to rigging the security feed and my private elevator the day Delia and I got trapped and no one could explain how it happened. As a tech whiz, he found a loophole and manipulated it to their advantage.

Their fake dating relationship became a true one over the last two years. Recently, he realized Delia was only using him for his skills. When she came back with The Twins and two goons she hired in exchange for some ransom money, they argued because Antonio couldn't stand by a kidnapping.

The "number" Haley referenced is a tech video that further proves my innocence she and a STEELE Cyber Security employee found on a camera Antonio didn't know about.

Finally, my name and STEELE get fully cleared because of Antonio's confession and Haley's findings.

Delia Shaw is in the dust, truly, as Malcolm once said!

LEONIE

$\mathcal{T}$he cries of seagulls soaring high above the waves of the Mediterranean Sea as they search for breakfast wake me in the early morning.

Roger, The Twins, and I arrived last night aboard the vintage steam yacht for the week I won my bid at the center gala's silent auction. Then we'll celebrate The Twins' birthday at our villa in Capri with the family and stay for a month.

After the kidnapping, we had to remain in Southampton for an additional week. We met with the FBI and local law enforcement to give statements and to press charges.

It was a straightforward investigation since Antonio confessed in order to gain immunity for the first-degree kidnapping felony and aggravated assault with a motor vehicle charge. They accused him for his involvement in the case against Roger and STEELE International. Regardless, he'll still get plenty of time behind bars.

The asshole!

She who shall not be named is another story. With her accomplishes, they received the highest charges and face life in prison without parole. When she entered the courtroom for their arraignment already in a prison jumpsuit, the defeated expression on her face proved she finally understood the ramifications of her heinous actions.

Roger had to hold his arm around my waist to keep me in my seat.

I wanted to launch myself at her and rip her to fucking pieces with my bare hands. Haley's whipping didn't satisfy my need to destroy she who shall not be named.

But like my mother told me, *"Mon Trésor, it is not for you to handle. The Divine has a way to right every wrong. So trust and let go."*

And that's what I did. I freed myself of the negativity through a soul-searching sunrise meditation, then a swim in the cleansing ocean waters. A new day dawned.

When I returned to shore, Roger was waiting for me. I loved that he gave me the space I needed to come to terms with my role in the kidnapping—or rather me acknowledging I did not have a role—and letting go of any ego-driven guilt.

Wordlessly, Roger held out an oversized beach towel and wrapped it around me when I stepped between his outstretched arms. He rested his chin on top of my head and sighed, content to hold me close. The warmth of his love dried me more than the plush Hermès terrycloth.

I told him how much I love him.

Roger kissed me senseless. My knees buckled from the

sensory overload. He picked me up and carried me home. When we arrived, he continued to carry me up the stairs to our bedroom.

I gave my body to him heart and soul as he made passionate love to me. The entire time he drove his massive dick between my slick folds, Roger murmured more words of love and devotion. All the while, I cried and clung to him like a human life preserver rocked by the waves in open water.

Roger completed my cleansing as he bathed my insides with his life essence repeatedly.

I had gone into self-isolation, but Roger refused to leave my side. The only outside contact I had was to scour the Internet for any word or developments outside of what our attorneys and law enforcement told me.

The media worldwide had a field day with the kidnapping, car crash, Antonio's confession, and the subsequent clearing of Roger's name. They dug up all sorts of sources who came forward to depict she who shall not be named as an amoral gold digger. Antonio became her boy toy who she conned into helping her attempt to destroy Roger and STEELE.

Funny how those "sources" weren't around when she started this whole fucking mess.

STEELE's communications team ran with it and provided the media with more positive stories and images of Roger as a devoted family man who's committed to his community. The team highlighted STEELE Foundation's philanthropic activities to show the company wasn't only about generating billions of dollars; it gives back to those in need.

Even Harris and Haley's STEELE Technology and Cyber Security received a boost from the coverage. Companies and high-net worth individuals reached out to them immediately. The Dynamic Duo's client roster increased tenfold.

Roger persuaded me to step away from my laptop and back into the real world to continue my healing.

So after a few days we rejoined our family. More support gave me additional strength to move forward and to leave the past in the rearview mirror.

When I flinched at the sight of stitches on my BBF's forehead, Lola insisted I let it go.

She didn't blame me for any of it. She said it gave her the chance to see a plastic surgeon about liposuction and a breast reduction.

Sebastian growled, and Lola burst out laughing. She admitted she was teasing him since he loves her curvy, petite body.

In the morning, she sat gingerly on her yoga mat and quipped Baz proved all night just how much he relishes her hourglass figure.

Even though the medic examined The Twins, Roger flew in the top pediatrician of the Tri-state area. The doctor put them through an extensive exam. The results on their bloodwork and other samples came back negative for any and every toxin imaginable.

We had the best child psychologist analyze The Twins. Again, the results we appropriate for their age with no signs of mental or emotional damage from the kidnapping. She assured us they didn't remember any of it and being so young they rebound quickly.

The testing proved our observations of normalcy were spot on. Roger and I were beyond relieved.

However, the psychologist Roger insisted I meet with suggested I revisit the site and drive. At first I balked at the idea. But she encouraged me to keep it in mind and to try when I was ready.

Before we left, I did it. Lola came with me and The Twins to recreate the situation, but more so for support.

We retraced our steps. The first time we passed the crash site on the way to the village, I tensed and broke out in a cold sweat. On the way back, we pulled over and stepped out of Haley's Cullinan to look around.

My heart constricted when we saw the damage to the tree and expressed our thanks we made it out alive.

Roger and Sebastian were waiting for us at the compound's entry gates. Lola hopped into the golf cart with Baz and Roger slid into the passenger seat. He kissed my cheek and told me how proud he was of me. I smiled and cupped his face for a proper kiss.

We took the Mediterranean cruise as a time to recharge before everyone joins us at our Villa dei Fiori in Capri for The Twins' first birthday party next week. The plans have been in place for months. We refuse to let she who shall not be named derail the joy of our sons' celebration!

"If you want something to think about so deeply, ponder how far down your throat my cock reaches as you take every one of the thick ten inches, Pretty Kitty."

I can't help but to giggle.

A few days ago, Roger said the psychologist suggested he treats me as he normally would and not with kid gloves. His interpretation: fuck my brains out as often as possible and then some more...

Two can play this carnal game.

I roll over to face him. Without looking away, I place my palm between his firm pecs and drag my fingernails straight down. The silky texture of his happy trail between eight-pack abs lets me know how close I am to my impressive, mouth-watering prize.

My teeth draw the corner of my bottom lip inwards when I graze his mushroom head.

Roger shudders. His head hits the pillows as he closes his hooded eyes, when I continue to use my nails along his turgid length. It jumps in my hands and hardens further.

I jerk his dick until Roger opens his eyes. My thumb swirls the bead of pre-cum around the swollen tip. More leaks out as I pinch the sides.

He grunts as his hips lift involuntarily and his fists grip the sheets.

"Are you asking me to swallow you whole, *Amoureux*?" I purr, continuing to jerk and release his dick in a leisurely rhythm.

He hisses when I lean over to lap a bead from his shiny tip.

"Mmmmmm, warm and salty," I moan, smacking my lips against him.

Roger growls and buries his hand in my hair, pushing

his tip into my mouth. He groans when I open my throat to his invasion.

Let's see how far he goes.

His girth stretches my mouth as my jaw lowers to accommodate his cock. The tip of my tongue swirls around his ridges and veins, then I flatten my tongue to massage underneath.

I get him down far, but not enough. One hand grips the base of his dick while the other kneads his heavy balls. My pussy clenches, jealous my hands and mouth are full. But my core is empty. I moan from the ache.

Roger sucks in air and lifts his hips. His hand tightens to wind my long strands around his fist. He uses the leverage to drive his dick deeper, then to guide my movement.

My swollen lips press against his groin—that silky happy trail now tickles my nose—as he holds me in place. I gag, caught off guard.

"Breathe, Pretty Kitty," Roger growls.

I lift my gaze to his darkened orbs.

"Fuck! You... are... so... damn... sexy..." he punctuates each word with a powerful thrust of his hips.

Roger returns me to my task, seeking to reach further down my throat. His cock pulses, but he's not ready to cum yet. Instead, he pulls out with a pop and groans when he sees a trail of saliva lead from my lips to his rock-hard dick.

"*Merci, Monsieur Steele,*" I utter in a raspy voice. "I want some more, *s'il te plait, Amoureux.*"

His eyes spark and his nostrils flare when I open my mouth wide to welcome him.

"As you wish, Pretty Kitty," Roger replies as he puts his dick on my waiting tongue.

I amp up my ministrations until he explodes with a roar, shooting his cum deep down my throat as my lips brush his heated skin.

Roger collapses onto the bed heaving and pulls me on top of him. He wraps his arms around my back and nuzzles my neck with his open mouth.

When he catches his breath, he thrums in my ear, "So, good you are to me, Mrs. Steele."

"I CAN SEE why you the design of this yacht piqued your interest. They did an excellent job with the restoration down to the minute details," Roger says as we stretch out on the deck.

Luxury of a bygone age abounds in its Edwardian elegance and glamour. Built in the early 1900s to amaze and entertain the highest echelons of society, it features a gleaming navy blue hull and a deckhouse. It has exquisite brass fixtures, polished timber, and sumptuous fabrics. Plus four lavish staterooms perfect for rest. It's a rare and original piece of history.

"I knew you'd love it!" I reply as Gaspard and I play patty-cake. "Can't you picture an opulent and formal Edwardian-themed party? I'd come as Gigi and you as Gaston. A chance to dress like my favorite movie!"

Roger laughs, which makes Rodolphe, who sits on the chaise between his father's legs, claps his hands and calls Dada, Dada.

"You'd like a party, too?" He asks as he tickles Rodolphe's tummy. "Who would you come as, my little one?"

I smile at my three boys.

This is just what we needed—family time floating from one secluded spot to the next, basking in the warmth of the Med.

We spend the rest of the week doing just that until we pull up near our Villa dei Fiori in Capri. We'll use the tender to reach the private dock.

As the crew helps us disembark, I turn to face the yacht once more. It floats majestically on the azure blue water as the sun hits its shiny surface.

"I hate to leave. The boat is so gorgeous, and we had such a good time," I sigh. "Do you think the owners will let us rent her again?"

Roger shrugs and raises his eyebrows.

"Hmmm... I don't know. You tell me," he responds as he shakes hands with the crew.

I frown at him and glance at the captain.

"Would you be so kind as to provide me with the owner's contact information, or I can give you mine," I say. "We really enjoyed ourselves. You and your crew treated us so well."

The captain looks at Roger, then back to me.

"Thank you, Madame Steele," he starts before looking once again at Roger.

I frown again. What is going on with these two?

"Roger—"

He starts to chuckle and points at the yacht.

"You tell me since we own her," he says.

"What??" I ask, shocked.

Roger continues, "You loved it. We have a dock, but no boat, so... I bought her for you. The previous owners signed the paperwork this morning."

"Whaaat?!?!" I screech. "Are you serious, Roger?"

As the captain hands binoculars to me, Roger says, "Look at her stern, baby."

The boat now faces away from us to show its rear end. Gigi Capri. The name and hailing port written in the same red color and font of the movie title.

"Whaaaat?!?!?!" I yell as I wrap my arms around Roger's neck, peppering his face with kisses. "When did you do all of this?"

He explains he couldn't help himself since I was so enthralled by it and it's the only one of its kind fully restored left in the world. So he couldn't buy another one.

I press my lips to his ear so only he can hear and say, "So, good you are to *me*, Mr. Steele."

ROGER

*T*he sight of my wife and sons splashing in the pool beneath the brilliant sun with the flowers around them and the Mediterranean Sea in the distance makes me want to ditch the conference call. It pays to be the boss and take off for a month on brief notice, but I still have obligations—this meeting included.

My Business Development Team has four properties they're presenting for approval to upper management after having shared it with the directors. Every year, STEELE Residential Properties expands its portfolio with twelve to twenty projects around the globe. This set has Kuala Lumpur in Malaysia, Buenos Aires in Argentina, Brussels in Belgium, and Sydney in Australia.

And each location requires site visits on my part— planned and unexpected.

Now with my family, I can't imagine just up and going when an emergency arises or staying for weeks on end. Before my time was my business. The drive to succeed at all costs was my top priority, as it is with all of my siblings.

The one of us who has slowed down if a tad bit is Sebastian, and only since he married Lola. She's as work focused as Baz. That's what drew them together—well, along with their palpable sexual attraction.

Leonie didn't become a megamodel on her beauty alone. She puts in the time and dedication—although in her easygoing way. A style that drove me mad and our clashing nearly ended us forever.

Her plate will be full more than before. With Leonie heading a division within STEELE, she must take time to build the new arm from scratch. Not to mention her spokesmodel contracts with Lola's Coterie, the global cosmetics company, and more recently with Van Cleef & Arpels.

Of course we'll share responsibility for The Twins and have support from Nanny Grace. Yeah, I'm the man of the house, but I respect her career goals as much as I respect mine. We'll coordinate our schedules and as Leonie said, *"We'll put date nights, family time, and getaways with The Twins or together on our calendars in pen!"*

"—concludes our presentation. Kindly share your feedback."

Back to business.

"HOW ARE THE PROPERTIES? Did you decide the next two developments?" Sebastian asks later via video conference.

We're in our weekly one-on-one during which I give

him status updates, review timelines, and discuss any concerns or feedback. It's part of the strategy he implemented when he took over as CEO from our father, along with spending a week at each of STEELE's offices worldwide. Baz wants to make sure every member of the staff can have a voice and know their leader. The response has been positive.

"All of them have potential for generating revenue. However, the ones in Sydney and Kuala Lumpur would expand STEELE's footprint in that part of the world significantly," I respond.

Sebastian nods and scans his laptop. When he finds what he's searching for, he turns his attention back to me.

"Malcolm is scouting locations in Kuala Lumpur, too. Let's patch him into the call," Baz says.

The three of us discuss the pros and cons of the sites Malcolm found and the feasibility to purchase property around the site my team selected. Combined with the Entertainment Properties, we would add a hotel and restaurants.

"You know, this project could benefit from Leonie's Children and Young Adults Division. Is she free to jump on the call?" Malcolm asks.

I glance out the window and see Leonie in a teeny orange bikini headed this way, a Twin holding each of her hands. A goofy grin spreads across my face. MILF Alert... Damn, I'm a lucky son of a gun!

"Earth to Roger... Come in, Roger," Baz teases. "I take it you see her. Hopefully she's dressed and available."

I tell them to hold on while I call her out the window.

She comes in and sets The Twins in their playpen filled with toys I have in my office to keep them occupied while I'm working.

"Hello gentleman," she says smiling. "How may I help you today?"

They laugh, and we fill her in on the project. We discuss her division's potential role in the development. She gives great recommendations that impress all three of us. Baz gives the green light to move forward on a plan for Kuala Lumpur and Sydney.

"I can't wait to see Lola and Starr! You're still set to arrive in a few days for Thanksgiving, *non?*" Leonie asks.

Baz and Malcolm confirm, and we end the video conference.

"You did an outstanding job off the cuff, babe. I'm so proud of you!" I tell Leonie as I pull her from her seat to my lap.

"Thank you, *Mon Cœur*, I want to make my division as successful as yours!" She responds. "Besides, who knew I'd take part in a STEELE meeting with a bikini on?!"

Her giggle turns into a mewl when I slide one triangular scrap of material to the side and suckle her brown nipple.

"Yeah, who knew?" I chuckle as I nip the tender bud. "Let's put The Twins down for their naps, then return for an in-depth one-on-one..."

LEONIE and I stand holding The Twins, waving as the second Sikorsky touches down on the helipad at the rear of the villa.

"Look, Rodolphe and Gaspard, Grandaddy and Grand-mommy!" I tell them as my parents alight from the back of the helicopter.

The Twins laugh and wave some more.

Sebastian and Lola disembark next, followed by Malcolm and Starr, then Harris and Haley. They wave and troop over.

"Hey, Little Pumpkins! Did you miss your favorite auntie?" Lola asks as Baz scoops Gaspard out of my arms.

"And your very favorite uncle?" He adds giving Malcolm and Harris the side eye with a grin.

We make our way around to the terrace where Guy and Josy sit. They flew in this morning. Everyone exchanges greetings before Leonie and I show the newest arrivals to their sumptuous bedroom suites.

Villa dei Fiori has fast become one of our most cher-ished homes. It's where we had our babymoon when Leonie was nineteen weeks pregnant and we'd been back together for nine months. She fell in love with Lucien's former home the moment she set eyes on it—another *coup de foudre*. So, I bought it for her.

The salmon-colored stucco exterior with white trim around the windows, columns, and roof lines blend beauti-fully with the lush greenery and stunning sea views from all sides. The sea-edge gardens, bountiful with camellias, magnolias, and palm trees prove as captivating as the impressive views of Mount Vesuvius, the Peninsula of

Sorrento, the entire Gulf of Naples, and Anacapri. Its private swimming pool set in the side garden's grass and its exclusive sea access with a second plunge pool below makes it a unique property.

We plan to spend more time here than the one time in the last year and a half. Guy and Josy and my siblings took advantage and stayed on different occasions. Since my parents have Villa Sogno across the Tyrrhenian Sea in Positano, this is their first visit.

"Oh! This is a stunning villa! I love the gardens with all the fragrant flowers," my mother gushes as we walk to their suite. "I'm surprised Lucien gave it up."

I chuckle and respond, "He drove a hard bargain. But it was worth it to see the smile on Leonie's face when I gave it to her."

My father nods, then adds, "I know the feeling, son. Nothing is better than your wife's happiness. Remember my words well."

As we pass through the villa, I point out the rooms for a mini tour. The antique furnishings, Murano glass fixtures, and unobstructed views charm both of them.

However, they're even more pleased with their enormous corner suite and balcony overlooking the sea. The cobalt blue, champagne, and gold color scheme with crystal chandeliers and wall sconces, silk fabrics, plus a bathroom in floor-to-ceiling travertine slabs make for a lavish set of rooms.

"Very nice indeed," My father says as he takes in the suite.

I leave them to get settled before we have lunch alfresco

in the seaside garden. A quick text to Leonie, and I find her with The Twins, Malcolm, Starr, and Haley seated on blankets in the grass near the lunch table.

"How was your flight?" I ask Starr since she traveled the farthest from Beverly Hills.

She smiles and her dimples pop in her lovely face. Malcolm certainly picked a beauty.

It always strikes me as funny how all of Leonie's girlfriends are so attractive, smart, and self-made multimillionaires. Even Blair who comes from a wealthy English family that owns a manufacturing company and Billie whose family are well-to-do Southern politicians. Given their status, neither of them has to be Lola's assistants; they love fashion and didn't want to follow in their families' footsteps.

But most of all, not a gold digger among them and not fazed by the men in their lives being multibillionaires. Well, aside from the gifts we happily bestow upon them...

"It was long and hard, but comfy on Malcolm's jet," Starr responds, winking at him.

He smirks and adds, "Yes, and rather palatable."

Leonie bursts out laughing, then starts to snort uncontrollably.

"What's so funny?"

We glance up to find Baz, Lola, and Harris behind us.

"Oh, just the rigors and demands of travel," Starr deadpans.

Malcolm sits back on his hands, all smug with a cocky grin on his face. The Alpha Dom took his carnal tastes to the skies for fifteen hours.

Sebastian snickers and Lola snorts.

"No comment..." Haley says, rolling her eyes, disgusted as usual with hearing about her brothers' sex lives, even as innuendos.

She glances down at her mobile and smiles. Then types a response at lightning speed. When she raises her head, her cheeks flush and her eyes shine. No longer wearing her glasses makes the dove gray orbs more expressive. Happy Haley, hmmm interesting.

"What's up, Baby Girl?" I ask, knowing the nickname drives her crazy.

Still in la-la land, Haley startles, then responds rushed, "Oh, uh... Callum's over in Sorrento."

When she doesn't continue, I prod her. He wants to take Haley to dinner. So I tell her he can come here if they want. He's more than welcome. They agree, and I arrange for the helicopter to pick him up in an hour.

As it turns out, my brothers and I think he could be an excellent match for our little sister. Callum proved himself during Labor Day weekend as a guy who's worthy of Haley, has his own fortune, and blends well with our family. We couldn't care less he's a Scottish duke. Baz hired his guy to conduct an extensive background check on Callum as soon as we met him while we were in Verbier for Christmas. Nothing in it caused concern.

Haley being with Callum and not with Lachlan sits better with Sebastian and with the rest of us. Baz can't get past his best friend with his younger sister. Baz had been suspicious since we were at Villa Sogno when he proposed to Lola. Then at our Labor Day party, he argued with Lach after he saw him in an intense conversation with Haley. It has strained things with the friends since.

My parents and in-laws appear. We gather around the table for a delicious lunch of flavorful local dishes prepared by the chef and served by the staff with wines from the villa's prized cellar.

The staff fell in love with Leonie the moment they saw her, so we kept them on after we bought the villa. Besides, they're familiar with it, and Lucien told us they're great.

Shortly after we finish eating, Callum touches down. Haley goes to greet him, and some time later they join us for Limoncello Gin Collins on the lawn furniture. Her lips appear swollen, and his eyes gleam.

Mmhmmm.

"How are things with you, Callum?" My father asks as he sips his digestif. "I read in the *Financial Times* renewable energy is on the rise for another year in a row for Scotland."

They get into a discussion on Callum's family's business, Graham Energy, Oil & Gas Company, based in Aberdeen, Scotland. His father still leads the company as CEO, but he's in the process of grooming Callum for the role in five years. His younger brother and sister hold positions, too.

The conversation flows easily with everyone's participation.

We grew up discussing business to prepare for joining our family's legacy. Balanced with volunteer work to help others and not to live as spoiled rich kids instilled in us by our mother, we're a well-rounded group. Again, having partners who are the same just adds more perspectives to the pot.I lean back in my chair and tuck Leonie under my arm, happy to relax with our family.

"THIS IS FANTASTIC! I agree we should have an opulent Edwardian-themed-*Gigi* party!"

Leonie and I finished giving a tour of the yacht to everyone, and Lola can't wait to plan the soiree.

They do their happy shimmy dance, then continue on to the bow where we'll have cocktails before Thanksgiving dinner begins.

The last few days have been full of swimming at our private beach or in the pool and excursions to the Blue Grotto, Monte Solaro, and Villa di Tiberio. The Blue Grotto thrilled The Twins when their laughter echoed inside of the water-filled cavern.

Leonie wanted to save *Gigi* for last as the highlight and setting for our Thanksgiving dinner as we cruise around Capri for three hours. We time it for cocktails at sunset and dinner by torchlight—electric since we don't want to risk damage to the boat.

We dress in semi-formal attire with the guys in suits and the women in dresses. The Twins wear shirt and shorts one-piece sets with socks that mimic shoes and outdo us all.

Once we're gathered at the bow with drinks in hand, my father leads us in expressing his thanks over the past year. Each of us takes a turn ending with me. I'm already emotional after Leonie's heartfelt words of gratitude for our lives no longer impacted by Delia and Antonio, and most of all for the safety of our sons.

Coming on the end of her touching speech and tears, I hold her close in my arms and address our family.

"Thanks can never express the depth of my feelings for all of you and others who are not present. Your love and support from the start of that fiasco to the joy of our wedding with the addition of my in-laws and the wonderful holidays we shared to the return of our sons mean more than you can imagine. Mom, Dad, all of our lives you raised us to be a close-knit clan. This past year proves you succeeded. I love you all beyond measure."

I lift my glass and proclaim, "Now let us enjoy this Thanksgiving dinner and here's to many, many more!"

"Hear, hear!!"

"Bravo, Roger! We love you, too!!"

"Happy Thanksgiving, everyone!!"

LEONIE

"$\mathcal{M}$mm hmmm... I made the appointment, *Mon Cœur*... Yes, yes, I'll call you right away. *Oui, je t'aime aussi.*"

Ugh...

I end Roger's call, drop my mobile, and rush from our bed to the bathroom, covering my mouth with my hands. I cannot believe I got food poisoning from the seafood dinner we ate last night. The dish must have had tainted shrimp.

Ughhh...

A queasy sensation came over me the moment I smelled it as I took the first bite. Never again will I ignore my senses and proceed to eat something regardless in my life! This is my third trip to the bathroom since I woke up this morning.

At first Roger insisted upon staying with me. But I know he has some important end-of-the-year meetings all day, and I won't cause him to miss any of them.

He relented after I agreed to go to the doctor, even though I told him the food poisoning just has to work its way out of my system. Given enough time, it should go away. But I promised Roger anyway.

Fortunately, Roger called Nanny Grace to come over earlier than usual. She's with The Twins. So I drag about getting showered and dressed. Then call my doctor's office. The next available appointment isn't until one in the afternoon.

Ughhhh…

I head down to the custom chef's kitchen—not that I use it for more than the basics, like boiling water—and fix some hot ginger tea. The smell is soothing and reminds me of the last time I drank copious amounts of iced lemon ginger tea. It was the only thing that kept the nausea at bay when I was pregnant with Rodolphe and Gaspard.

Merde! Mais non… I just had my period, and my birth control shot isn't due anytime soon.

As I stand staring out at the snow blanketing Paris below, my mind drifts to Verbier. Roger and I leave in a couple of weeks to celebrate our first wedding anniversary while The Twins stay with my parents. They'll bring them when they fly in the day before Christmas Eve, along with the rest of our family.

An entire year has passed. I smile as I reminisce about our Winter Wonderland Wedding. Roger made my fairy-tale dream come true, and every day since. I love him so very much!

Tears fill my eyes and my vision blurs.

Good grief. Get it together, Leonie!

For the moment, my stomach doesn't roil. I munch on a few crackers from the well-stocked pantry, as I go back upstairs to The Twins' five-room suite.

We expanded by making the original nursery with bathroom Rodolphe's bedroom and converting the two rooms next to it into a connecting playroom and a bedroom for Gaspard with his bathroom. At fifteen months, they need their own space. They'll continue to use their suite as they get older. So it's worth the effort.

"Bonjour, mes beaux fils!" I call to them as I walk into their playroom. *"Comment vas-tu aujourd'hui?"*

They're understanding French and English and get the gist of me saying good morning and asking how they're doing today.

I greet Nanny Grace, too. We read to them and play developmental games for a couple of hours. Then I give them kisses and go to my home office to check on some projects.

Hilarie Roux, my personal assistant, amazes me with her ability to keep track of all the details and my schedule given we have seven projects my division currently has in the works. But I should not expect any less from her, given Françoise helped to find Hilarie for me. Only the best will get past Roger's assistant!

The reminder alarm goes off on my mobile. I finish up the spreadsheet I'm working on and text Eric. He responds right away that he's in the garage ready for me to arrive. Then I go upstairs to tell The Twins goodbye.

As I ride in the back of the Rolls-Royce Phantom, a text message from Roger pops up. I smile as I read it.

Hey, babe. Eric texted to let me know you're on your way to the doctor (on time, I might add). Call when you find out what's wrong.. I love you.

Oui, Monsieur Steele. I love you more.

Fortunately, the wait isn't long at my doctor's office. The nurse checks my vitals and notes my temperature is slightly higher than normal. She takes my urine sample and leaves the exam room, saying the doctor will be in shortly.

I answer some emails while I wait. Then glance up when the door opens, and the doctor walks in with the nurse.

"Madame Steele, congratulations! You're pregnant!"

I sit on the exam table in shock.

When the doctor suggests I make an appointment with my OB-GYN, I snap to attention. After he assures me there's no mistake, I call Dr. Berger, who just so happens to have an appointment in twenty minutes.

While I put off Roger's texts stating the doctor had an emergency that delayed my appointment, Eric rushes me over. I ask Eric not to tell Roger I left the doctor's office or where we're headed. He understands and agrees with a smile.

Dr. Berger confirms my pregnancy of eighteen weeks, and the ultrasound shows one perfectly healthy baby. He gives me copies of the scan and anti-nausea medicine along with my prenatal pills.

I laugh and say see you next month!

My mobile rings as Eric opens the car door for me —Roger.

"Leonie, what did the doctor say?" He asks worriedly.

Roger still has two more meetings, so I tell him the doctor gave me medicine to stop the queasiness. Since it's the truth—albeit partially—I don't feel bad. When he gets home, I'll tell him everything.

"Hi, baby, how are you feeling now?"

I suppress a giggle at Roger's mention of "baby," and wrap my arms around his neck, flattening my body against his to give him a passionate kiss.

"Wow! That good, huh?" He chuckles and grinds his hips against me. "Well, I know what will make you feel even better, Pretty Kitty."

Putting my palm on his chest, I smile up at Roger, then step away. The gift wrapped with shiny silver paper and tied with a French Rose pink ribbon sits on the coffee table. I turn to Roger and beckon for him to sit down on the sofa.

He cocks his head to the side, but does as I ask.

I tuck my legs beneath me as I sit beside him. With a smile, I hand the box to Roger.

"Merry Early Christmas, *Mon Cœur*," I tell him softly.

Roger's eyebrows draw together as he looks at the gift, then at me. He holds it to his ear and shakes it.

I nudge his shoulder and nod for him to open it. Without him noticing, I slip my mobile from behind me and hit the video record button. I want to capture his reaction.

He removes the ribbon and ties it around my neck in a

pussy cat bow. Then chuckles as he murmurs, "Here, Pretty Kitty, Kitty. Here."

Roger's laughter stops when he pushes the tissue paper aside to find the ultrasound scan image. His eyes widen and fly to mine as his mouth hangs open in muted surprise.

I fill the sudden void with, "Remember our night of fireworks during Labor Day weekend, *Mon Cœur*? Well, all those hours of passionate lovemaking resulted in my pregnancy. We're having a baby girl! *Félicitations, Papa!*"

The most beatific smile spreads across Roger's face.

My heart swells with love for my man. Then races when he jumps off the couch with a whoop and scoops me into his arms.

Between kisses, he buries his face in my hair, murmuring words of love.

"And how are you, my love? What did Dr. Berger say?" Roger asks as he holds me aloft with his eyes full of concern.

It reminds me of his words when we first learned of my pregnancy with The Twins and my mother's experiences scared me.

"Leonie, understand me clearly. If for any reason I have to choose between you and this baby or any other, I choose you always. You mean everything to me. We can try for another baby, or we can adopt a baby in need of a wonderful home. But you... You are irreplaceable, my love. Call me selfish. But I will not live without you, Leonie."

I love Roger with all of my heart and can understand his concern. But we're good.

"Our baby and I are perfectly healthy. The nausea

comes from morning sickness, nothing more. So, he really gave me the medication along with my prenatal pills," I answer smiling happily. "My regular physician told me I'm pregnant based on the urine test results. Dr. Berger confirmed eighteen weeks. Right around Labor Day. She'll be born mid-May next year!"

Roger places me on my feet and drops to his knees. He lifts the hem of my pink cashmere maxi lounge dress to kiss my belly. His lips move as he whispers to our daughter.

I stroke his silky hair, massaging his scalp as I continue to record him.

"What are you saying to our Baby Girl, *Mon Cœur*?" I ask, expecting sweet words of love and joy.

"I told her I love her and can't wait to hold her in my arms," He responds, then his mouth moves lower to brush against my bare mons and slit. "Then I told her I am going to make love to her *Maman*. Right. Now."

ROGER

Leonie's giggles morph into moans as I grip her round ass cheek with one hand and slip the fingers of my other inside the crotch of her pink lacy briefs.

She's gone all out with the little girl pink.

Fuck, I love my woman!

All day I found it strange Leonie circumvented my text messages and phone calls. Eric was even mum about their whereabouts. If it weren't for my end-of-the-year meetings and me wanting to clear my schedule so we can leave earlier for Verbier, I would have used the tracker app to find her.

Now I know why.

What's crazy is me being so distracted I hadn't noticed the subtle changes in Leonie's body: her nipples a deeper shade of chocolate and more sensitive to my caresses; the swell to her normally flat belly; how brightly her eyes and skin glow. The sudden nausea should have clued both of us in.

My heart races as joy pumps through me. Another baby and so soon! Rodolphe and Gaspard will turn fifteen months in a couple of weeks. They'll be just shy of two years old when Leonie gives birth to our Baby Girl.

I hadn't wanted to mention my desire for more children since Leonie's fearful of her mother's miscarriages and the pain from their losses. Although The Twins satisfy me plenty, I'd love to have a daughter.

And now I will! What a blessing just in time for Christmas! I give a silent prayer.

Then, turn my attention to the task well in hand—fucking Leonie until she's hoarse from screaming my name. Hell... I may even put another baby inside of her womb! That's how hard I'm going to give it to her.

My tongue slides along her moist slit, lapping at her pussy juices. The enticing scent of her arousal fills my nostrils, and I inhale deeply. Delicious.

Leonie's legs quiver as she tugs on my hair.

The bite of pain caused by her pleasure hardens my cock against the zipper of my trousers painfully. I put her thigh onto my shoulder and lower my grip to hold the other one in place. Then rip her panties off.

Opened up to me, I devour her pussy.

"Rogeeerrr... Ahhh... Ahhh... Fuck!" Leonie cries as she tosses her head back, gripping my hair to ride my face through her orgasm. "Mmmmmm... so good, *Amoureux*..."

I run the flat of my tongue from her puckered back hole past her slick folds to her swollen clit, claiming every drop of her pussy juices. Her clit gets special attention as I flick the tip of my tongue at it, then wrap it around the engorged nub to tug at it.

Leonie convulses and bends over my head as a second orgasm takes ahold of her. She whimpers as she pants through the waves of pleasure. A thud to the floor, and I notice her mobile fell.

I wipe my wet mouth and chin on her inner thigh and rise to my full height, bringing her to stand on jelly knees.

"Off!" I command, as I lift the dress over her head to bare her to me completely.

Leonie scrambles to get her arms and head through the holes and tosses the garment to the floor. She glances up at me in expectation of my next move. She senses I'm in one of my controlling moods.

I shrug out of my jacket, and eagerly she reaches to undo my tie and shirt buttons. Finally, I free my turgid length from the confining trousers, then stroke it as I stare at my woman.

Leonie gracefully drops to her knees and reaches for my cock.

"No," I say, lifting her back up. "I want to feel your tight, soaked pussy wrapped around my dick, Pretty Kitty. Not that hot little mouth of yours. At least not now…"

Leonie shudders as a frisson of erotic energy sweeps through her at my passionate dominance.

I may not be a full Dom, but I am a demanding Alpha male. Leonie's no sub, but she likes for me to control her in our sex lives. And now is no exception. The caveman comes to the forefront.

Her pupils dilate further as I lead her to the sofa. A soft cry comes from her lips when I command her on her knees spread wide and her hands on the back of the sofa. Once in position, Leonie peeks at me from over her shoulder, her long hair skims her ass. With hooded eyes, she scans my body from head to toe, returning to my fat cock gripped in my fist. Slowly, she licks her lips.

And I'm on her.

One sizable hand grips her hip while the other lines my dick with her pussy.

"*Oh! Baise moi! Oooh!*" She screams when I plunge into her tight channel in one unyielding thrust. "Fuuuck! You're… so… big… Ooohhh!"

My hips take on a mind of their own as I drill Leonie into the sofa repeatedly.

Her head lolls forward, and she pants.

"You are mine. Mine to fuck and mine to give me babies. You know that, do you not, Pretty Kitty?" I demand driving up onto my toes to go deeper within Leonie's core.

The angle hits her G-spot to make her wail, and her nails to dig into the silk fabric. Her pussy walls flutter up and down my dick as she writhes against me through another orgasm.

I use her curvy hips as leverage to piston her body back and forth on my cock. Leonie feels so good I close my eyes and hum as my orgasm starts at my toes and runs up the backs of my thighs. The zing at the base of my spine shoots to my heavy balls as they slap against Leonie's clit.

As much as I want to keep going to increase our pleasure, my body demands release.

I glide my fingers along Leonie's spine to place one hand on her neck to lower her torso parallel to the sofa seat, opening up the length of her channel even more.

Leaning over Leonie, I shift my hold around to her throat and growl in her ear, "Tell me how much you get off from my giant dick wrecking your tight pussy, Pretty Kitty."

Leonie mewls as another climax takes over her. She arches her back like a good little pet and takes me deeper.

In a voice hoarse from her screams, Leonie moans, "Too much to express, *Amoureux!*"

With a dark chuckle, I speed up my thrusts as I buck against her. Our sweaty bodies slip and slide as our sensual scent surrounds us.

Leonie's strangled cry from another climax triggers my release.

I wrap my arms around her waist and pound into her as I roar through my mind-blowing orgasm.

"FUUUCK!!!!"

We collapse to the sofa. I'm careful to hold my weight

off Leonie and pull her to lie in front of me as my cock slips from her pussy, dripping with our combined essence.

Leonie purrs as we spoon together, and I pull the oversized cashmere throw around us.

"Thank you for my Baby Girl, sweetheart. I love you both and our sons more than you can imagine," I murmur against her damp hair.

"I love you, too, *Mon Cœur*. So, so very much..." Leonie rasps as she falls asleep.

While her breathing evens out, I think about how so, so very lucky I am to have her as my wife, lover, and mother of my children.

This Christmas will be even more special than the last.

ROGER

"*I*'m so glad we're back, *Mon Cœur*! The village is so enchanting with the snow falling and the Swiss Alps in the background. It seems like we're inside of a snow globe just shaken with the flakes falling all around us gently!"

Leonie exclaims as we drive through Verbier towards our *Chalet de la Joie*.

I glance at her and smile at her excitement. She's been pumping her favorite Christmas songs all week, even through the jet's sound system on the way here.

She turns to me and sings how all she wants for Christmas is me. Her eyes sparkle with golden flecks as she bounces in her seat, clapping her hands in sheer delight.

Since we learned about Leonie's pregnancy, all the signs are obvious to me now. I place my hand on her baby bump —single, now that we're only having a girl—and rub it lovingly. Mine!

Nothing compares to a man knowing he made his mate

pregnant with his seed in her fertile womb. I haven't stopped grinning in weeks.

During a video conference with Malcolm, he asked me why I was all goofy. But I didn't tell him since Leonie and I choose to wait until everyone gathers at the chalet. They're in for a big surprise!

She's twenty weeks along. So Dr. Berger assures us we're in the clear when I insisted upon a follow-up appointment where I was present to hear all the details for myself. What a relief it is for us to know.

My mission to complete all of my work early redoubled. Now we're here three days before our anniversary. One year and two plus babies. We couldn't get any busier even if we tried!

"Roger, I'm starving! Do you think we can stop by that chocolate shop off Place Centrale and get some of those truffles and the delicious hot cocoa? Oh, and some chocolate chip scones?"

I chuckle at Leonie's request. Yup, she's preggie all right.

"Sure, babe, whatever you want," I respond as I flick the signal to turn right for the shop. "But don't you want to eat some actual food, too? The chef stocked the pantry with your favorites and can come by to fix something for you real quick."

Leonie ponders my suggestion, then brightens as she faces me.

"How about we get the chocolate, then she can cook some steaks frites... Or chicken paillard? *Non, non...* French onion soup! Yummy, yummy for my tummy,

tummy!" She says rubbing her belly and smacking her lips.

I crack up, and we call the chef to put in Leonie's smorgasbord. Why pick only one when she can have it all?

As Lola once wisely said, *"Happy wife, happy life..."*

* * *

FOLLOWING the directions Leonie left for me, I step out of the bathroom from a shower wrapped in my Loro Piana cashmere robe.

My eyes scan our bedroom. It's lit by dozens of white candles of all shapes and sizes placed around the space. A roaring fire makes it toasty, filling the air with the fragrant scent of pine.

A heated smile crosses my face when I spot Leonie lying on her back naked on top of the large faux-fur blanket before the stone fireplace. Her naked skin glows in the ambient red and orange light.

When she senses my presence, Leonie bows her back and cups her fuller breasts, kneading them and plucking the beaded nipples. Her head thrown back as she moans deep in her throat.

Fuck. Me.

My cock tents the robe, pushing past the opening. Like a divining rod, it seeks out her wet, warm pussy. I shed the robe with a quickness and stalk over to her. My eager dick bobs up and down in agreement.

"Joyeux Anniversaire, Amoureux," Leonie purrs seductively, her eyes at half-mast.

As she licks her plump lower lip, she widens her bent knees. Fully on display for my viewing pleasure, her juicy pussy glistens and her puckered hole winks at me.

I sink down between Leonie's welcoming thighs, placing my hands on her knees. Then I bend over her so her pebbled nipples graze my hard chest.

"Happy Anniversary, Mrs. Steele" I croon against her luscious lips.

Leonie moans when I nip them and nudge my dick at her already slippery folds. Then we both groan when I sink myself inside her slowly.

I still to allow her body to accommodate my girth and deepen our kiss. Then shift my hips for long and even strokes, going further with each movement.

On a sigh, I trail open-mouthed kisses along Leonie's neck down to her soft mounds. My lips latch onto her sensitized nipple and suckle strongly until she mewls and writhes beneath me, her hand pushing my head closer to her bosom.

My mouth glides across the hollow between her breasts to reach the other turgid nipple. Sucking hard on the bud until she squirms some more.

Leonie cries out and lifts her hips to meet my thrusts as I change to slow, shallow strokes. She wants it fast and deep.

But not tonight. No pounding into her. Tonight I make sweet love to my wife.

I quiet Leonie with a toe-curling kiss as I continue to rock into her hot, wet pussy in a gentle, steady rhythm. Her small hands clutch my thick biceps while her full breasts flatten between us and her pelvis cradles mine. Our legs intertwine to bring us as close as possible intimately.

We continue to lose ourselves in the other as our climaxes build with the heat of our bodies, now warmer than the blazing fire beside us.

Leonie gasps as her pussy clamps on my cock, sending an electric current up my length and through my body, zipping to my limbs. When her walls flutter and she begs for more, I increase my pace to thrust faster and deeper.

"Cum with me, baby! Cum hard with me now!" I thrum in her ear.

Leonie bucks, then tightens all around me as her orgasm overtakes her.

The soft cries make my dick throb and pulse as I unleash a torrent of jizz deep into her womb.

Together we ride out our pleasure with kisses and words of love forever.

Later, after we stoke our desires, Leonie sits between my legs as we soak in the clawfoot tub. We stare out the window that faces the massive snow-covered Swiss peaks. The sound of more Christmas songs plays in the background softly as the fire crackles in the bathroom side of the hearth.

"We should name her Daphne Beaulieu Steele," Leonie says as she runs her fingertips along my forearms around her waist. "Daphne means laurel tree and Beaulieu lovely place, like the trees around *Le Beaulieu Manoir*."

She shifts to glance back at me and quirks her elegantly arched eyebrow.

"What do you think?" She asks.

I squeeze her and kiss her forehead.

"Sounds good to me, my love," I respond. "Feminine and strong as steel, just like her *Maman Lionne*."

Leonie grins and nuzzles into my chest.

"Thank you, *Chéri*," she says, kissing my pecs.

I place a kiss atop her head, and we sit a few moments more before we climb out and go to bed.

Tomorrow we'll celebrate our news with our family.

"HEY, hey, hey! The gang's all here!! Merry Christmas Eve!"

Leonie and I laugh as Harris makes his way through the front door after Sebastian and Lola, arms laden with gifts. We tease he looks like a young Santa Claus.

He rejoins with, "A sexy AF one, no doubt! And no last-minute presents for me, Roger dear! Let's see if you get coal in your stocking this year..."

Malcolm and Starr enter behind him, and the girls hug while Malcolm and I bro hug.

"Good to see you, man!" I tell him.

"Still looking goofy, bro!" He teases.

Haley walks in looking glum, and I pull her into a bear hug, lifting her off her feet.

Leonie mentioned Haley was going through some relationship issues, so I know I had to cheer my baby sister up posthaste.

"You better have brought your, A game or I'm going to leave you in the powder tomorrow morning for our

Christmas Eve run!" I tease her. "Don't blame me when your googles get covered in snow!"

Haley rolls her eyes and retorts, "Even on my worse day, I can outrace you, Roger!"

Guy and Josy come in carrying The Twins.

Leonie and I scoop them up and hold them close. These past few days are the longest we've been apart from them. They laugh at our overzealous kisses and pat our faces with their chubby hands.

My parents are the last to enter, and we greet them warmly.

"This tree is even bigger than last year's," my mother says, smiling as she takes a glass of hot mulled wine. "I love the new decorations!"

Everyone makes their way to their suites while Leonie and I tend to The Twins.

"When should we tell them?" She asks once we're in the nursery.

I think about it for a moment as I wrangle Gaspard out of his snowsuit.

"After we eat dinner and exchange gifts. She'll be another present," I respond, tickling him on his tummy when his shirt lifts.

I still can't believe we have another baby on the way and a girl to boot!

Leonie says we should get a dog so The Twins get used to another being in our home that will share our love.

I told her I don't know. But really have two female Bichon Frise puppies I'll give to her and to The Twins as their presents for tonight. The little balls of white fluff stole my heart when the Parisian breeder sent photos and when I met them last week. They came along with my parents and wait with Nanny Grace in her suite of rooms above the garage.

We head back downstairs to the dining room where Josy chats with the chef she favored about tonight's dinner. It's like last year's in honor of the French tradition of le *Réveillon de Noël* for the Christmas meal.

Leonie made requests for some of her favorites since her pregnancy urges dictate her meal choices these days. The chef was more than happy to oblige her and promised to follow Dr. Berger's recommendations for foods.

We relish in each other's company as we dine on fine dishes and excellent wines. The conversation flows easily.

No one notices Leonie drinks iced lemon ginger tea since it's in a crystal glass like everyone else's wine. She smiles secretly at me throughout our dinner.

Once we're gathered in the great room and exchanged our first gifts as our tradition for Christmas Eve, I stand and pull Leonie to her feet with me. The puppies scamper around our feet, playing with a toy.

"Well everyone, Leonie and I have some news to share with you," I start gazing from one smiling face to the other before my eyes turn to my wife's gorgeous face.

"We're twenty weeks pregnant with a baby girl!!" She announces, grinning like the Cheshire Cat.

Everyone whoops and hollers.

"Congratulations!!"

"*Oh, Mon Dieu!*"

"Awesome news, Roger and Leonie!!"

"Fantastique, Mon Trésor!"

When the well-wishing ends, Sebastian clears his throat and stands, too.

"Roger and Leonie, Lola and I are so thrilled for you! Once again you'll make us an aunt and an uncle—the most favorites, of course," he pauses to pull Lola into his side. "And we will make you an aunt and uncle, too. The most favorite is up to the others."

At first everyone smiles and nods. Then the room erupts when we realize what he means.

He and Lola are expecting a baby, too!

"We're twenty weeks, too!" Lola gushes as she rubs her belly covered by an oversized sweater. "Can you believe it, BFF?!"

"Oh, Lola, Sebastian! We're so happy for you, too!!" Leonie exclaims as she hugs her bestie and they start to cry.

Undoubtedly they remember Lola being upset this time last year as she sat in the windowed walkway in the early morning debating having children with Baz then or later.

Now here we are a year later, and we're both expecting. I knew this Christmas was going to be even more special than the last!

The doorbell chimes, and my mother waves me off as she heads to the entryway to answer. Everyone is present, so I'm not sure who it could be.

I glance down at Leonie, and she shrugs her shoulders.

My mother returns to the great room with Lachlan behind her. She glances at Haley questioningly, then at Sebastian worriedly.

Lachlan strides right in and stops in front of Haley,

clasping her hands in his. Without his emerald green eyes leaving her dove gray ones, he addresses my father and Baz.

"No disrespect, Uncle Morgan. We're like brothers, Sebastian. But Haley is mine, and I won't go another day without her for anyone."

Silence descends on the great room. Talk about the other shoe drops, rather the third...

* * *

Roger & Leonie's Story Concludes for Now...

Turn the page for the Steele Family, Author's Note, and a Preview of *Deepen My Desires Sebastian & Lola Part III*

THE STEELE FAMILY

STEELE INTERNATIONAL, INC

Multigenerational, multibillion-dollar business luxury real estate development and management corporation

Headquarters & Family's Primary Residences:

The STEELE Tower, New York City

A modern, gray-tinted glass fifty-seven story mixed-use skyscraper on southwest corner of Fifty-Seventh Street and Fifth Avenue within Billionaires' Row

Global Offices:

- The United States of America (New York City, New Jersey, Chicago, California, Miami, Las Vegas)
- The Caribbean (St. Maarten, St. Barth's, St. Lucia)
- The French & Italian Rivieras (Nice, Cannes, Positano, Capri)
- Monaco (Monte Carlo)
- The United Arab Emirates (Abu Dhabi, Dubai)

STEELE FOUNDATION: A STRONG AND SUPPORTIVE HOUSE

Builds and manages attractive, affordable housing for urban, lower-income families

Available for download at **bit.ly/STEELEFamily**

Author's Note

Thank you for reading Part III of Roger and Leonie's sexy, sizzling romance! I hope that you enjoyed the Happy For Now conclusion of their passionate love affair. If so, I'd love to hear your thoughts, please share a review at **http://bit.ly/CLBooksSI5Review** and tell your friends.

Wow! *Justify* gave lots of hints at what's next for the Steele clan in the Desires Series!

Click below for the answers to one steamy story featuring Power Couple Alpha Dom Sebastian and Independent Woman-cum-sub Lola as their scintillating trilogy concludes:

Deepen My Desires Sebastian & Lola Part III

At **CharmaineLouise.com** take the *Four types of lovers. Which are you?* **Quiz** to match your Sexy Fantasy: sub, Voyeur, Dominatrix, or Dominatrix sub Switch.

Follow me on social media including my CLBooks Coterie Fan Club below or on your favorite channels below and subscribe to my newsletter at **bit.ly/CLBooksNewsletter** for a **Free Book**.

Fulfill Your Desires.

xoxo

Charmaine Louise

STEELE International, Inc.
A Billionaires Romance Series Book 6

Deepen My Desires Sebastian & Lola Part III

Click on the link below or visit books2read.com/u/
bo2enV to get your copy.

Deepen My Desires Sebastian & Lola Part III

Books in the Series:

Discover My Desires Sebastian & Lola Prequel
(Available Exclusively to Subscribers)

COMING NEXT: DEEPEN MY DESIRES SEBASTIAN & LOLA PART III PREVIEW

"*I* want to have a baby with you, Lola."

Sebastian Steele—the former multibillion-aire playboy now my husband of eighteen months—murmurs to me as he traces shapes with his fingertips on my bare, flat belly.

Shocked to hear his words, I stiffen. An ice bucket of water douses the fiery heat swirling around our post-climax bodies.

We just made passionate love, and my core still buzzes from Baz's skillful touch—mouth, lips, tongue, fingers, ten-inches...

I roll over to face him in bed at my best friend turned sister-in-law Leonie Steele, formerly Beaulieu, and Baz's second younger brother Roger's new, multimillion-dollar chalet in Verbier, Switzerland. I need to know how serious Baz is about a baby.

As I stare into his dove gray eyes that shine in the moonlight from the wall of windows in our suite, I search his handsome face for any sign of a joke. No guile, only earnestness, and dare I think hopefulness show.

Damn.

Why now?

I thought we addressed this issue months ago.

First Baz only hinted at a baby all nonchalant like. A reference to the need for the next head of STEELE International, Inc., his family's multigenerational, multibillionaire dollar luxury real estate development and management corporation based in New York City.

Baz, previously president of the Retail Properties Division, earned the CEO role when his father Morgan announced his retirement and named Baz his successor at our wedding, as Morgan's father named him. Each of his siblings works at STEELE: Malcolm, second oldest, president of the Entertainment Properties Division; Roger, president of the Residential Properties Division; Harris and Haley, youngest and fraternal twins, co-founders of the subsidiary STEELE Technology and Cyber Security.

Who needs "the next head of STEELE" only eighteen months after being appointed and Baz is only thirty-seven years old now, nowhere near retirement age? Really? Cue the biggest eye roll of the millennia...

I didn't open my mouth.

Then a couple of months passed, and he mentioned having a baby outright.

I told him we should spend our first few years as a couple, no need to rush into a family. We'd rushed enough —meeting one week; living tougher the next week; a couple for four months before our disastrous breakup...

Plus, we have our career goals that dominate our focus. The growth of Lola's Coterie my luxury lingerie and now evening wear collection boutiques and Baz as CEO and Chairman of the Board. We're both driven and acknowledge the importance of our businesses. Particularly since my growth ties in with STEELE as their retail spaces serve as my boutique locations around the globe.

Baz agreed. That is, until he brought it up again just now...

I blame Leonie and Roger for running around proud parents of identical twin boys, Rodolphe Beaulieu Steele and Gaspard Beaulieu Steele. They just turned three-months old and nothing is more adorable than The Twins. To see my bestie so ecstatic with her husband of four days, Roger, and her *beaux fils*—beautiful sons as the Parisian and Tunisian beauty in her own right calls them—makes my heart swell with love.

Since Leonie and Roger prove a young couple can successfully balance a family while they excel in their careers—Leonie as a megamodel turned interior designer with her newly created division at STEELE—influenced Sebastian clearly. Not to mention how they cannot keep their hands off each other. Who said babies end a steamy sex life?

Can I see Baz and me like Leonie and Roger living their best lives? Hell yes! But...

I can't get over the loss of my parents in a tragic car accident when I was seventeen years old and left all alone in the world.

The thought of having children only to leave them

makes me violently ill. Sweat breaks out on my skin and dry heaves rack my body, dizziness overtakes me. Realistically I know there's no way to see the future, and no one has kids expecting their own deaths, but it's hard for me, even fifteen years later.

The upside came from my friendships with Luc Montaigne and Leonie, who he introduced to me eight years ago. Luc became my mentor, Vice Chair of Lola's Coterie, and a father figure. That is after I literally bumped into him one evening in Paris where I was an apprentice at a lace atelier after graduating from the Fashion Institute of Technology in my native New York City.

Le Renard Argenté, fifty-two and the multibillionaire CEO and Chairman of the Board of his family's multigenerational banking empire Banque Montaigne headquartered in Paris with branches worldwide, took me under his wing. The Silver Fox lives up to his name as a sexy and fit older man who is the last *duc* of his family's noble line.

When he introduced me to Leonie, she agreed to become the spokesmodel for Lola's Coterie. It was one move that skyrocketed my company to the stratosphere. To have *The Lion*—the world renown face of fashion houses and cosmetics companies—represent my lingerie brand made Lola's Coterie a household name.

Luc and Leonie became my surrogate family along with Leonie's parents, *Papa* Guy and *Maman* Joséphine. Sadly, Luc lost his wife and son in childbirth one year before he met me. We helped each other to survive our shared grief of losing loved ones unexpectedly.

So while I'm super happy for Leonie and Roger, I'm still

hesitant to move forward with a child. I've put off thinking about it. But they influenced me, too. Especially since we arrived in Verbier yesterday to celebrate not only their marriage, but Christmas and New Year's. Spending time at the Christmas market and at dinner makes me want what they have for Baz and me.

"Babe, don't look so stricken. Just think more about it. For me, for us. Okay?"

Baz's softly spoken request pulls me from my musings. His eyes now fill with concern and a touch of sadness.

My throat clogs, and my chest constricts. I can only nod in response.

"Words, Little Pet. I will have your words," Baz corrects me in his commanding Alpha Dom voice.

I shiver and bite my lower lip as a thrill rushes through me.

To think just over three years ago I was first introduced to a D/s relationship by my onetime lover Simon Blanchett. The hot AF Alpha Dom spanked me before giving me the most intense orgasms and sense of release I'd ever experienced. He awakened the need in me.

Until Baz... The only man I submit to now after my Independent Woman realizes I can still roar in the boardroom, but purr in the bedroom. I give Sebastian control with our fucking willingly, but with enough sass I'll forever need a spanking. Indeed, a total win-win situation. Give it to me, baby!

"Yes, Sir," I answer firmly.

"Good. Now go to sleep, you earned your rest, Little Pet," Baz says with a smirk.

He kisses my lips, but ends with a nip for a touch of pain with the pleasure before he rolls me back over to spoon again.

I lie wrapped in his warm, loving embrace as my mind continues to work over the issue.

Once his breathing evens out, and his hold lessens, I slip from our bed.

I pad to the bathroom to clean up, then put on one of Lola's Coterie cashmere lounge suits and matching slippers. A quick peek at Sebastian assures me he's still fast asleep. For a moment, I stare at his gorgeous face, so peaceful. I love this man with all of my heart and soul and want both of us happy.

With a sad smile, I turn for the suite's main door.

The massive chalet sits quietly. How's the Christmas tale go? Not even a mouse stirs. Dim lighting from wall sconces and ceiling pots make my way visible. It's a comfy and chic custom-built chalet with all the top amenities and accoutrements expected by a posh family.

Roger gifted it to his new bride as one of his wedding presents. Leonie whose favorite holiday is Christmas named it *Chalet de le Joie* since it's the time of year most filled with joy.

Verbs, as the in-the-know jet-set call Verbier, is a town in the Swiss Alps. A part of the Valais canton in the southwest of Switzerland, France borders Verbier to the west with Italy to the south. It's the most exclusive ski destination in the world.

It's the winter version of Monaco, with the difference being people who go to Monaco want to watch or be watched. Whereas Verbier has an understated style where wealth is glamorous, stylish and tasteful. People are here for the reasons one goes to a ski resort—the superb skiing. Not to mention the phenomenal bars and restaurants; the après-ski is perfect for party lovers. Verbier is a glamorous winter playground.

Leonie and Roger's luxury chalet occupies the area south of the Médran lift. They're slightly away from town along Rue de Médran, where the extra space means they are rarely overlooked and have a private, exclusive vibe. The residential compound is opposite to the STEELE Verbier Hotel & Resort that's closer to the heart of the village square. The concept is for the STEELE Verbier Chalets to access the resort for its five-star amenities. The most important include the luxury thermal bath spa and the three Jackson Corporation restaurants headed by the Steele siblings' cousin Lucien the *Sexy Chef* as he's known by his millions of followers.

The STEELE Verbier had its grand opening during last year's ski season. They planned the Residential Properties Division's completion of the by-application-only compound of ten state-of-the-art chalets and private club-house to take occupancy for this year's season. As always, both top-notch properties deserve the STEELE stamp.

I make my way down the back set of stairs that open out on a windowed walkway. It connects the huge chef's kitchen and butler's pantry with a cluster of rooms.

Not that Leonie cooks! Over the years, *Maman* Josy taught their Tunisian family's traditional recipes to me since cooking is one of my favorite pastimes.

A giggle bubbles up as I think about the time Leonie burned water... Yeah, she boiled it right out of the pot and burnt the whole kit and caboodle! *Maman* Josy banned her from *Le Beaulieu Manoir's* kitchen for a week. It's surprising Leonie didn't burn down her family's ancestral mansion on the westernmost part of the outskirts of Paris in Neuilly-Auteuil-Passy. The majestic property features manicured park-like grounds, stables, tennis court, swimming pool and cabana, and a palatial French Rococo mansion. A part of the 16th arrondissement, it's in the wealthiest neighborhood.

They built the hamlet between the thirteenth and seventeenth centuries. Later, during the reign of Louis XV, it became a fashionable country retreat for French elites. The Beaulieu's twenty acres of land border Bois de Boulogne with parts of the acreage awarded to their ancestors by the monarch.

So growing up überwealthy, Leonie really does not need to cook at *Le Manoir* or here. Not that I did either with a mother who was a high-powered medical attorney and my father was one of the world's top cardiologists. They were multimillionaires. I just love to cook and enjoy the fruits of my labor, and Baz loves my curves.

The fully stocked pantry offers tons of options for a warm cuppa; I opt for chamomile tea. Once it's ready, I return to the walkway and curl up on a settee. Then bundle an oversized cashmere throw around me; it engulfs my petite body.

Listlessly, I gaze out the windows as the early morning

light sparks beyond the Swiss Alps. So lost in thought, I don't hear anyone approach.

"Hey. What are you doing up so early?"

I glance over my shoulder to find Leonie.

The sad expression on my face makes her pause.

"What's wrong?!" She asks urgently as she sits beside me hurriedly. "Why are you out here and not upstairs with Sebastian? Did something happen?"

Her feline amber eyes narrow as she searches my face for the cause of my distress. We've become one another's defenders over the years. To take on boyfriends and touchy-feely fans in a heartbeat.

I sigh and wipe a hand over my heart-shaped face. With a smile, I shake my head. The glossy raven tresses sway with the movement. "Sebastian and I—"

"I'll kick his ass! I don't care if he's Roger's brother! What did he do to you?!" Leonie demands, her French accent thickening with her emotions as her eyes glow fiercely.

Another giggle surfaces through the pain, and I hold up my hands to stop her.

"No. It's not what you guess," I say. "He wants to have a baby for a while now. At first he only hinted at it, later he mentioned it outright. Now, being around The Twins and seeing how happy you and Roger are and how you're making the family thing work, Baz brought it up again earlier this morning. I couldn't fall sleep. I stayed up thinking long after he fell asleep. So I came down here for some chamomile tea."

I twirl a strand of hair around my fingers. My gaze goes

back out the floor-to-ceiling windows and to the beauty of the snow-covered Swiss Alps beyond. Puffs of snow fall from a leaden sky.

It's Christmas morning and a picturesque wintry day. My best friend knows I should enjoy a cuddle with my hubby instead of sitting down here all alone. She waits for me to continue.

Moments later, I shift on the settee to face Leonie.

"I do want children, and I know we can make it work, too," I start. Again, I look away. "But I'm scared about them losing one of us like I lost my parents at seventeen. It's really so hard…"

My voice cracks and tears fill my hazel eyes as my lower lip trembles.

Leonie scoots closer and pulls me into an embrace. Her maternal instincts make her rock me and hum softly as she rubs my back soothingly.

I'm sure she's thinking about how I felt that night when the police came to my family's apartment on Manhattan's Upper East Side. Only a few hours before, I'd wished my parents a good time at dinner with their out-of-town friends.

I give Leonie a squeeze before I sit up, drying my eyes with the backs of my hands. I take a deep cleansing breath like Starr Knight—our close friend and yogi, who helped me get through the rough patch after I left Baz early on— taught us. On the exhale, I nod, the decision made.

Again, Leonie waits for me to speak, knowing her BFF so well and how I like to think things through unin- terrupted.

"I can't not live because of a what may happen. I want what you and Roger have just as much as Sebastian. Hell, probably even more"—I chuckle and clasp her hands in mine—"What do you think? Am I being silly?"

Leonie squeezes my hands and shakes her head. Her long mahogany waves settle around her like a lion's mane.

"Absolutely not! You had a traumatic experience that's not so easily overcome. Luc and I helped you and being around my parents did, too. But it still had to be hard"— she squeezes my hands again and continues—"But now, you have a man who loves you madly and an even bigger family with the entire Steele clan. You have the support of many loved ones. 'Live. Live. Live' as Auntie Mame says!"

I giggle again at her reference to one of her favorite movies about the eccentric, carefree socialite who let nothing or anyone make her change course—much like Leonie.

"There you are!"

"We've been looking all over for the two of you!"

Sebastian and Roger stride down the hallway, their long legs make quick work of the distance between us. Baz cocks his head to the side and narrows his eyes when he notices my tear-stained face.

"What's wrong, baby? What happened? Are you sick?" He asks rapidly as he rushes to kneel before me.

Leonie pats his shoulder and squeezes it. He glances at her, puzzled.

"Take her upstairs. Despite how nice it is for us to have some BFF alone time, I'm positive Lola would rather be with you than in this walkway with me," she says grinning.

Baz nods and scoops me in a bride-like hold. I wrap my arms around his neck as I nuzzle against him, breathing in his sexy cologne that's imprinted on my brain as love and safety. Creed Aventus. The iconic name derived from ventus—the wind—illustrating the Aventus man as destined to live a driven life, ever galloping with the wind at his back toward success. How apropos.

Roger claps him on the back as we pass.

Sebastian acknowledges him barely as he murmurs soothing words in my ear.

In what seems like no time, we're back in our suite. Baz stands me by the bed and strips the lounge suit from my body, then tucks me under the covers. He takes off his long-sleeved t-shirt and sweatpants.

My body instantly responds to his muscular six-foot-four-inch frame and massive cock, even flaccid it's major.

He catches sight of my hungry gaze—knowing how my other favorite pastime is to suck him off—and smirks.

"First, tell me why you left our bed and ended up in the walkway in tears, babe," Baz says as he scoots under the bedding beside me.

We promised one another honesty above all, a lesson we learned after our breakup.

"I'm scared to have children only for them to lose me or you like I lost my parents," the words tumble from my mouth in a rush.

Baz nods and cups my face to pin me with his intense gaze.

"My love, I cannot imagine your pain. I can only try to ease it with my love for you"— he says then kisses me deeply—"But we have to live our lives and not let the past, no matter how tragic, stop us. Yes?"

I take another cleansing breath as I say a silent prayer to my parents for their strength.

"Yes, Baz. Let's have a baby, my love."

The most beatific smile crosses Sebastian's face, lighting his gray eyes to the color of molten platinum.

"Second, let's get started right. Now."

* * *

Click the Link Below for Your Copy

Deepen My Desires Sebastian & Lola Part III

I dedicate this novel to those who would love a life of happiness, good times with family, and fantastic sex with your most treasured one!

Fulfill Your Desires.

xoxo
Charmaine Louise

WELCOME TO CHARMAINELOUISE — THE SENSUAL LIFESTYLE

GLITZY. GLAMOROUS. STEAMY.

CharmaineLouise New York, Inc. invites you to indulge in *The Sensual Lifestyle* through **CharmaineLouise Books** and **CharmaineLouise Intimates**. CLBrands immerse you in *Sexy Fantasies* with CLBooks contemporary romance novels and give you *Sexy Under Things & Loungewear* with CLIntimates.

Charmaine Louise Shelton the Founder, CEO & Author of CLNY loves all things classic, elegant, feminine, and of course with an erotic edge! Favorite outfit of choice is a cashmere cardigan, leather pencil skirt, and seamed silk stockings with stiletto heels. Sexy Fantasy Type: sub with a dash of Voyeur. When not writing and designing, Charmaine Louise travels and spends time with her Maltese buddies, ZIGGY and Jynger.

CharmaineLouise — *The Sensual Lifestyle*

~ Visit online at **CharmaineLouise.com**

~ Subscribe to **CharmaineLouise Newsletter**

~ Find us on Facebook **@CharmaineLouiseNewYork**

~ Instagram **@CharLouNY**

CharmaineLouise Books *Sexy Fantasies* launched summer 2020. Sizzling, contemporary romance with your soon-to-be favorite Alpha Doms, Powerful Billionaires, and the women they lust after and love for second chances, insta-love, enemies-to-lovers, and more.

Want to chat it up and share your thoughts with other CLBooks Lovers? Read our blog, join our Charmaine-Louise Books Coterie Fan Club and follow us on my author pages and social media to be in the know about the book release dates, exclusive content, giveaways, contests, and more!

~ **Purchase your eBook and paperback novels from my Author Page by clicking here!**

~ Read and subscribe to our blog *The World of Sex*

~ Connect on **Amazon Author Page**

~ Goodreads Author Profile

~ Bookbub Author Profile

CharmaineLouise Intimates *Sexy Under Things &*
Loungewear debuted in 2003. Inspired by the sensuous
sirens and sylph swans of the past and present, the hand
crochet cashmere and silk collections are for the sexy:
hence, the line names Ginger — Bombshell; Diana —
Showstopper; Jackie — Timeless; Lena — Classic. Also
known as The Movie-Star from Gilligan's Island; Ms. Ross
The Boss; Mrs. Kennedy Onassis; Ms. Horne.

Do you thrive on seduction and being sexy lounging at
home? Read our blog and follow us on social media to
receive the tips, the latest additions to the collections,
private sales, and more!

~ Read and subscribe to our blog *The Art of Seduction*

~ Find us on Facebook **@CharmaineLousieIntimates**

~ Instagram **@CharmaineLouiseIntimates**

Fulfill Your Desires.